KNIGHT'S HONOUR

by Stephen Wheeler

Text © Stephen Wheeler

Cover photograph of William Marshal's tomb © Philip Moore

By the same author

THE SILENT AND THE DEAD

Brother Walter Mysteries:
UNHOLY INNOCENCE
ABBOT'S PASSION
WALTER'S GHOST
MONK'S CURSE
BLOOD MOON
NINE NUNS
FALLEN ANGEL
DEVIL'S ACRE

Prologue

Mention the name "Arthur" to any English man or woman and their eyes will instantly glaze over. They will froth at the mouth and start muttering about Holy Grails, ladies in lakes and mystical magicians. To them, King Arthur is the very embodiment of romantic love, honour and chivalry. The truth, alas, is rather more prosaic. Arthur was simply the saviour of the nation, neither more nor less. Certainly at the time England could have done with such a hero for it was a period of tremendous struggle against terrible foes.

Everyone knows the story of Arthur, how he was the product of an illicit liaison between Uther Pendragon and Ingraine, the wife of Duke Gorlois of Cornwall. To save Ingraine's blushes she was tricked by the wizard Merlin into thinking Uther was her husband although Gorlois was actually away fighting at the time. Later, Gorlois was killed and Uther and Ingraine married thus legitimizing Arthur who became King of Britain having proven his worthiness by drawing the sword Excalibur from the stone. He then went on to win glorious battles dying only when his life's work was done and the country was secure and at peace.

So far so improbable. But there is another part to the legend of Arthur that he never really died but sleeps on the mystical Isle of Avalon awaiting the day when he will be called upon to save his people again. That time is now, for in this year of 1217 England is once again in great peril, probably greater than at any time since Arthur's day and in need of a saviour at least as heroic. And as luck would have it we have one. I am Walter de Ixworth, physician to the monks and good people of Saint Edmundsbury. What I am about to unfold is the story of how Arthur did indeed rise from his slumbers to don the mantle of Saviour of the Nation once more - and my part in it.

Part One

THE JOURNEY OUT

Chapter One
LET BATTLE COMMENCE

So, England is at war again. What else is new? We seem to have been at war with someone or other more or less constantly for decades - the French, the Scots, the Saracens - or just with each other. We just can't seem to stop ourselves. Let's face it, the English are a belligerent race - but then, so are all the others.

I'm not making excuses. War is a terrible thing. I've never been directly involved in one myself but as a child I witnessed the aftermath of the battle at Fornham just outside Bury when old King Harry put down the rebellion of his eldest son, the Young King. I saw the dreadful wounds and mutilations inflicted then - it was one of the reasons I decided to become a medic. But even that is not the worst of it for wars are not won by armies on the battlefield. They are won by depriving the enemy of his means to continue fighting. To that end crops are burned, villages levelled and every living thing in them - men, women, children and beasts – are killed so that there is no-one left to pay the soldiers and nothing for them to plunder. That is the greatest tragedy of war and its greatest crime: the murder of innocents.

But Fornham was a mere squabble between a father and his son. This latest struggle is far more serious for upon its outcome rests the very soul of England. Nothing so fundamental has been known since the

Conquest a hundred and fifty years ago. Whoever wins this one will determine the direction the country takes for decades, possibly centuries, to come. Let me explain:

Two years ago King John put his seal to a concordat that was supposed to bring to an end years of strife between him and his barons. It didn't. Neither side was happy with the result. The king thought the concordat - lately known as the Great Charter or *Magna Carta* - had gone too far while the barons thought it hadn't gone far enough. Both sides withdrew and prepared for further trouble which wasn't long in coming.

The first thing John did was to get his overlord, the pope, to declare the charter void which he was happy to do. The last thing Pope Innocent wanted was his fiefdom run by a bunch of laymen no matter how noble. In response the barons revoked their oaths of loyalty to the king and started looking around for a replacement.

That was easier said than done. The obvious choice was John's eldest son. But Henry was a child of seven, hardly a suitable leader in time of war. Besides, he was in John's hands safely out of the barons' reach.

If not Henry then who else was there? Of John's four brothers only Geoffrey had had a legitimate son named, prophetically, Arthur. Indeed, Arthur had been John's main rival for the throne at the start of his reign but then had mysteriously disappeared - it is assumed murdered by John although this has never been proved. Had he lived Arthur would now be a man of thirty and an ideal choice to replace his uncle. Unfortunately Arthur is dead – or at any rate, hasn't been seen these past fourteen years.

That left who? The only other realistic choice was John's niece, Blanche. But no woman has ever ruled England in her own right. The last time it was attempted we ended up with the Anarchy – a civil war that lasted nineteen years and left the country in ruins. No-one wanted to risk that again. However, Blanche did have a husband: Prince Louis, the son of King Philip of France. Although not of English royal blood, Louis did have a legitimate claim to the throne through his wife. For his part, Louis was only too delighted at the prospect of uniting the two crowns of England and France under him – his father, King Philip, even more so. Whether the rebel barons were quite so enthusiastic about this aspect of the proposal is debatable, but there was no-one else. It was therefore to Louis the barons turned as fighting broke out again.

All that was eighteen months ago. Since then a desultory civil war has raged back and forth between John and the rebel barons neither side managing to land the knock-out blow. For a while it looked as though John might just have the edge, but then Louis landed in Kent with fresh troops and money and that tipped the balance back in favour of the rebels again. It was then that John did the one thing that was certain to secure him victory: he died. Overnight Louis went from being England's white knight saving the nation from a tyrant king to being a foreign interloper intent on stealing the throne from its rightful inheritor: the young Prince Henry. Being a child, Henry was a total innocent untainted by his father's excesses and support quickly rallied around him. As their final *coup de grâce* the new regency government re-issued Magna Carta thus removing at a stroke the chief cause of the rebellion. There was now no longer any need to carry on fighting.

Unfortunately matters didn't end there. Prince Louis is still in England, still hoping to be king although rapidly running out of money and support, while the regency council has the legitimacy but lacks the resources to deal the final blow. Result: stalemate. The fighting may have subsided for now but that is not the same thing as peace. That will only come when one side is victorious over the other.

And what of the rest of us ordinary folk while all this is going on? We carry on with our lives as normal. At least that is what I would like to do. Yet where am I? As I write these words you find me seated on a covered wagon travelling along Ermine Street, that great north road built by a previous invader of these islands: the Romans. Behind me lying prone in the back of the wagon is a high-born lady, Mistress Maude de la Haye by name, and her manservant. Also along for the ride is my old friend and Brother in Christ, Jocelin of Brackland. How this ragbag little band came to be bumping along the rutted and decaying Ermine Street and not secure behind the walls of Saint Edmund's abbey needs some explaining. It was at the behest of our prior, Brother Herbert. To those of you who have followed these jottings of mine in the past, that fact alone will be enough to start you nodding. So, let us go back a few days and see how this sorry state of affairs arose...

'Walter, my dear fellow! Thank you for coming. Have a seat.'

Herbert came round to my side of his desk in his palatial office above the prior's house and plumped up the cushion on the chair he'd placed there specifically for me.

I am always a little suspicious when the prior is being this friendly. Usually when I'm summoned before him there is no chair, certainly no cushion, and I have to stand before him like a recalcitrant schoolboy. My suspicions therefore alerted, I sat with caution as he adopted the nearest thing to a smile his beaky visage could manage.

'Would you care for some refreshment? A cup of spiced wine perhaps?'

'That's very kind of you, brother. But no, thank you.' I wanted to keep a clear head for whatever was coming.

'As you wish,' Herbert continued to beam. He returned to his side of the desk and started tapping his nails on his teeth – a habit I always find irritating. The silence continued. I waited.

'Your laboratorium,' he said at last. 'How's everything there? I don't seem to get over there as much as I would like. All in order is it?'

'The roof leaks. I've run out of my supply of balsam. Mice have gnawed through from the stable next door, and last week my cat died. Apart from that, everything is fine.'

'Good, good,' he nodded absently.

There followed a further uneasy silence which this time I broke:

'Was there something specific, brother? Only I am rather busy.'

'No no. Just a friendly chat between colleagues.'

'In that case…' I started to rise.

'Well yes, actually there is something. I want you to go to Lincoln.'

I was half-way up out of my chair and stopped. 'Lincoln?'

'Yes. You know where that is?'

'In Lincolnshire?'

'Spot on!' he beamed. 'Lincolnshire is exactly where it is.' And chuckled at his joke.

I sat down again. 'Brother Prior, why do you want me to go to Lincoln?'

His brow furrowed, he lowered his voice and his face adopted a look of studied concern. 'We've a very important guest staying in the abbey at the moment, Walter - Lady Maude de la Haye. You've heard of her?'

'Should I have done?'

'It's a tragic case. You see she's dying. Some ... women's trouble.' He flapped a dismissive hand in the air. 'I won't go into details. It's a terrible shame, but there it is. She has to go to Lincoln and can hardly go on her own. She needs an escort, someone with medical training.'

'I sympathize of course, brother. But since I'm not familiar with the lady much less examined her, and she's not a patient of mine...'

'Ah, well, that's because she has her own physicians.'

'Then if she has physicians of her own why can't they take her to Lincoln?'

'Because they're already there.'

This was becoming more and more bizarre.

'Brother Prior, if the lady's physicians are in Lincoln how did they manage to diagnose her symptoms?'

He grimaced. 'Don't start getting technical, Walter. The fact is they are there and you are here and you're the best person to take her.'

I frowned. 'I do have other concerns, brother.'

'Like what?'

'There's been an outbreak of bedbugs in the novice dormitory.'

'Your assistant can handle that, surely?'

'I don't have an assistant at the moment.'

'That's right,' he frowned. 'You terrified your last one, didn't you? The infirmarer then.'

I pouted. 'Brother Thomas is having the same problem. It's the bedlinen. It didn't get boiled properly last month. Not enough hot water. More precisely, there's no wood to burn in order to heat the water.'

Herbert adopted a defensive pose. 'I can't help that. It's the war. All our wood has been commandeered by the army.' He shook his head and shrugged helplessly.

Now, that I knew was a lie. Among my few trusted acquaintances at the abbey I happen to count Brother Durant whose job it is to collect lumber from our own abbey woods located outside the town. He told me there was plenty of fuel available but it was being sold off at inflated prices to rogue traders who then sell it on to the army at an even greater price. It was a situation that could only happen with Herbert's connivance – or at least his acquiescence. This was just Herbert trying to profit from another's misfortunes as usual.

'Besides,' Herbert went on. 'It's hardly a reason to keep you in the abbey.'

'As abbey physician I have a duty of care. Surely you'd agree it is part of my function to relieve sickness, however it is caused.'

'Bedbugs is not a sickness.'

'But they cause great distress. Itching which leads to scratching and sores.'

He frowned. 'Don't you think you're exaggerating the problem just a little?'

'I didn't invent the bedbugs, brother.'

'No, but you're making the most of them. If it wasn't that it'd be something else. You see, this is you all over, Walter. Whenever I ask you to do something you put obstacles in the way. There's no reason why you can't go to Lincoln. This bedbugs excuse. It's ... obfuscation.'

'Is that the right word, brother?'

'It'll do till I think of a better one.'

I clearly wasn't getting anywhere with this line of argument. I'd have to try another:

'Isn't travel a bit risky just at the moment? There is a war on you know?'

'War!' he scoffed. 'There hasn't been any fighting in months. And now that King John is dead – God rest his soul - the war is as good as over.'

'I thought a moment ago the army was stockpiling fuel?'

'For armies to clash they have to be within striking distance of each other – you'd agree with that, at least. And I happen to know the earl marshal is in Oxford at the moment and the dauphin is in Dover. Miles apart.'

'Lincoln is half way between the two. And they could come together again at any time. I'd be caught in the middle.'

'Not if you're quick. Lincoln's what, fifty miles from Bury? Easily manageable in three days.'

I snorted. 'On a fast horse with a following wind, maybe. But a wagon drawn by oxen? With a sick patient on board?'

'Call it four, then. Break the journey at Thetford. The nuns of Saint George will look after you.' He gave a wry wink. 'You'll like that, all those women fussing over you. You can stay at Lynn priory the next day - I've already had a word with the bishop.'

I bet he had.

'I'm still not sure.'

'Well I am. You're going and that's an end to it. I've promised Mistress Maude and I can't go back on my word.' He waited. 'Anything else?'

'No Brother Prior.'

'Right then. Off you go. I leave you to make the necessary arrangements.'

It sounded as though the arrangements had already been made. I don't know why I even bother arguing. Once Herbert had made up his mind on something there was no shifting it. And as he was my superior at the abbey I had no option but to obey him.

It's at times like this that I wish Abbot Hugh were here a little more often. Not that he'd be a particular ally of mine, but he might bring some semblance of reason into the argument. Unfortunately Hugh was still in Rome trying to drum up support for the new regency council. So like it or not Prior Herbert was in charge. The question was, why was he so keen on this trip? Maybe he was hoping there would be fighting of some kind along the way and I would get caught up in it. I wouldn't put it past him. As far as Herbert was concerned I was an expendable nuisance. Maybe it was as simple as that.

Downstairs Herbert's clerk, the very excellent and ever-attentive Jephthet, was seated at his desk as usual. The man is a diabolus with a permanent sneer on his face. His greatest pleasure in life is the discomfort of others, a condition for which he has plenty of opportunity with me. From the look on his face today he obviously knew what the interview had been about and was looking even more pleased with himself than usual. I didn't want to get into another unpleasant exchange so I gave him a brief nod of my head as I made for the door.

'Have a good journey north, master,' he called out in his nasally twang and sniggered.

I stopped and beamed back at him. 'Why thank you Jephthet. I am looking forward to it as a matter of fact. A chance to get away for a while. Sample the delights of the countryside.'

He gave a little sneer. I'm sure he wasn't fooled by my phony bravado. But then I had another thought:

'By the way, I've been meaning to ask, are you cold in bed at night?'

'Cold in bed, brother?'

'Yes. These wintry nights can't be very comfortable.'

'It's May, master.'

'May can be unpredictable. Roasting one minute, freezing the next.'

'I can't say I've noticed. Why do you ask?'

'I have some spare bedlinen that I thought you might like.'

He looked at me suspiciously. 'That's very thoughtful of you, master.'

'Not at all. Looking after my flock among whom I count you, dear Jephthet, is my purpose in life,' I smiled. 'I'll have some blankets sent over. I've lots available at the moment.'

'Thank you, master.'

'Don't mention it.'

I went away with a smile on my face. A couple of blankets to keep him warm – and a few little added companions for company. They should keep him busy for a while. Well, one has to have some pleasures in life.

Chapter Two
STEPPING OUT

Despite Prior Herbert's diktat, I was determined to get out of this trip if I possibly could if for no other reason than to thwart one of his suspect schemes. And suspect I was certain it was. He was being altogether too charming - like the fox in that fable by Aesop. To get the crow to drop the lump of cheese it was holding in its beak the fox flatters the crow's singing voice until the stupid bird opens its beak to sing and out drops the cheese – straight into the fox's mouth. In this case I am the crow and Herbert is the fox. Except I have no intention of dropping my lump of cheese by agreeing to his little game if I can possibly help it. At least, that was my initial intention. Two things changed my mind – or rather, two people: the first was my old friend Jocelin of Brackland.

Leaving the prior's house, I saw him being led across the yard by a novice. It is a sight that always fills me with sadness for I have a particular fondness for this man. We go back a long way and have shared many an adventure together. But time has not been kind to Jocelin. Now in his seventh decade of life he is practically blind and has to be led around like a latter-day Bartimaeus, the blind beggar whose sight Jesus restored on account of his unshakable faith. Jocelin has faith but unlike Bartimaeus so far it has not healed him.

Sad as it was to see him so reduced, the greatest cruelty is that his eyesight is now so bad that he can no longer see well enough to write. Writing has been Jocelin's greatest love and something at which he particularly excelled. He has produced one of the abbey's finest chronicles which I am sure will endure for many future generations to enjoy. He would like to write more but alas, failing eyesight has ambushed that desire and Prior Herbert is too mean to give him an amanuensis. The novice he's been allocated, biddable and accommodating though he is, cannot write. I suspect that's the reason he was chosen for Jocelin's writing could at times be provocative; (he was very rude about Herbert when he was first made prior – but then, weren't we all?). Maybe this was his way of getting his own back. And so Jocelin must remain mute, on parchment at least, frustrated in his yearnings and to the world's impoverishment.

But at least his stammer has improved since he retired from abbey duties and is able to relax a little more. As I approached he stopped and squinted in my direction.

'Walter? Is that you?'

'Hello old thing,' I said going up to him. 'How are you getting along?'

He shrugged resigned shoulders. 'I live - with the help of my young f-friend here.' He patted the shoulder of the novice. The boy smiled but I was sure he'd rather be doing almost anything rather than leading an old man around all day.

Jocelin took his hand off the boy's shoulder and put it firmly on my arm. 'Come, walk with me a little. Thank you Osbert, you may go. Master Walter will look after me now.'

The boy looked relieved to be set free and walked off rapidly before Jocelin could change his mind. Once out of earshot he began:

'I hear you're off to L-Lincoln, Walter.'

'Good news travels fast. How did you find out? I've only just heard myself.'

'You know the abbey. N-nothing remains a s-secret for long. What have you decided?'

'I was hoping to get out of it. I don't know the real reason Herbert wants me to go to Lincoln and frankly I don't care. He's made up some ridiculous excuse about taking some matron to see her aunt there. Whatever the real reason it will all be for nothing. Lincoln's half way to Scotland. With the country the state it's in at the moment we'd be lucky to get there unscathed. I mean, who would be stupid enough to want to travel all that way at such a time?'

'Actually, I would.'

I looked at him aghast. 'What? *You* want to go to Lincoln? Why?'

'I have f-family there.'

'But I thought you were a Buryman through and through. And an only child with no other family – or so you've always led me to believe.'

'C-close family, no. But these are c-cousins. D-distant c-cousins.'

'Very distant by the sounds of things. How come I've never heard of these cousins before?'

'I d-don't t-tell you everything, Walter,' he frowned. 'Anyway, I haven't s-seen them for years – d-decades in f-fact. They are c-cousins on my m-mother's s-side. A s-sister, or f-first c-cousin, I f-forget which.'

I looked at him doubtfully. Jocelin has never been a very good liar. And his stammer had returned which is always a sure sign he's uncomfortable.

'Lincoln's a long way away,' I reminded him again. 'The roads will be in a terrible state especially after the winter storms. And there's no-one at the moment to repair them. It won't be a comfortable ride. Are you sure you're up to it? You're not getting any younger.'

'All the more r-reason to go n-now while I still c-can. B-but thank you for reminding me of m-my mortality.'

'And then there are your eyes,' I continued. 'You won't be able to take Osbert with you, you know? I won't be able to look after you and the Lady Maude.'

'I d-don't really n-need the boy. He's more for c-company than anything else. It'll be an adventure.'

'Not if we get attacked by a band of cut-throats it won't!'

'We won't get attacked.'

'You hope. It's a dangerous world out there especially at the moment.'

He was getting flustered again. 'Look Walter, it's quite s-simple. I have c-cousins who I would like to have this l-last chance to v-visit before I d-die and I would very much appreciate it if we could t-travel there together. Is it s-so much to ask?'

He seemed determined to go whatever I said.

'You'll need the prior's permission to leave the abbey.'

He flapped a dismissive hand. 'Herbert won't say no. He'll be happy to be r-rid of me for a while. I am n-nothing but a b-burden these days, a useless appendage - like a w-withered hand.'

'That's nonsense and you know it.'

'S-so what's your answer? Will you t-take me with you or n-not?'

'I still haven't said I'm going yet.'

'But you haven't s-said you won't.'

'Not yet.'

'Good. That's s-settled then. I'll make the n-necessary arrangements.'

Before I could raise further objections, he turned on his heel and shuffled off – without the aid of his young assistant I noticed. Maybe he wasn't as blind as he made out after all.

The second person to induce me to take the Mistress Maude to Lincoln was the lady herself – though not for the reasons you might think. I called her a matron. She was anything but. I'd freely admit she was a fine-looking woman, in her early thirties at a guess, but it wasn't just her physical appearance that aroused my interest. Call me vain, but after forty years of dealing with sick people I like to think I had developed a nose for these things and Lady M just did not smell ill to me. But that was clearly the impression she was trying to give. I discovered her lying on her cot with the blanket pulled up under her chin and her eyes firmly closed. She was slightly breathless which made me suspect she had only just managed to get under the blanket before I arrived. She was obviously faking, but why? For the moment I decided to play along.

'Dear lady, how are you?'

'Hm? What's that?' She opened her eyes with exaggerated difficulty, her voice weak and pathetic. 'Oh it's you, Brother Walter. So good of you to come. I'm sorry, I was asleep.'

That, too, was interesting for how did she know who I was? As far as I knew we had never met before. There's nothing to distinguish me from any of the other monks. Perhaps I'm being over-cautious but that's the trouble with any proposal of Prior Herbert's, suspicion lurks around every corner - and under every blanket.

'I was asking how you are feeling?'

'Not too badly today, thank you,' she replied laboriously. 'Some days I am better than others. Alas, I do not know how many I have left.' She gave a pathetic cough.

'Would you like me to examine you?'

'No need. I have been examined by my own doctors. And my complaint is a delicate one.'

I gave her my most avuncular smile. 'Dear lady let me reassure you, I have been in this profession for more years than I care to remember. There is nothing you can reveal to me that I have not seen a hundred times before.' I started to tug gently at the blanket.

She held on to it tightly. 'I'd really rather not.'

I tugged back. 'It will only take a moment. I promise not to embarrass you. I just want to look at your feet.'

She frowned. 'My *feet?* What have my feet to do with anything?'

I smiled again. 'Indulge me, I beg you. It's a new form of diagnosis I am currently developing. It won't hurt. Just your feet. I promise I won't venture any higher. I won't even touch them. I just want to look at them.'

Reluctantly she allowed me to pull the blanket up – just enough to expose a shapely pair of ankles.

Why did I want to see her feet? Simple really. I'd already noticed that the bedlinen was the same as that used in both the novice dormitory and the infirmary. I was looking for signs of insect bites. If she had been as bedridden as she was trying to pretend she would have several on her ankles. There were none. They were perfectly white and clear, which meant she can't have been in the bed for long. As I suspected, she was faking. The question was, why?

'So?' she asked when I'd finished. 'What is your prognosis? Will I live?'

'It's too early to say,' I said carefully replacing the blanket. 'I dare say I will gain a better understanding of your condition on our journey. May I ask, is there any particular reason you wish to go to Lincoln?'

'Did the prior not tell you? The chatelaine of Lincoln Castle is my aunt. Lady Nicola de la Haye. A very dear and favourite aunt. Perhaps you've heard of her?'

As a matter of fact I had. Lady Nicola de la Haye was famous, indeed something of a legend. I can remember my father telling me about her. The post of chatelaine – the name given to a female constable of a castle – is a very rare honour. Few women are granted such responsibility. Lady Nicola had held the post for some decades. But she must be getting on a bit now. I was surprised to hear she was still in command of such a prestigious and important castle as Lincoln.

'It's a long way for a fit person never mind someone in your condition, my lady. As your physician I'm not sure I can sanction such a hazardous adventure.'

'I'm not so ill that I cannot travel, brother.'

I gave an indulgent smile. 'Forgive me, but I'm the best judge of that. As your physician – albeit physician *in locum* - I would feel happier for you to remain here at the abbey. Good morning.' I turned to leave.

'But my aunt is expecting me. I cannot disappoint her.'

'In that case would it not be easier for her to come here?'

'She is elderly and not in the best of health herself. I really must go now while I have the chance. In fact, I *insist* you take me!'

Insist, eh? Hm. A very determined young woman.

There didn't seem any point in arguing. The lady, Herbert, Jocelin – everyone seemed determined on this accursed trip. And if I'm honest my curiosity was beginning to become aroused. Why was everybody being to furtive? Couldn't they just come out with the real reason for wanting this journey? Someone wasn't telling me the full story and it seemed the only way I was going to find that out was by agreeing to go on this trip. In any case, I didn't really have much choice. Prior Herbert had spoken and my duty as a cloister monk, as I avowed when I first joined the Order so many long decades ago, was to obey my superiors without question. Not that I always had.

As I was leaving I noticed a young man hovering in the shadows. He was so furtively hidden that I almost missed him. I would have greeted him except he withdrew even further at my approach. Who was this? I wondered. Was he expecting to come on this trip too?

I have to admit I was intrigued. I'd been on other journeys away from the abbey before, of course, and some of them with unforeseen, even dangerous, consequences. Like a blind man about to take a leap off a cliff I couldn't resist the temptation to find out what lay at the bottom of this particular precipice. Whatever the truth of it, the following day we set off on the road north – myself, the Lady Maude, Jocelin and, as I had suspected, the mysterious young man in the shadows. And a fine spring morning it was too with not a hint of the tempest that was about to engulf us.

Chapter Three
BUMPS IN THE ROAD

Travelling through open country is dangerous at the best of times. We know all about that in Bury. Barely a week goes by than some poor wretch isn't brought in to the abbey having been found lying dead on the roadside. We never know who they are as they are stripped of everything they possessed – their clothes, their valuables, even their dignity - and left naked in a ditch like a piece of discarded offal. Maybe some time later someone might come looking for a missing husband or son but by then it would be too late; the body would already have been buried in the abbey cemetery.

That's in peacetime. During a civil war travel is even more dangerous. In fact it's positively suicidal. Not only are there the usual hazards of highwaymen to contend with but now there are bands of penniless soldiers as well roaming the country foraging for food and anything else that might take their fancy with few to stop them. With most of East Anglia in rebel hands at the moment there is the further problem of free-booting Frenchmen to contend with who have few qualms about assailing the native population. We had the small comfort of a truce during Pentecost, but truces rarely hold. There are always rogue elements willing to break them especially if they are starving. If you do have to travel the sensible thing is to do so in a group, if you can find anyone else foolhardy enough to join you, never alone. Yet that is precisely what Prior Herbert was asking us to do.

The first leg of our journey to Lincoln, the twelve miles to Thetford, is the shortest but possibly the most hazardous. The road is forested on either side all the way providing plenty of cover for any would-be assassin to leap out and surprise innocent travellers. Indeed, I was once assaulted in this very same piece of forest by the dread Geoffrey de Saye, may his soul rot in hell, and very nearly lost my life. But that's another story.

What makes this stretch of road particularly dangerous is St Edmund's connection with the convent of Saint George in Thetford. Saint George's is a daughter house of the abbey and life there has always been precarious. Being but few in number the nuns there aren't able to provide for themselves and rely on the abbey to supply them with most of their basic needs. Every week without fail, therefore, thirty loaves of bread, a hundred gallons of beer and a good deal of cooked meat have to be carted along this route making it an easy target for robbers. Assaults on our servants and theft of our goods are a common occurrence.

We took what precautions we could travelling on a day when deliveries are not normally made, but that was no guarantee we would pass entirely unnoticed. I did ask Prior Herbert for an escort if only for this part of the journey but he pooh-poohed the request. The only escort we needed, he declared, was prayer:

'The Lord will protect those he loves best, brother.'

'Yes, but can't we give the Lord a helping hand by providing an outrider or two? Just to be on the safe side.'

'And draw attention to yourselves? Escorts by their very existence suggest you have something worth escorting. Naked suggests you have nothing to steal. No no, I think you'll find my solution is by far the safest and most sensible. Remember the words of the psalm brother, "the robbery of the wicked shall destroy them!"'

'I'll try to remember it when I'm lying on the roadside with my throat cut, Brother Prior.'

Herbert was right about one thing, however: I was looking forward to my visit to the nuns of Saint George's, though not for the reasons he thought. At least, not entirely. I admit, I do like being fussed over by women, but that wasn't it. I was eager to renew old acquaintances. It's been fifteen years since I was last there accompanying Abbot Samson. That visit was not a great success and we had left under a cloud.

I did, however, make one firm friend among the nuns there: Sister Monica-Jerome. My clumsy antics seemed to amuse her and we formed a sort of impromptu alliance against one of her more severe sisters: the formidable Sister Benjamin. I wondered if either of these ladies, or indeed any of the nuns I met then, were still at the convent today. I supposed I would find out soon enough – that's if we arrived at all. I was still convinced we'd all be murdered before we reached Thetford. I could almost wish we were just to prove Herbert wrong. However, after an uneventful journey during which we met not another living soul, bandit or otherwise, we arrived at the gates of Saint George's shortly before vespers. I do hate it when Prior Herbert is proved right.

The nuns had clearly been expecting us. Herbert must have sent them notice of our visit weeks earlier which makes me wonder why he even bothered discussing the trip with me. Whilst we were welcomed in a spirit of Christian charity there was no great ceremony, unlike the last time I was here with Abbot Samson when they went down on their knees in the mud to laud him. I suppose this time there was no abbot for them to impress only a couple of elderly common-or-garden monks and two laymen of doubtful import.

I would hesitate to say that a change of regime had anything to do with this more workaday approach, but the prioress who was here last time, Odell, was an entirely different animal from the present one. Odell died some years ago, sadly, and her successor is – wouldn't you know it? - Sister Benjamin. No great surprises there. With so few nuns to choose from the field was limited and whatever else I might think of Benjamin she is a very capable woman. Still, I was slightly nervous about meeting her again. We hadn't exactly hit it off the last time and I wondered how we would get along this time. But I was determined to do my best to pour oil on any troubled waters. The only problem with that image is that oil burns.

'It is good to see you again Sister – or should I say *Mother* Benjamin?' I gave her my most obsequious smile. 'Congratulations on your elevation, by the way.'

'That was some time ago,' she sniffed. 'But thank you anyway. Much has happened since you were last here. I trust the intervening years have been kind to you. You look in fine fettle.'

The last time I was here Benjamin was the convent's apothecary, among all her other responsibilities, and was keen to display the fact and show off her skills. She considered herself at least my equal in the field of medicine. Nonsense of course. Her amateurish quackery could not compare with my lengthy, and I might add, expensive schooling in the intricate art of anatomical physick at one of Europe's most prestigious universities. Her manner hadn't changed much either. "Looking in fine fettle" is something you'd say about a horse.

'I have a touch of rheumatism in my left shoulder,' I told her rotating it a few times. 'But apart from that my limbs work reasonably well. Thank you for asking.'

'Rheumatics eh? I have a remedy for that. Remind me to give it you before you leave.'

'I will indeed. Er, have you met my brother monk, Jocelin of Brackland?'

Jocelin had been skulking behind me hoping not to be noticed. I now pulled him forward into the full glare of Benjamin's critical eye.

'D-delighted, M-mother P-p-p-prioress,' he stammered furiously.

Benjamin wrinkled her nose at the bobbing figure before her as though she'd just detected a bad smell. Jocelin grinned back like an idiotic ape.

'Dom Jocelin had your job at the abbey for a while,' I told her conversationally.

Her brow knitted. 'Prioress?'

'Guest-master. You once held that post along with all your duties I seem to recall. In fact, you could say the two of us together would make one of you. Guest-master *and* physician.'

It was meant as a compliment. But I'm not sure the comparison impressed her very much. Only *two* men to equal her? Surely it would take three at least!

'I've given you your old room in the guest wing, Brother Walter,' she continued without comment. 'You remember where that is. Dom Jocelin can have the room next to it.'

'Oh, you needn't have gone to so much trouble,' I smiled. 'One room would have been sufficient.'

She shook her head. 'We have a rule at the convent that male visitors, particularly monks, do not share rooms. That way we avoid ... problems.'

'Ah,' I nodded. 'Very wise. However, in this case you may have noticed Dom Jocelin's eyesight is not what it once was. I'm not sure he can navigate strange surroundings unaided.' I lowered my voice. 'And between you and me, mother, the dom is not fully *compos mentis*, if you take my meaning. He gets confused.' I tapped the side of my head and then shook it sadly. 'It could get embarrassing if he wanders into the wrong room - the nuns' dormitory say - by accident. Could you not make an exception just this once and permit us to share? Separate beds, naturally.'

Benjamin pursed her lips but reluctantly took us to a room that had two beds – separated of course, as far apart as possible on opposite sides of the room.

'Will this do?'

'This will do splendidly!' I smiled. 'Thank you mother.'

She grunted. 'Is there anything else you require before I leave?'

'Cornflowers.'

Benjamin looked at me blank. 'Cornflowers brother?'

'Yes. The last time I was here there was a wonderful display of them - beautifully-crafted lace ones on the dresser. The work of Sister Angelina I believe. I was hoping they would still be here. And perhaps I could meet her?'

Benjamin drew herself up. 'Sister Angelina is no longer with us.'

'Oh dear. What happened to her? Not expired I hope?'

Benjamin shook her head. 'Worse. She married. One of our gardeners. She and her husband now run a stall on the market.'

'Successfully I'm sure.'

'I wouldn't know. I've never been.'

'What about that other nun, Sister Monica erm ... something or other?' I kneaded my forehead trying to remember Monica-Jerome's name.

'Monica-Jerome is still here. Doubtless you will see her at supper.'

'I shall look forward to it. Now, about our two companions - Mistress Maude and her manservant? May I ask, where might they be ensconced?'

'I have given Lady Maude the lodge. Her man will sleep with the other servants in the kitchen.'

'Erm,' Jocelin raised a hesitant finger. 'M-m-may I just interject here? I b-b-believe L-lady Maude prefers G-Gelyn to s-sleep with her – that is to s-say in the s-s-same r-r-room as her. F-for s-s-s-security reasons you, er, understand, ahem, er, hm, yes…' His voice trailed away.

Benjamin shook her head. 'That will not be possible. We have even stricter rules when it comes to males and females cohabiting than we do with males. They will not be … ensconced … together. Now, if there is nothing more I have other matters to attend to. Vespers will begin momentarily and supper immediately after that. The dining hall is -'

'- out this door, across the courtyard and to our left,' I smiled. 'Yes, I remember.'

Benjamin grunted. 'Until later then.'

'Well, that went better than I was expecting,' I said once she'd gone.

Jocelin glared at me. 'C-confused? Not f-fully *compos mentis?* Apt to w-wander about?'

I grimaced. 'I had to say something. She would never have permitted us to share otherwise. Sister Benjamin is as unbendable as she is unbending. But you can't fault her competency. She's managed to keep this place going for the past twenty years despite having so few numbers and virtually no income. That takes some doing.'

'A f-formidable woman. B-but I think she may have met her m-match with the L-Lady Maude.'

'Yes,' I nodded with a wry smile. 'Wouldn't you like to be a fly on that wall when those two meet!'

We started unpacking our belongings.

'Speaking of our two companions, now that we've been with them a while, what do you make of them?'

'I don't th-think Lady Maude is all that she seems.'

'Yes, I'd come to a similar conclusion. She certainly isn't ill. At least, not as ill as she likes to pretend. Why do you suppose she's faking? Just to get a free ride to Lincoln?'

'There m-must be easier ways.'

'And that manservant of hers. Unusual for a noblewoman to have a male servant rather than a maid, don't you think? One so close to her own age, too.'

'I hope you're not intimating there m-may be more to their relationship than m-mistress and s-servant, Walter.'

'I don't know. But it is a little suspicious. Maybe Benjamin is right to insist on separate rooms.'

'She will have her w-work c-cut out if she tries.'

'That would indeed be a terrible thing,' I grinned. 'Truly terrible.'

Jocelin shook his head. 'You're a w-wicked person sometimes, Walter de Ixworth.'

I finished unpacking my meagre belongings and sat down on the bed.

'So we agree the lady isn't all she makes out to be. What about the boy? You were with him in the back of the wagon. What did you make of him?'

'His n-name is Gelyn. He speaks a s-strange dialect of French I'm not f-familiar with. He d-doesn't speak any English – at least, he pretends not to.'

'You don't sound very convinced.'

'It's d-difficult to be c-certain. From his intonation I th-thought he might be Welsh. S-so I t-tried some on him just to see.'

'I didn't know you spoke Welsh.'

'I d-don't. I just g-gabbled at him with a lot of ch's and sh's. He p-pretended to understand me. B-but he couldn't have done. I was s-speaking gibberish.'

'Nothing new there then,' I grinned.

What were we to make of them? A lady who is ill but isn't and a young man who is a servant but who clearly wasn't. The mystery deepened. And we were not able to quiz them further as neither appeared at supper. Lady M ate in her room and Gelyn never left her side. It was thus left to Jocelin and me to join the prioress at high table alone.

At least I managed to enter the dining hall by the correct door this time and not make a fool of myself as I had last time with Abbot Samson. Just as then, the nuns were already present waiting for us to arrive. I have to say I was shocked at how few in number there were – only four fully-fledged nuns and one novice. Maybe Angelina wasn't the only one to reject the new regime. I recognised Monica-Jerome instantly - you could hardly miss her with her prominent teeth. She managed a brief smile of recognition before Benjamin stood up and addressed the assembly:

'Sisters, we have the great good fortune to be able to welcome today two brothers from our mother house in Bury. Master Walter who some of you may remember from the last time he was here, and Dom Jocelin. I am sure you will all be delighted and honoured that they have chosen to stay with us. If any of you wishes to air any grievances or indeed, take advantage of their presence for confession, then I am sure they would be only too pleased to attend. And now, Brother Walter would like to say a few words to you,' whereupon she sat down.

Say a few words? This took me completely by surprise. I hadn't intended addressing the sisters. I looked down at the half dozen expectant faces all turned to me waiting for my pearls of wisdom.

I slowly stood up trying to summon something. 'Erm, well I…' I surveyed my audience, made a quick sign of the Cross, muttered, '*Dominus vobiscum* – enjoy your supper ladies,' and sat down again.

I thought I heard someone - Monica-Jerome I expect – giggle from the floor below. Benjamin looked livid but said nothing. We ate the rest of the meal in silence.

After supper I was able to intercept Monica-Jerome as we were leaving. She had hung back for the same reason:

'Dear Monica-Jerome,' I said taking both her hands in mine. 'It is good to see you again.'

'You too, brother,' she giggled. 'You haven't changed.'

'Neither have you.'

Despite the intervening fifteen years, she didn't look a day older than when we last met– not a wrinkle or a grey hair. Mind you, with her wimple tied so tightly around her face there wasn't really much of either to see.

'Mother Benjamin looked as though she just swallowed a wasp when you sat down.'

'Brave wasp if she did.'

She giggled again.

'How have you been? How is the school?'

At that her smile dropped. 'I no longer teach. Mother Benjamin thought I was too lenient with the girls. I refused to whip them. I'm the convent archivist now, though not a very good one. I get so muddled with all those lists,' she frowned.

'Would you like me to have a word with her?'

She shook her head. 'It would do no good. The reverend mother would not be dissuaded. I fear we must obey our superiors and be content with our lot as our founder, Saint Benedict, directed,' she sighed.

'Amen to that, sister.'

After supper Jocelin and I retired to our room to await the bell for compline. There was still no sign of Lady Maude or Gelyn, but then I wouldn't really expect them to join in one of our offices. In the chapel there was no sign of the prioress either - no doubt busy with other more important matters. However the next morning I was in for a shock. Jocelin and I had just finished loading up the wagon ready for the off and were waiting for our charges to appear. The entire troupe of nuns and novices - all seven of them - was there to see us off, including Benjamin who was sporting a large bruise over one eye. No prizes for guessing how she got it. I had to cover my mouth in case she saw me grinning.

'Why, Mother Superior,' I said forcing a frown of concern. 'Are you well? Have you had an accident?'

Her hand went to her eye. 'It is nothing. A cupboard door was left open.'

'Well I hope you punished the lax offender. That eye looks painful. Would you like me to prepare a poultice?'

'Thank you, no.'

I shrugged. 'As you wish.'

Just then Lady Maude and Gelyn appeared. Maude was looking stern. She kept her eyes fixed straight ahead as the pair of them clambered aboard the wagon and disappeared beneath the canvass without a word. When I turned back I saw that Benjamin had also vanished back inside the convent. Jocelin and I exchanged quizzical looks. It was Monica-Jerome who put me straight:

'Last night the prioress went to discuss something with your lady. It seems there was a difference of opinion on certain matters, but I have no idea what. I only heard the accompanying raised voices.' She giggled. 'We all did.'

'Who won the argument I wonder?'

'Can't you guess?' Monica beamed.

'Interesting. So we can rule out Gelyn as being *non compos mentis*.'

'I don't follow.'

I shook my head. 'Never mind. A private joke.'

Maude had suddenly shot up in my estimation. Anyone who can get the better of Benjamin deserved respect. I was only glad I hadn't yet got on the wrong side of the lady myself. But all that was about to change.

Chapter Four
COMING UP FOR AIR

We didn't see much of our passengers for the rest of that day both mistress and servant keeping out of sight beneath the canvass on the back of the wagon. That suited me fine. It was a warm sunny day and Jocelin joined me up on the driver's bench with the excuse that two pairs of eyes were better than one for keeping a lookout for brigands, though quite what use a blind man's eyes were was debatable. We stopped by a small brook at midday to eat and let the oxen drink. Jocelin and I ate our meal seated on the ground with our backs against the wheel while Maude and Gelyn remained under canvass. Soon we were off again. And so passed the second day.

Our next port of call was Lynn – or Bishop's Lynn I suppose I should call it after the town's one-time owner, Bishop Losinga, the founder of Norwich cathedral. Here we stayed at Saint Margaret's priory - quite a minor house with just a handful of monks. The prior there, Magnus, had been expecting us having been forewarned by Prior Herbert, but was a little at a loss to understand our purpose. I didn't understand it either so I was unable to enlighten him. The conversation over dinner was therefore a little stinted and made worse by Lady Maude who once again kept to her room feigning ill-health and requesting that her manservant remain with her. Prior Magnus was no more comfortable with this arrangement than Mother Benjamin had been, but once again the lady insisted.

'De la Haye,' he said scratching his beard. 'Don't I know that name?'

'My aunt is Lady Nicola de la Haye,' replied Maude. 'The chatelaine of Lincoln Castle.'

'Ah yes, of course,' nodded Magnus. 'Lady Nicola. A very capable lady.'

'And an influential one, in the spiritual as well as secular world.'

The prior recognised a veiled threat when he heard one.

'Indeed,' he nodded. 'Well, I suppose under the circumstances it will be all right just this once.'

Maude grunted and disappeared with Gelyn to their room. He nodded towards the door through which had Maude and Gelyn had exited.

'Quite a determined young lady.'

'Oh yes,' I agreed. 'I wouldn't want to tangle with her.'

'I'll bear it in mind.'

We settled down for a cosy chat and a cup of ale.

'So tell me,' said Magnus. 'How goes the war? We don't hear too much stuck up here at the end of the world. You're down in the thick of it in Suffolk. You must know.'

'I wouldn't say we know much more than you,' I replied. 'But as far as anyone can tell it's stalemate at the moment. At least, that's what I'm told – and hopefully it will remain so until Brother Jocelin and I have completed our task of delivering our charges and returned to Bury.'

'But it can't stay like that, surely? One side or the other must eventually get the upper hand. My money would be on the dauphin.'

At that Jocelin looked up. 'Isn't that a bit d-disloyal? S-surely we should all be ch-cheering for the king?'

'Oh, I do cheer for him - heartily. But cheering doesn't win battles. One has to face facts. The French are better equipped than us. They have more money and more men. The king's forces are split between the rebel barons on one side and those barons still loyal to King John on the other. Not many of them either, I have to say.'

'B-but the dauphin's f-forces are also split,' insisted Jocelin. 'Half in the s-south and h-half in the north with the k-king's men in between.' He made a cutting motion with his hand to demonstrate the point.

'Ah, but you are forgetting one vital factor,' said Magnus. 'King Henry is but a child.'

'A ch-child with a c-competent r-regency council acting for him,' Jocelin pointed out.

Magnus gave him a pitying look. 'Councils can't fight wars, brother. They soon start squabbling amongst themselves and instead of a horse you end up with a camel. To win a war you need bold and decisive action. That's why it's always better to have a single strong man at the top making the decisions.'

'L-like Prince L-Louis you mean?'

'Precisely.'

'B-but it is you who are f-forgetting that Pope Honorius has excommunicated all the r-rebels. That p-puts them in opposition to God. With G-God and the p-pope on Henry's side how can he l-lose? Or d-do you not believe in d-divine intervention, B-Brother P-Prior?'

'Of course I do. But so far the pope's words haven't had much effect, have they? Maybe God isn't listening,' he chuckled.

Jocelin took a sharp intake of breath. 'Brother Prior, that's bordering on the blasphemous! Henry is God's ch-chosen one, therefore he c-cannot f-fail.'

'If you say so,' smiled Magnus.

'I d-don't trust that man,' said Jocelin when we were alone again in our room. 'He sounds like a r-renegade to me.'

'Oh I shouldn't take too much notice of that. I think he just enjoys a good argument. I don't suppose he gets much opportunity stuck out here "at the end of the world".'

'End of the w-world!' scoffed Jocelin. 'It'll b-be the end of him if he d-doesn't learn to c-curb his t-tongue and show a little more l-l-loyalty.'

I wasn't going to argue with him. Magnus was generous enough to give us a bed and that was good enough for me.

Next on our itinerary was Saint Botolph's Town – or "Boston" as the locals call it. There were even fewer monks here than at Lynn. Prior Francis was was a totally different animal from Magnus. A much younger man, he had fewer qualms about letting Gelyn sleep in the same room as Lady Maude. I got the impression he wanted our stay to have as little fuss as possible - probably with good reason.

Bostonians have always been a rebellious bunch. At the start of the war they had been firm supporters of the rebel side and during King John's final retreat across the marshes they had refused to give him sanctuary. Hardly surprising really. With eighty monks, Bury would have felt the impact of the king and his entourage. A community as small as Saint Botolph's would never have survived. Whether it was this or because of their earlier affiliations, John had had to continue on to

Swineshead Abbey and thence to Newark where he died. As a result the priory had received the reprobation of the legate and for a while the entire house had been excommunicated. I imagined Prior Francis was still nervous as a result and didn't want the same thing to happen again.

'Do you think the king will win?' he asked nervously. 'The new king I mean. Henry.'

'Of c-course he'll w-win!' insisted Jocelin. 'With God on his side, how can he l-lose? The d-dauphin will give up and return to F-France. You m-mark my w-word!'

Francis nodded resignedly. 'I'm sure you're right.'

That was the summation of the conversation. Supper was eaten in silence. Later when we joined the other brothers for compline, Francis was notably absent.

'I don't trust that man,' Jocelin said.

'You said the same about Prior Magnus.'

'And d-do you w-wonder? These are d-dangerous times. Treachery is everywhere. We n-never know who our f-friends are from one day to the n-next. Francis was with the rebels when he thought they were w-winning. N-now he's with the king. How long will it be before he changes s-sides again?'

'Just until tomorrow morning would suit me.'

'You should t-take these things more seriously, Walter. What if we get our throats c-cut in the middle of the night?'

'Then you have my permission to tell me you told me so,' I grinned.

We managed to get through the night without our throats being cut. But next morning Jocelin was no happier.

'Did you h-hear them?'
'Who?'

'Th-those two n-next d-door.' He nodded towards Maude and Gelyn. 'I th-think M-Mother B-Benjamin was r-right to try to k-keep them apart.'

I glanced across at our two charges. They were in a corner laughing together in a very intimate way.

'I sleep like a log these days. Little wakes me.'

'I'm surprised you m-managed to sleep at all the r-racket they were m-making.'

'Why, what were they doing?'

'I d-don't kn-know, but it was chatter chatter all n-night long.'

'Well, if chatter was all they were doing.'

He frowned. 'It's the boy's morals I am concerned about, the l-lady clearly has none. S-so far we've ignored them. B-but they are young and we have a d-duty of c-care to their souls as well as their b-bodies.'

I sighed. 'What do you want me to do about it?'

'T-talk to them. Remind them of their ch-chastity.'

'Why don't you do it if you're that concerned?'

He grimaced. 'You're b-better at that sort of thing th-than I am. I'd only get t-tongue t-tied.'

'Moral lecturing is not something I do very often either. Hush now, Lady Maude's coming over.'

'Are we leaving today brother? Only time is pressing. I'd like to be on the road again as soon as possible. It's my aunt, you see. She is not long for this world and wishes to see me before she expires.'

'I thought *you* were the one who was ill and wished to see your aunt before *you* expired,' I smiled.

'Both.'

'We will be under way as soon as I've said farewell to our host and thanked him for his hospitality. You may wish to do the same.'

'I'll leave the etiquette side of things to you. Anything else before we get aboard?'

I shook my head. 'No no. You carry on. I'll only be a few moments.'

She grunted and went back to Gelyn.

Jocelin sidled up to me. 'C-coward!'

'Well you won't have to worry about her for much longer,' I told him. 'Our next stop is Lincoln. Then we can bid farewell to them both and return to Bury.'

And so we were off again for the final leg of our journey. There should just be just enough time to make it to Lincoln in daylight, assuming no mishaps. So far our journey had been remarkably uneventful. Of course it couldn't last.

Chapter Five
HIDDEN TALENTS

I know I said I'd tackle Lady Maude about her relationship with her "manservant" but the truth is I don't like bad feeling if I can possibly avoid it. We were manacled together for just a few more hours and I didn't want to spend them in silent resentment. Besides, so far there was only the *suspicion* of inappropriate goings-on, no actual proof. At least, that's what I told myself. Still, it would do no harm to keep a discreet eye on things to which end I asked Jocelin to remain in the back of the wagon - *pour décourager les autres* as the French never say. In any case, I had enough to do navigating a safe course along the highway without worrying about what was going on in the wagon behind me. As I had suspected, the road here was in a terrible state, potholes and deep ruts everywhere – another consequence of the civil war, I supposed. I needed all my wits about me if we were to progress safely. A broken axle out here in the middle of nowhere was no laughing matter. My mind being on other things, therefore, I gave little thought to our two guests and their machinations.

However, after a while I did become aware that it had gone quiet in the back. I could usually hear Jocelin or Lady Maude's voices but now there was silence. I tried calling out but got no reply. Where had they gone? Had they all fallen asleep?

Eventually curiosity got the better of me and I turned around to see what was happening. What I saw shocked and horrified me. Lady M and Gelyn were locked in what I can only describe as a lover's embrace with Jocelin looking on wide-eyed and staring back at me in silent horror.

'What the -?' I began but got no further. There was a bump in the road followed by a sickening crunch. The front of the wagon dropped violently and we came to a sudden halt nearly propelling me from my seat. A quick glance over the side of the wagon confirmed my worst fears: the right front wheel had gone down into one of the ruts I'd been trying so hard to avoid. We were stuck fast.

I turned around angrily in my seat. 'What in God's name are you playing at, woman!'

She looked back equally angrily: 'How dare you speak to me like that!'

'I'll speak to you how I wish, madam, when I see such goings on. I don't know what the social mores are in the part of the world you come from, but this is England and that sort of behaviour is not tolerated here – at least, not on my ox-wagon.'

I was aware that I was sounding pompous but I couldn't help it. I was so shocked by the sheer blatancy of their behaviour that for once I was lost for words. Not so the lady:

'You forget my condition, *mon frère.* The surface of the road aggravates it. Occasionally I need a little support. What you saw – whatever you *think* you saw - Gelyn was cradling me against the tawdriness of your English roads and the discomfort of your driving - which, I might add, is at times reckless to the point of being dangerous. And clearly he was right to do so.' She nodded towards the sunken wheel.

I glanced at the wheel then back at her: 'That wouldn't have happened, madam, if you hadn't been doing … whatever it was you were doing.'

'And it wouldn't have been necessary at all if you had been concentrating on the road instead of ogling me.'

My jaw dropped open. '*Ogling* you? I was not ogling you!' I turned to Jocelin: 'Brother, you saw what was going on. Tell the lady.'

Jocelin said nothing.

'Jocelin?'

He squirmed uncomfortably. 'I h-had my eyes c-closed, Walter. I d-didn't s-see anything.'

I couldn't believe my ears. Keeping an eye on Maude and Gelyn had been his idea and now he was trying to get out of it. But why was I surprised? That was Jocelin all over, always squeamish about intimacy. Even the mildest handshake had him wincing with embarrassment.

'Well brother?' smirked the lady. 'Are you just going to sit there with your mouth opening closing like a fish or are you going to dig us out?'

I snapped my mouth shut and glowered at Jocelin, but what could I do? I angrily climbed down off the wagon to examine the wheel. It wasn't broken, God be thanked, but getting the wagon back onto the road was going to be a Herculean task. It had sunk into the rut nearly up to the axle and no amount of coaxing could get our two oxen to move us. We were going to have to uncouple them and somehow lift the wagon ourselves.

'And that means all of you,' I growled at the others. 'Lady as well as men.'

Maude gave a haughty laugh. 'What? You expect me in my condition to help pull a wagon out of a ditch? I think not!'

Her condition! There was nothing wrong with her – nothing physical at any rate.

'Madam, if you want to get to Lincoln today you're going to have to.'

She shook her head firmly. 'Out of the question!'

'Then we will remain here,' I said folding my arms.

'Suits me.' She folded hers.

We glared at each other like a couple of squabbling infants neither willing to give way. Eventually Jocelin's was the voice of reason:

'Surely the th-three of us men can d-do it between us, Walter?' he said to me quietly.

I continued to glower at him. 'Oh, so *now* you have something to say, brother.'

He blushed, shamefaced. 'There are only s-so many things anyone can s-see in a lifetime, Walter, and I am r-rapidly using up m-my q-quota. Why else do you th-think I am l-losing m-my eyesight? I h-have to p-preserve what I h-have l-left.'

I was speechless. 'Jocelin, you -!'

But he was right of course. I mean about the wagon. It would have to be us three men. I doubted if Maude would have been much use in any case. With as little grace as I could muster, therefore, I uncoupled Hyperion and Helios from their harnesses and together Jocelin, Gelyn and I put our shoulders against the wheel. But we barely managed to move it more than a few inches before it rolled back again. At one point it nearly went over Gelyn's foot. I yelled at him to move it which he did just in the nick of time.

'So, you do understand English when it suits you.'

'A little,' he agreed shyly.

We tried again but to no avail.

'It's no good. It's still to heavy. We will have to unload.'

Once again the lady refused. 'No no no, you will damage my property. My baggage stays on the wagon.'

'It was probably your baggage that caused us to flounder in the first place. What have you got in them anyway? King John's lost jewels?'

This time it was Gelyn who had a quiet word with his mistress. At last she relented and allowed us to unload her trunks fussing over each one in turn like a mother hen. Even then she refused to get off the wagon herself. I couldn't be bothered arguing with her and let her be.

It took us a while but we managed to empty the wagon of the dozen heavy bags and trunks. It would all have to go back on again of course once the wheel was free – assuming it ever was. The whole process was going to add hours to our journey. It was then just as I didn't think things couldn't get any worse, they did: four horsemen suddenly appeared on the slope above us. My heart sank. Were these the renegade soldiers I had long feared?

The lead rider snorted his destrier to a halt before us. I have to admit he didn't *look* like a bandit. But then what do bandits look like? They don't usually leave witnesses to describe them. He walked his horse slowly around the wagon before coming back to me again.

'Having trouble, brother?'

'As you see, my son. The roads in these parts…' I shook my head and rolled my eyes to heaven despairingly. 'Thank goodness you've arrived in time to help us.'

He continued to study me coldly. 'You the one in charge?'

'Walter de Ixworth, from the abbey of Saint Edmundsbury in Suffolk. And you are?'

He didn't reply but nodded to Jocelin. 'You?'

'J-J-J-,' Jocelin began. 'J-J-J-. J-J-J-J -'

'Jocelin de Brackland,' I answered for him. 'From the same abbey. And you haven't answered my question.'

He still didn't. But I'd decided by now these were not bandits but troops of some description though what they were doing out here miles from any town or castle was anybody's guess.

'How many?' he asked.

I was about to answer "four" but out of the corner of my eye I could see Jocelin frantically flashing three fingers at me.

'F-f-f - three,' I managed at last.

The man raised a speculative eyebrow. 'You seem to have developed a stammer too, brother.'

'It's catching.'

I glowered at Jocelin. What was he up to?

The man then signalled to one of the other men who slid smartly off his horse, leapt up onto the side of the wagon and pulled back the canvass. As he did so he whistled through his teeth.

'Sssssh! Well now, what have we here?'

I spun round and was shocked to see Lady Maude lying in the back with a veil covering her face. I could feel my pulse quicken. I knew only too well what can happen to women in situations like this. Much as I disliked the woman I wouldn't have wished that on her.

'That is the Lady Maude de la Haye,' I said quickly. 'A very important lady - and a very sick one. We are on our way to Lincoln to consult with her doctors.'

Right on cue Maude began to moan. It was a good act. It almost convinced me. She "accidentally" let slip her veil to expose her face which had become deathly white, her eyes blackened and her lips blue. For once she really did look genuinely ill. But where was Gelyn? He seemed to have vanished. Was he now adding cowardice to his list of iniquities?

Maude put out a shaky hand towards the trooper. 'Pierre? Is that you Pierre?'

The startled man jumped back down from the wagon.

'Captain,' he said quietly. 'I think we should go.' He lowered his voice further. 'Lepers!'

Captain, eh? So I was right, they were soldiers. He leaned forward on his horse to get a better look for himself.

Maude opened her eyes to him. 'Pierre? Is that you?'

'Who's Pierre?' he asked.

'Her husband,' I replied. 'He died of the same affliction. It's a tragic tale.'

'Perhaps we should kill them all,' said the trooper unsheathing his dagger.

'Do that and you will be cursed in this world and the next,' I said to him. 'Can you not see the woman is touched?'

Maude moaned again.

The captain jerked his head and the trooper re-sheathed his dagger and returned to his mount.

'You shouldn't be on the road, brother. These are dangerous times.' He started to turn his horse's head.

'Eh, before you go,' I said nodding to the moribund wheel. 'Could you, erm…?'

He signalled to his other two men who dismounted and between them managed to lift the wagon back up onto the road. I was genuinely grateful.

'Thank you, captain. You've saved us half a day.'

'Like I said, brother. Dangerous times. Get to where you are going and quickly.'

'Oh, we will. And thank you again.'

With one last look around he nodded to his men and they all galloped off.

'Phew! That was c-close,' said Jocelin watching them go. 'Wh-what do you suppose they wanted?'

'What these people always want,' Maude replied sitting up and wiping the make-up from her face. 'Money of course.'

I shook my head. 'Not this time. They were looking for something – or some*one*.'

'Whatever it was they didn't get it, thanks to my quick thinking.'

'Yes, I admit you were good,' I told her. 'You've obviously done this sort of thing before.'

'So were you. Maybe we should work together.'

I thought about that for a moment before shaking my head. 'I don't think so.'

Once the coast was clear Gelyn emerged from beneath the folds of bedding where he'd been hiding.

'Ha!' I said. 'Gallant to the last.'

He continued to pretend not to understand me but I knew now that he did.

'Right,' I said to Jocelin. 'You re-harness Helios and Hyperion while our disappearing friend and I reload the baggage. The sooner we get away from here the better.'

Once the baggage was safely stowed I had one final look over the wagon. There didn't seem to be any major damage though you can never tell. I had to pray that the wheel and the axle remained solid.

'Given up chaperoning our guests, brother?' I said to Jocelin once he had rejoined me on the driving seat.

'There d-doesn't seem much p-point my b-being back there. They d-do whatever they want in front of me.'

'I'm surprised you even noticed. Eyes shut indeed!'

He grimaced. 'Who w-were those m-men do you think? They l-looked like real s-soldiers to me.'

'They were. But whose? The rebels or the king's?'

'D-does it matter? Once they r-realise they've b-been duped they'll b-be back.'

'By which time, failing any more mishaps, we'll be at Lincoln's gates.'

'G-God w-willing,' said Jocelin.

But we were not quite done yet. Suddenly from the behind me there was a blood-curdling cry. I thought for a moment we'd gone down another pothole and rapidly pulled the wagon to a halt again.

'Whoa, Hyperion!' I looked at Jocelin. 'Now what?'

Lady M clambered noisily across the back of the wagon.

'What's happened?' I asked her. 'Are you in pain again?'

She glared at me. 'First you accuse me of impropriety with my manservant. Then you force me to submit to your will. Now you conspire to rob me!'

I frowned. 'Rob you? What are you talking about?'

'My jewels! They are gone!'

'I thought that was a joke. Who could ...?'

Even before the words were fully out of my mouth I knew the answer. Of course, it had to have been the trooper who searched the wagon. He may have been afraid of catching a nasty disease, but not enough to overcome his love of gold.

Lady Maude had come to the same conclusion. 'We must go back and find this man.'

'Don't be absurd! We only just got away with our lives. If we went back we'd definitely be murdered. For the sake of a few trinkets?'

'They are not trinkets! I wouldn't be surprised if you haven't colluded with those men to rob me!'

I shook my head sadly. 'I'm beginning to think you really are touched in the head.'

'I demand you turn this wagon around this instant!'

'And I'm telling you no.'

I was about to turn away again when she did something totally unexpected. She slapped my face - hard. I was speechless. I haven't been struck like that since I was a child. Jocelin must have been shocked too for he gasped. It was a cathartic moment. She may be a woman of nobility accustomed to having her every whim obeyed, but this was different. Something else had crept into her voice – an arrogance I hadn't heard there before.

At last I found my voice again: 'Who are you really and what is the true purpose for your journey? You're not ill and Gelyn isn't your manservant. I think it's time you told us the truth.'

Her eyes were on fire. She opened her mouth to say something but then closed it again. Without another word she returned to the rear of the wagon and pulled the canvass partition aggressively between us.

The delay over the wheel meant there was not enough time to get to Lincoln that day. We were going to have to have an unscheduled overnight stop at the side of the road. Dangerous under any circumstances, but we had no choice, there was nowhere to put up for the night. We just had to pray that there were no more marauding soldiers or brigands in the area. And our prayers were answered. We passed the night undisturbed other than by the snuffling of night creatures and were moving again the following day as soon as it was light. At least the weather was with us. Saturday the 20th of May dawned sunny, dry and warm. Portents for a peaceful end to our odyssey? I hoped so.

Chapter Six
AN OX IN THE BARGATE

The last few miles of our journey were traversed in silence, a situation which suited me fine. I was seething with anger over that slap in the face and was in no hurry to speak to her. At least all pretence had finally gone even if I didn't yet know the truth of who she was or why she was so desperate to get to Lincoln.

'Maybe she's right,' I said to Jocelin. 'Maybe we should go back - not to look for Maude's jewels but all the way to Bury. Abandon the entire project.'

'And wh-what would happen if we d-did?' he asked. 'The lady would simply get s-some other poor wretches to accompany her, P-Prior Herbert would p-punish us for disobedience, and – m-most importantly of all - we would n-never know the real p-purpose of Lady Maude's journey.'

'Huh! Do we even want to know?'

'Y-yes. You do.'

He was right of course. In spite of everything I did want to know the truth of who Maude really was and why she was so determined to get to Lincoln. We wouldn't have too long to wait now to find out.

Not knowing Lincoln at all, I assumed the best route in would be to continue the way we had been coming along Ermine Street and up into the town. We could see the town wall up ahead on the bluff rising above us but the road down here was hemmed in on all sides. To our left was a river and to our right some kind of canal which cut across our path. In front of us and bridging the canal was a gate through which we would have to pass if we were to get any closer to the town. This I later discovered is called the Bargate, and "bar" is a very good word for it. The entire contraption seemed to be designed to thwart any movement across the canal.

Let me describe this evil contrivance for you: it consisted of a swing barrier with portcullis and drawbridge, counterweights and beams. I'd never come across anything quite so elaborate before and stood scratching my head in bewilderment as to how it operated. It seemed you had to raise one barrier in order to get on which action then lowered another barrier. Then in order to get off again you had to raise the second barrier which lowered the first thus restricting the available space to one person at a time. There was no way that I could see we were going to get the wagon through without dismantling it and passing through each element at a time. Needless to say Maude was no help.

'You should have gone around another way.'

'That's easy to say now. I didn't know this infernal contraption was here - did you?'

'No of course I didn't. But I'm not surprised. You English, you make everything so difficult.'

'Maybe it was designed to keep out undesirables.'

'Like who precisely?'

I didn't say.

I still wasn't sure what to do. It reminded me of that old riddle about how to cross a river with a chicken, a fox and a bag of wheat without one eating the other. I could see I was going to have to go back and forth across the bridge several times before we were all through.

I decided in the end that Hyperion should go through first being the most docile of our two beasts of burden. He could be left alone on the far side while Jocelin loaded Helios. Unfortunately we didn't get that far. Having uncoupled Hyperion we managed to get him into the gate all right, but no further. Somehow he got stuck between the barriers and try as we might we could not move him either forward or back. Until he did neither we nor anyone else was going any further.

Lady Maude was soon tutting again.

'Useless! Absolutely useless!'

'If you think you can do better, madam, you're welcome to try.'

'You're the one in charge. You sort it out.'

I tried again to coax Hyperion forward, to no avail. Fortunately just at that moment a shepherd appeared guiding a sheep with a stick.

I went over to him. 'Ah, there you are my man. I wonder, can you help us? I know this sounds ridiculous but we can't seem to get through the gate,' I laughed nonchalantly.

'That's because there be a ox blocking it,' he said helpfully.

'Indeed. Do you have any suggestions?'

'Aye. You need to get the ox off first.'

'Thank you. I've tried. He's stuck fast.'

'Not surprised. Gate weren't built for oxes. 'Twas built for folks. Only one, see? One at a time. That's the rule.'

'Yes, I think I managed to work that much out for myself.'

'Should'na let that critter onto the bridge,' he said shaking his head. 'That were your mistake.'

'Well he's there now. The thing is how do we get him off and us across it?'

'You won't. Not with a ox in it.'

'Why are you wasting time with this fool?' said Maude impatiently. 'He's obviously an imbecile.'

'Please madam,' I said to her. 'You're not helping.'

She snorted and marched off.

'Feisty en't she?' grinned the shepherd. 'I likes a woman wi' spirit.'

'Is there another way into the town?' I asked him.

The man looked bemused. 'You want to get into the town?'

'We do.'

'Today?'

'Yes.'

He shrugged. 'In that case you have to go round across the marsh to the castle gate.'

I squinted. 'How far is that?'

'A mile, mebbe more. It be steep, mind. You won't drag that four-wheeler up it with just that one critter.'

I frowned. 'Is there no other road we can use?'

'Oh, there be plenty of rids.'

'Good.'

'But none that go into the town.'

Maude was right. The man was an imbecile. I thanked him for his help and he went on his way still prodding his sheep with his stick.

Maude glared at me. 'A mile? You expect me to walk a mile? In my condition?'

'Madam, you're no iller than I am.' I sighed. 'All right. For the sake of a bit of peace you can ride in the back – but if it's as steep as our friend says you'll have to get off and push like everybody else.'

'Hmph!'

'Wh-what about Hyperion?' said Jocelin. 'We c-can't just l-leave him.'

'We have no choice. Just hope someone comes along who knows how that infernal contraption works and lets him out. We'll come back for him later.'

'If he doesn't end up as someone's l-lunch first.'

We trudged across the wet meadows. The shepherd was right. The land rose suddenly and very steeply so that Helios, shorn of his companion, was unable to drag the cart by himself. I applied the brake.

'It's no good. We'll have to walk. Everyone off – and no arguments this time.'

'I shan't forget this,' Maude growled clambering down.

With the wagon now lighter again we were able to make better progress. Even so it was still hard going. The light was slowly coming up across the meadows but there was no sign of anyone in the fields. Even the birds seemed to have left the sky. There was an eerie silence about the place.

'I d-don't like this,' frowned Jocelin. 'S-something's wrong.'

We could see the outline of the castle looming above us. It looked intimidating but at the same time somehow reassuring. I was longing to get inside and put an end to all this. Then as we rounded the final bend in the hill we came across another sight that fair took my breath away.

I stopped dead in my tracks. 'Good God!'

Spread out before us were hundreds of men, horses, wagons. It looked like an entire army was assembled just below the crest of the hill, the steel of their armour glinting in the early morning sunlight and steam coming from the backs of the animals. No wonder that shepherd queried our intention of going into Lincoln. He must have known all this was here. Why on earth didn't he tell us?

A knight spotted us and galloped over.

'What are you doing here, brother?' he demanded angrily.

'I er -'

But before I could answer he grabbed the hood of my robe and pushed me to the ground.

'Aow!' I yelled. 'You've broken my arm!'

'Lucky it wasn't your neck!'

More soldiers arrived. They quickly took charge of the wagon hastily leading it away while another grabbed hold of Jocelin. But where were Maude and Gelyn? Of course. At the first sign of trouble they'd disappeared back inside the wagon. The wagon with our two companions went one way while Jocelin and I went another.

'Wait!' I protested. 'You can't -'

'Shut it!' barked the knight.

There was no arguing with him. I had no idea what was happening or where we were going as I half ran, half stumbled down the slope propelled by our captors.

Chapter Seven
THE ONCE AND FUTURE KING

We found ourselves inside a military field tent. I say "tent". I've been in houses that were less substantial. It was a vast edifice and carefully guarded. Set up in the middle was a table around which stood three burly men dressed in armour. But these were no ordinary soldiers. Two looked like grandees of some kind while the third, incongruously, wore a priest's tonsure. I had no idea who they were although the oldest of them looked vaguely familiar. He was a giant of a man standing head and shoulders above the rest. He too was armoured but he looked far too old to be a fighting man. I felt sure I'd seen him before but I couldn't think where.

Laid out on the table between them was a crudely-drawn map of a town – Lincoln presumably - which they had evidently been studying before Jocelin and were bundled in. It was the tonsured man who spoke first:

'Well now, what have we here?'

'I could ask the same thing,' I replied before I could stop myself. That brought a sharp slap of rebuke on the back of my head from the guard who was holding me.

'Mind your manners.'

'I should answer my lord bishop's question,' the giant said. 'If you want to keep your head, that is.'

Did he say *bishop*? That at least explained the tonsure. But why was a bishop dressed like a soldier?

'Sir, forgive me, but with my arms thrust up behind me like this the blood is cut off to the brain and I'm finding it somewhat difficult to think. I'm sure he's broken my arm.'

'I haven't broken it,' said the guard. 'Yet.'

That brought a slight smile to the giant's lips. He signalled to the guards holding us to release us – much to my relief.

'Well?' said the giant.

'Brother Walter de Ixworth,' I replied rubbing my wrists. 'And this is Brother Jocelin de Brackland. We are monks of Saint Edmund's Abbey in Suffolk.'

Jocelin gave a slight bob of his head.

'What are monks doing in the middle of a battle field?' growled the bishop.

'I didn't realise we were.'

'Really? What did you think it was out there? A May dance?'

'My lords,' interrupted the third man. 'We don't have time for this. They are clearly spies. Let me run them through have done with it.' He made to draw his sword.

'Spies don't generally turn up on wagons,' said the giant putting out a restraining hand. 'No, they are what they say they are. Monks of Saint Edmund's.'

'How can you be so sure?'

'Because I've met them before. This one at any rate,' he said indicating me. 'At the abbey in Bury.'

'Thank you, my lord,' I said not without relief. 'But I'm afraid you have the advantage of me.'

'Then allow me to introduce you.' He pointed to the tonsured man first. 'This is my lord Peter des Roches, the bishop of Winchester. The gentleman who nearly ran you through is the earl of Salisbury. And I …' he smiled. 'I'm the one asking the questions.'

'That still doesn't answer *my* question,' said the bishop. 'Why are they here? God rot them, they've probably given us away!'

'I think our presence was already known, my lord. Four hundred knights and two hundred bowmen are difficult to keep secret.'

I was aghast. 'So many?'

The earl looked up. 'You see? I told you. Spies.'

'We are not spies,' I said irritably. 'We are monks.'

'Then tell us why are you here,' said the giant.

I took a deep breath. 'We are on our way to Lincoln Castle. To visit the chatelaine there, Lady Nicola de la Haye.'

The earl snorted. 'The hell you are!'

'What Earl William means,' said the giant amiably, 'is that Lady Nicola is a little busy at present. Not exactly receiving visitors, if you take my meaning. She's holed up in the castle under siege.'

'Under siege from whom?'

'From the French of course,' said the earl. 'Who do you think?'

'But I understood the French were far to the south of here. We've just come from that direction. We saw no Frenchmen – did we Jocelin?'

Jocelin shook his head rapidly from side to side grinning like a frightened baboon.

'That's good hearing at least,' nodded the giant.

'If it's true,' growled the earl.

'Their compatriots are inside the town,' explained the giant. 'Lady Nicola has been gallantly keeping them and their rebel allies at bay for us for the past year, and we three gentlemen have come to relieve her – with the help of our four hundred knights and two hundred bowmen of course,' he added with a smile.

'Meaning a battle?' I said.

'That's the general idea.'

I was horrified. Memories of the carnage I'd witnessed at Fornham came flooding back to me.

'Oh, but that means blood will be spilt.'

'Unless you know of another way of slicing a man in two,' said the bishop.

'Let me explain,' said the giant. 'You see, the king's enemies -'

'You mean the French,' interrupted the earl.

'- at the moment they are split. Half their army are in the south, the other half are here, within Lincoln's walls. Our job is to winkle them out. If we don't and they link up with those in the south then England is lost. It's as simple as that.'

'Can't you just get them to surrender? Surely once they see how many men you have they will.'

'We've tried but for some reason they are reluctant to come out.'

'Aye,' said the earl. 'Afraid they'll get thrashed!'

Just then there was a distant crash followed by the sound of cheering.

The giant raised a finger. 'You hear that? That's the French *perrièrre*. It's a sort of giant catapult that lobs boulders as big as a man's head. Every time they release it another section of the castle wall comes down. Pretty soon they'll have breached it entirely and once they do that we might as well pack up and go home. So you see, my friend, we don't have a lot of choice in the matter. We have to act now if we are to save Lady Nicola - and England.'

'Why are we wasting time explaining the rudiments of war to these clerics?' growled the earl. 'We should be already mounted.'

'My lord Salisbury is right,' said the bishop. 'We should get moving.'

They started picking up their weapons, but before they could leave we were interrupted by more raised voices outside the tent:

'Take your hands off me you filthy English *pig!*'

'God save us, what now?' growled the earl.

Inwardly I groaned too. I recognised the voice and I could guess what was coming. A heavily armoured soldier then entered the tent pushing a struggling Lady Maude and Gelyn before him.

'I found these two hiding on the wagon, my lord,' he said sucking blood from his hand. 'This one I think is a cat judging by her teeth and claws.'

'We were not hiding, you oaf!' said Maude slapping the man on his breastplate. 'And you're lucky I didn't bite your hand off!'

The earl guffawed: 'Ha! Maybe we should launch this one at the French. Worth two *perrièrres* wouldn't you say?'

The giant turned to Maude: 'Who are you and why were you hiding?'

'I just told you. I was not hiding!'

'I can tell you who she is,' I sighed. 'She's the Lady Maude de la Haye, niece to Lady Nicola. She's the reason we're here. She's come to visit her aunt. She's also very ill – even if she doesn't look it.'

'I didn't know Lady Nicola had a niece,' said the earl.

'She doesn't,' growled the bishop.

'Is that right?' asked the giant. 'Are you Lady Nicola's niece?'

Maude smirked. 'No I'm not.'

Inwardly I groaned again. What was she playing at now?

'Then who are you really?'

She raised her chin, drew back her shoulders and held herself regally erect. 'I am Eleanor, daughter of Duke Geoffrey of Brittany. And this,' she indicated Gelyn, 'is my brother Arthur. That's right my lords, the *Prince* Arthur, lost these past fourteen years but now returned and ready to reclaim his rightful place on the throne of England.'

At this, Gelyn stepped forward and held out his hand for homage. '*Enchanté, mes seigneurs.*'

For a moment there was not a sound to be heard other than the distant crash of the *perrièrre,* unless you count my jaw hitting the ground. I didn't know whether to laugh or cry. We all just stared at the couple. Was this some kind of joke? Princess Eleanor? And Prince Arthur? Really?

At last the giant spoke: 'Are you, indeed? And I am Neptune, monarch of the seas.'

'Ha!' chuckled the earl.

But Maude wasn't laughing. She was deadly serious. She looked the giant straight in the eyes.

'No you're not. You're William Marshal, the Earl Regent.'

I slapped a metaphorical hand to my brow. Of course! That's where I'd seen him before. William Marshal. He was at Bury Abbey when King John visited in 1199. That's how he knew me. He looked different back then of course. He wasn't dressed in a suit of armour for one thing. His beard was also black, not grey as it was now. Already in those days he was a major influence in the land having served all the kings back to Henry II. But now he was Regent of England, the single most powerful man in the land. And I had just been crossing verbal swords with him. Worse, if Maude and Gelyn really were who she said they were then I had also been fighting with two princes of the blood royal. God, what had I done?

'You're remarkably well-informed,' the Marshal said to Maude.

'More than that, my lord. We have come to relieve you of your command and demand that you defer immediately to our authority.'

'*Our* authority?' asked the Marshal.

'I mean my brother's.'

The earl of Salisbury snorted with contempt: 'Surely you don't believe any of this tosh, William?'

The Marshal didn't reply. Fortunately he didn't have to. Outside there came the sound of more cheering but much closer this time and then a messenger rushed in. Seeing so many people he stopped abruptly but looked anxiously at the Marshal barely able to contain himself.

'What is it John? What's happened?'

'The earl of Chester, my lord. He has broken through. The north gate is down.'

'By God it is!' said Lord Salisbury thumping the table.

'William, we must go!' said the bishop jumping up. 'Now!'

Suddenly everyone was making for the exit at once.

'Sir, sir!' shouted a servant. 'Your helm!'

So intent had the Marshal been to leave that he'd forgotten to put on his helmet. He reluctantly came back and waited while the servant laced him up.

Maude was looking at him expectantly. 'Well, my lord?'

The Marshal frowned. 'We'll continue this later.'

'Hm!' she nodded.

'What do you want me to do with them in the meantime?' asked the guard.

'Take them away and guard them well. No – better still, give them into the care of Lady Nicola.'

'And the monks?'

He thought for a moment. 'They can go.'

So saying, William Marshal, earl of Pembroke and Regent of England, stepped out of the tent – and into destiny.

Part Two

IN LINCOLN TOWN

Chapter Eight
LINCOLN FAIR

Jocelin sat down heavily on one of the vacated benches and wiped the sweat from his face with a rag. 'Who w-would have thought it?' he kept saying. 'Gelyn a p-prince, and Maude a p-princess. And we h-had them b-both on our w-wagon!' He shook his head in amazement. 'Who would have th-thought it?'

But I wasn't thinking about it. I was more interested in the map left on the table. I studied it for a few minutes trying to get my bearings.

'Come on!' I said to him at last.

He looked at me in alarm. 'Where are we g-going?'

'To the castle.'

'Wh-what? After everything the M-Marshal just s-said about it?'

'You don't want to miss all the fun, do you?'

'Yes. N-no.' He frowned. 'I th-thought you d-didn't l-like war?'

'I don't. But we're doing no good here. Maybe inside the castle we can be of help.'

'H-help to do wh-what?'

'I don't know. But we can't stay here and do nothing.'

Outside hundreds of foot soldiers and knights on horseback were already charging up the slope towards the town walls and yelling "For God and the Marshal!"

at the tops of their voices. Some were hurling missiles, some were raising assault ladders, but most were piling in through the west gate just north of the castle. It was impossible for Jocelin and me to try to get in amongst them so we made instead for the castle's own gate. This was the route our crossbowmen were taking and we went after them.

Once inside the castle we followed them up onto the castle ramparts looking down into the town. I have to admit that despite my misgivings it was thrilling to be there. I could feel my heart racing and not just because I was breathless from running up so many flights of steps. Everywhere down below was noise, chaos and confusion. Men were running, horses were charging, banners flying.

And so the battle that would become known as Lincoln Fair began and it was surely not at all what the rebels and their French allies had been anticipating. Like everyone else they had thought the town impregnable behind its walls never dreaming the royalists would be able to get in. No doubt they were remembering what happened the last time Lincoln was attacked seventy-six years earlier during the Anarchy. Then it was King Stephen who held the town when a large enemy force arrived at the gates. Stephen took the fatal decision to go out and meet them on the battlefield. It was a risky gamble which he lost and was himself captured as a result.

The French and their rebel allies were determined not to make the same mistake this time preferring to remain secure within the town. They had sufficient stocks of food and could last out a long siege. The royalists on the other hand were camped out in the open air. The country for miles around the town had long been cleared of any shelter and anything that might be useful to a besieging army. Even the wells had been poisoned. If sickness and the bloody flux didn't get them, they calculated, starvation would.

At least, that was the rebel hope. They certainly hadn't been anticipating a full-on assault within hours of the royalists arriving. But then they hadn't reckoned on Lady Nicola de la Haye. The rebels thought they had the main north gate of the town well covered, but there was also a west gate that they knew nothing about and which had been hidden for decades beneath the town ramparts. For the past year Lady Nicola had been carefully protecting this gate picking off any rebels who came too close to investigate. But when the earl of Chester broke through the north gate Lady Nicola immediately flung it open. Royalist soldiers were now pouring into the town from two sides at once.

From our vantage point up on the castle battlements Jocelin and I could see all this unfolding below us. The rebels and their French allies had been taken completely by surprise by the speed and ferocity of the assault and fell back in disarray. So fast had the onslaught been that few rebels knew what was happening. An early casualty was the French perrièrre master. Thinking the knight who was descending upon him was one of his own, he carried on casually loading his infernal machine in order to have another shot at the castle only to have his head lopped off with a single sword stroke. His lifeless body then toppled into his machine releasing the mechanism so that the last thing he did on this earth was to launch his own head against the castle wall - to the cheers of our arbalestriers watching from above.

And that wasn't the only piece of farce. To add to the mayhem our crossbowmen on the castle ramparts had been ordered to target the rebel horses down below. Not a pleasant thing to witness but it had the desired effect.

As their horses fell beneath them the knights were quickly reduced from cavalry to mere foot-soldiers, and knights on foot make clumsy infantrymen. Encumbered by their armour and the narrow streets they could not manoeuvre and made easy pickings for our lighter-armoured troops. Seeing their confusion the man in charge of our bowmen, a mercenary leader called Fawkes de Bréauté, rushed out of the castle to take hostages. But he was too eager and was himself captured and had to be rescued by his own men.

And so the battle raged. Slowly the French were driven back towards the cathedral in front of which was a cemetery. In the mêlée, graves were trampled and the bones of those buried in the cemetery were being disinterred so that the dead themselves seemed to be rising up to fight. But the rebels were soon joining them in eternity as our men systematically wore them down.

By now my initial thrill had given way to revulsion as I saw the reality of warfare. Limbs were being severed, bellies ripped open and men were slipping on the gore of their comrades on the cobblestones. The screams of the injured were becoming too much to bear. At last I could stand it no longer.

'Come on!' I said to Jocelin.

'N-now where are we going?'

'Down.'

He gasped. 'Down there? Are you m-mad? We'll be k-killed!'

'Others are already being killed. Show some backbone! What are you, man or mouse?'

'M-m-m-m-m…'

I didn't wait to hear the answer, I was already half-way down the stairs. Enemy or not these men were dying and as a priest and physician I knew my duty.

By now most of the fighting had moved away from the castle but there were still some stragglers and we were nearly thwarted even before we started. As we rounded one corner we were brought to a sudden halt by a band of rebel soldiers all with weapons drawn. As soon as they saw us they charged. There was no time to run or hide. We were moments away from being cut to ribbons.

But then something extraordinary happened. As suddenly as they started the men stopped dead in their tracks. They dropped their weapons and started dancing – yes *dancing,* hopping from one leg to the other, whooping and pulling faces. I couldn't believe what I was seeing. Was I dreaming?

'T-triboli,' said Jocelin.

I frowned. 'Trib-what?'

'Triboli. Three-pronged t-traps. Look!'

He picked one up from the ground to show me. It was like a piece of the children's game of five-stones. Except these weren't toys. They had vicious metal spikes sticking out at all angles so that however they fell one spike always stood vertically proud. Tread on one of these and you too would be hopping mad. Dozens had been scattered about the street to thwart any charge. And they worked. You could stop an army in its tracks with a field strewn with these. They gave us just the time we needed to escape.

'Quick!' said Jocelin. 'B-back the way we c-came!'

We rushed back round the corner only to run headlong into more trouble. A rebel knight, splendidly decked out in gleaming silver armour levelled his lance at us. This time I was certain we were done for. But before he could start his charge a gang of royalist troops jumped out of hiding waving their arms in the air and hollering. The knight's startled horse reared up on its hind legs toppling the knight to the ground whereupon he was immediately pounced upon and dragged away in chains.

Not so fortunate were the foot soldiers. Once downed they were dispatched without mercy. I watched with horror as gangs of our squires, boys not more than fifteen or sixteen years old, pounced on them and slit their throats without a second thought. We came across one young varlet no older than the novices in the abbey who had one poor wretch at his mercy. The man was badly injured, blood streaming from his head. The lad had his knee in the man's back and was in the process of pulling back his hair to expose his throat.

'Stop!' I yelled at the lad. 'Where is your Christian charity? This man is wounded. Look at him. His arm is broken. He can do no more harm. Let him live!'

The boy hesitated, his knife poised in mid-air. I was confident his natural humanity would prevail and he would release the man. I was wrong. With one deft movement he sliced through the man's gullet and let his semi-decapitated head drop.

'Sorry brother. Orders is orders. No prisoners to be taken.'

'May God forgive you!'

I fell on my knees beside the man and made the sign of the Cross over him. As I did so I heard the sound of a horse's hooves on the cobbles. I looked up to see another knight. When he raised his visor I saw it was none other than Bishop Peter himself. He didn't speak but the look on his face was eloquent enough. He stared at me for a moment before snorting in disgust and riding away. I couldn't help that. I was determined that if I could do nothing to save the man's life I could at least do something for his soul. But Jocelin wasn't so sure:

'C-come away Walter,' he said pulling at my arm. 'It's t-too d-dangerous. He was a r-rebel s-soldier after all.'

'He may have been. But he was also a Christian. He deserves the comfort of the Church.'

'No-one will th-thank you.'

'Do we do it for thanks?'

I quickly muttered the prayers for the dead before covering his face and making the sign again.

'Amen.'

By now it was early afternoon. The impetus of the battle had largely abated and most of the rebel leaders were captured or killed. Shorn of their leaders the rebel resistance finally broke. They started fleeing down the hill closely pursued by our men. I heard later there was a last stand made half way down the hill but it was not enough. Faced with a frontal onslaught of overwhelming force they broke again and were in full flight all the way down the hill to the river still pursued by our men. Thus ended the second Battle of Lincoln.

Oh, and why did they call all this butchery "Lincoln Fair"? As a kind of joke I suppose, one that I singularly fail to find funny.

Chapter Nine
AFTER THE FAIR

And so the conquering heroes returned full of the hubris of battle like the winning side of one of Bury's football matches – though possibly less bloody. We had graduated from a field tent to the castle and were up in the Lucy tower, the castle's main residence. Present was the same trio as before: William Marshal, Bishop Peter des Roches and Earl William of Salisbury but now joined by Earl Ranulf of Chester whose breach of the north gate had started the action. Wine was flowing freely as were the boasts, the men slapping each other on the back and guffawing like excited schoolboys. Except these weren't schoolboys, this wasn't a game of football and the points scored were not goals but smashed heads and severed limbs. Not that you'd think it listening to them:

'By Christ's holy lance!' laughed Earl Ranulf dropping heavily onto a chair. 'What an entertainment!'

'A dogfight to be sure!' agreed Earl William. 'Did ye see me? I must have bagged fifty of the devils!'

'Ten,' said the Marshal.

'Huh? You were counting?'

'No, my lord. But if you'd had fifty there'd have been forty fewer for the rest of us.'

The others guffawed their appreciation.

'What? Oh I s'pose so. Ten then. That's ten fewer Frenchies shitting on our grass – what? By the Mass, we were a band of brothers, were we not?' He frowned at me. 'What's that monk still doing here?'

I was on my own this time, doing my best to blend with the wall tapestries and clearly failing. Bishop Peter had dragged me along, I presume in order to humiliate me – or worse.

'I caught him giving succour to one of the rebels,' said the bishop. 'Seems we have a Judas in the camp.'

The earl's eyebrows shot up. 'Do we, by Christ? Then you should have throttled the treacherous swine.'

'Is this true, brother?' the Marshal asked me.

'No, my lord,' I replied firmly. 'It is not.'

'Don't lie!' growled the bishop. 'I saw you with my own eyes. You were kneeling next to a rebel soldier giving him comfort.'

'I was administering the last rites to a dying man, lord bishop – as is my calling. I am, after all, a man of God.'

He leaned closer. 'In case you haven't noticed, monk, so am I.'

'Is that why you carry a sword, my lord?'

His eyes narrowed. 'Why you -'

'I heard there was an ox lodged in the Bargate,' interrupted the Marshal.

Bishop Peter faltered. 'The what?'

'The Bargate, lord bishop. That's the gate leading south out of the town.' He turned to me: 'Brother, you came on a wagon drawn by oxen I seem to recall.'

'We did, my lord. Two.'

'But you arrived with only one. What happened to the other?'

'We lost it.'

Earl William snorted. '*Lost* it? How do you *lose* an ox?'

'It wasn't easy.'

'Am I right in thinking, then,' the Marshal continued, 'that it was your ox that was blocking the Bargate?'

I was beginning to see see where this was leading. 'It was.'

'So no-one could pass through the gate, in or out of the town?'

'No, not until the ox was released.'

'Which is how you came to be on the battlefield when you should have been inside the town wall?'

'I'm afraid so, my lord.'

'This is all very interesting,' growled Bishop Peter. 'But what has it to with him giving comfort to the enemy?'

'The rebels were trying to escape through the Bargate,' explained the Marshal. 'The ox prevented them. That doesn't sound like the action of a traitor to me. And when you think about it, one dead Frenchman isn't going to alter the final outcome, is it?'

'Not unless he could rise from the dead!' snorted Earl William. 'Ha!'

'Indeed,' grinned the Marshal. 'But enough talk of oxes and traitors. Time to take stock. Does anyone know the tally? John?'

His sergeant stepped forward. 'Forty-six magnates in all were taken captive, my lord.'

'How many killed?'

'Two: Count Thomas the French commander, and one of their sergeants.'

'And on our side?'

'Only the one. Sir Reginald Croc.'

'Croc?' frowned Earl Ranulf. 'Wasn't he the one who did for the count?'

'Aye. Stabbed him through the visor,' said Earl William shaking his head. 'Rum business that.'

'The fool refused to give up,' said Earl Ranulf. 'He'd have done for the Marshal if Croc hadn't stopped him.'

'I still say Croc should have taken him alive,' said Earl William. 'The count shouldn't have been killed like that. It wasn't right.'

Earl Ranulf shook his head. 'It was a lucky strike, that's all. It wasn't deliberate.'

'Unlucky for the count,' said Earl William.

'And for Croc. He too got killed for his trouble.'

'Do we know how Sir Reginald died?' the Marshal asked his sergeant.

'No, my lord.'

'A revenge killing I expect,' said Bishop Peter helping himself to more wine. 'One of the count's own men no doubt.'

'Still, only three dead. Not a bad tally.'

The others nodded their satisfaction.

I had been listening to all this with a growing sense of outrage. I must have muttered something under my breath, I don't know what. Unfortunately the Marshal heard me.

'You have something to add, brother?'

'Forgive me. I spoke out of turn.'

'Oh now, don't be shy,' said Bishop Peter coming over. 'If you have something to say, monk, let's hear it. I'm sure we're all eager to hear the appraisal of a Judas.'

'Yes, come on lad,' said Earl William. 'Speak up.'

'Aye, let's hear him,' said Earl Ranulf.

All eyes were suddenly on me. It seemed I had no choice.

'Well, my lords, only three dead, you say? Were we at different battles? I counted hundreds of dead and many more injured.'

'He's talking about the common rabble,' said Earl Ranulf.

'We don't count the ordinary soldiery, lad,' Earl William informed me.

'You think perhaps we should?' asked the Marshal.

'Given the amount of blood spilt, yes I would.'

'Told you,' said the bishop refilling his wine goblet. 'A Judas.' He leaned towards me again so that I could smell the wine on his breath. 'You needn't think you've gotten away with this, monk.'

The Marshal gave me an indulgent smile. 'What you have to understand, my friend, is that what happened today is not the end of the affair. If we are to carry on this struggle we have to pay our troops. Captured knights are an important source of revenue. Their ransoms help to refill the nation's coffers.'

'Ordinary soldiers aren't ransomed because they have no value,' said Earl William.

'God might disagree with you, my, lord,' I said.

'Then God can pay their wages.'

I could see I wasn't going to win this argument. And now they were all looking at me with hostility, not just the bishop. It was an awkward moment which to my relief was interrupted by the sound of voices out in the passageway. The door suddenly burst open and in blustered Maude followed by Gelyn and Lady Nicola.

'I'm sorry William,' said Lady Nicola breathlessly. 'She insisted.'

Maude stood with her hands on her hips glaring ferociously round the room.

'So, this is where the victors gather is it? Dividing up the spoils are we?'

'Lady Maude,' sighed the Marshal. 'How kind of you to join us.'

'I told you. I am Eleanor.'

The Marshal made a mock bow. 'What do you want?'

'Why, to congratulate you of course.'

'That's very kind.'

'And to say this: Now that you have won your great victory it is time to think to the future.'

'I assure you, madam, I think of little else.'

Earl William snorted.

'With the usurper dead and the dauphin on the run the throne stands empty,' she continued undeterred. 'That can't be allowed to continue. England needs a king. Your rightful king, Arthur, stands ready to reclaim his inheritance that was stolen from him.'

'Who's she talking about?' said Earl William. 'What usurper?'

'She's talking about King John,' replied the bishop.

'We already have a king,' said Earl William. 'Henry.'

'The bastard son of a bastard king?' said Maude.

'King John was no bastard,' the earl growled. 'He may have been many things but he was never that.'

'He was to me, his niece!'

'Ah, well now,' said Lady Nicola, 'only this morning you were *my* niece. Now you are a king's sister. What will you be tomorrow, I wonder? Empress perhaps?'

The others laughed appreciatively at the jest.

'A convenient ruse, Lady Nicola, that was all.'

'You mean a lie. Which makes me wonder what other lies you might be telling.'

'Not about my brother. He is next in line to the throne. Or do you dispute it?'

'We have yet to establish that he is Arthur,' said the Marshal equably.

'Then satisfy yourself,' said Maude. 'Go on. Question him. He will answer anything you put to him.'

'Very well.' He signalled to a trooper.

The man went out and came back with Gelyn. The Marshal beckoned him over. 'Come here boy.'

Gelyn went and stood in front of him. The Marshal looked him up and down critically.

'Well, you certainly look the part. You're the right age. There is something of a family resemblance, I suppose. The trouble is no-one has seen you for the past fourteen years. So tell us Highness, if that is indeed what you are, where have you been in all that time?'

'I should have thought that was obvious, *Seigneur,*' Gelyn replied. 'I have been in hiding. My uncle John did try to kill me more than once – or had you forgotten?'

'As I heard it last time he succeeded,' drawled Lady Nicola. 'Drowned you in the Seine didn't he? Or have you sprung gills now?'

Earl William snorted. 'Ha! Gills! Very good!'

'The trouble is,' said the Marshal, 'that after so long an absence few would recognize you. I for one do not.'

Gelyn looked a little startled by his words. 'Have we met before, *Seigneur?* I do not remember you.'

'Maybe not. But you do know this man.' The Marshal indicated Earl Ranulf who had been skulking quietly in the corner.

Gelyn looked at the earl. For a moment he seemed to hesitate. But then he smiled. 'Yes of course I know him. He is my mother's husband. How are you, stepfather?'

Earl Ranulf stared hard at Gelyn. 'It's possible I suppose. I married Arthur's mother when Duke Geoffrey died. But it didn't last. The woman was a virago. We were soon separated. I hardly knew the boy. It might be him. The girl, however, I do recognize. I can vouch for her. She's her mother's daughter all right. I'd recognise that hectoring tone in a melee.'

'Kind of you to remember me, stepfather,' smiled Maude sweetly – or Eleanor as I suppose I should now call her. 'Well, my lords? My lord Chester confirms it. Is that good enough for you or do you need further proof?'

Gelyn was starting to look more relaxed, but the Marshal hadn't quite finished with him:

'I'm disappointed you don't remember me, lad, because I remember you. We did meet once – briefly.'

Gelyn shook his head. 'I still don't remember.'

The Marshal made a conciliatory bow. 'Understandable. You were young. There were a great many other people around at the time. But you must remember the occasion at least. Sicily? Your uncle, King Richard, was on his way to the Holy Land to fight the infidel.'

Gelyn continued to look vague.

'And you cannot possibly have forgotten the gift he gave you.'

'Gift?'

The Marshal nodded. 'It created quite a stir at the time. Richard had already declared you to be his adopted son and heir -'

'There!' said Eleanor triumphantly. 'I told you so!'

'And to seal the occasion,' the Marshal continued, 'he presented you with a sword. A very special sword. Excalibur no less. King Arthur's sword.'

A murmur of appreciation went round the room.

'Excalibur,' Gelyn repeated slowly. 'Yes of course I remember it. How could I forget such a thing?'

'How indeed? So - where is it? Surely you kept it, an item of such profundity?'

There was a pause while we awaited his answer.

'I - lost it,' said Gelyn at last.

This time Earl William scoffed incredulously: 'You *lost* Excalibur?'

'I had constantly to be on the move, *Seigneur,* rarely in one place for very long. Things got ... *égaré.*' He looked at Eleanor for help.

'Mislaid,' she supplied.

'*Oui*,' he nodded. 'Mislaid. But I remember now. It will be in Paris with King Philip. Yes, that's right. King Philip will have care of it.'

'That seems reasonable,' nodded the Marshal. 'Well my lords, how say you? Is he Arthur or not?'

Earl Ranulf was non-committal. Lady Nicola shrugged. Earl William said nothing. If Bishop Peter had an opinion he kept it to himself. He had fallen asleep, drunk.

'Of course there is just one final test we could try,' said the Marshal. He turned to Gelyn again. 'Take off your shirt.'

Gelyn looked startled. 'My shirt? Why?'

'Arthur had a birthmark under his left arm. A very distinct birthmark in the shape of a heart. Once we've seen that the matter will be settled.'

'But there are ladies present.'

'Oh, Lady Nicola won't mind. Do you mind, Lady Nicola?'

'Not in the least.'

'And your sister will have seen you naked before many times I'm sure. So, I say again: take off your shirt.'

We all waited. Still Gelyn hesitated. He glanced at Eleanor.

'This is an outrage!' she growled. 'Asking a prince to expose his naked flesh before commoners!'

'It's for his own good. It will finally resolve the matter. Afterwards no-one will be in any more doubt.'

Eleanor opened her mouth to speak again, but closed it and lowered her eyes.

There was no alternative. Gelyn slowly began to remove his shirt - but then his nerve finally broke. He made a dash for the door but was caught by two of the guards. They dragged him back and roughly pulled his shirt over his head lifting up his left arm for all to see.

'Oh dear,' tutted the Marshal.

Panicking now, Gelyn turned to his mistress with frightened eyes. 'Maude? Eleanor?'

But Eleanor kept her own eyes lowered. Then she did something truly shocking. She drew a knife from her sleeve and slashed Gelyn once across the throat. Blood immediately spurted out of the boy in a great arc spattering Earl William's feet.

'Good God woman!' said the earl jumping back.

Guards rushed to restrain her but she'd already thrown the dagger to the floor. Everyone else stood back as Gelyn's hands went to his throat, his mouth opening and closing as though trying to speak, but no words came out. The expression on his face was more of surprise than anything. He staggered forward, sank to his knees, then onto his side where he lay for a few moments juddering convulsively. Finally he stopped moving altogether.

I gasped. Since nobody else was going to, I rushed to the boy's side. But there was nothing I could do. He was dead. I made the sign of the Cross over his face and closed his eyes.

Everybody was now glaring in horror at Eleanor. She glared impassively back at them.

'What are you all looking at me like that for? He claimed to be the King of England, didn't he? That's treason, isn't it? I executed him.'

'*You* were the one who claimed he was Arthur!' I managed through my angry tears.

'I only told you what he told me,' she replied calmly. 'How would I know if he was Arthur or not? I haven't seen my brother in fourteen years. He could have been Arthur. He looked the part - the Marshal himself said so. He knew the details of my brother's early life. I believed him.'

'Yes, and who coached him?' I asked.

'Well I hope you're not suggesting it was me.'

'Who better?'

She shook her head. 'We must face facts. Gelyn wasn't Arthur – the Marshal has proved that now. But I am Eleanor – my stepfather confirmed it.'

Earl Ranulf gasped. He looked round at the faces staring at him. 'You surely don't think that I had a hand in this?'

The Marshal held up a hand. 'Nobody doubts your loyalty, my lord.'

'So where does that leave us?' Eleanor went on. 'I should have thought the answer was obvious. Arthur is dead – finally and irrefutably - which means only one thing. *I* am next in line.'

Earl William snorted. 'To what?'

'The throne of course.'

'God's teeth!' he growled. 'We haven't just fought a war to put a woman on the throne!'

'You'd put a nine-year-old child there instead?' she snapped back. 'Face it, my lords. I am your best bet. A child cannot rule a kingdom.'

'That's true enough,' agreed the Marshal.

'So you accept my claim?'

'No madam, we do not. Henry is king - not to rule, at least, not yet. Until he's old enough to assume the mantle of kingship proper there will have to be a regency.'

'Oh, I see,' she nodded. 'That's your game is it? And how long will this regency last? Ten years? Twenty? And what will happen to sweet innocent Henry in the meantime? Maybe he'll disappear like my brother did. Maybe you desire the throne for yourself, Lord Marshal. How will you style yourself? King William Marshal the First?'

The Marshal sighed heavily. 'Madam, I have spent a lifetime serving kings. I know what kingship involves and believe me this is one cup I would gladly pass over. For now the matter is settled. Until the country is free of the French there can be no further discussion.'

'You need me!' she scowled.

'We were managing perfectly well before. No doubt we shall again.'

He signalled to the guards to escort the lady out. Give her her due, Eleanor knew when to give up – for the present at least. She started to leave but stopped at the door.

'This isn't over, Lord Marshal.'

'For you, madam, it is.'

'We'll see.'

So saying, she swept out closely followed by Lady Nicola.

The noise of her departure disturbed Bishop Peter who snorted awake: 'Hm? What's that? Have I missed something?'

'No bishop. Nothing at all.'

And thus the meeting ended in some disarray. Gelyn's body was carried out by two guards. Bishop Peter, too, was half-carried, half stumbled out between the arms of the two earls. I started to follow them when the Marshal stopped me.

'Where are you going?'

'To say prayers for the boy, my lord. As well as being a monk I am an ordained priest.'

'No need. We have priests of our own. I want you to stay a moment.'

The Marshal waited until the room was completely empty then poured himself a cup of wine and offered me one.

'You look shocked, brother.'

'Do you wonder after what we've just witnessed?'

'Here. Have a drink. It will steady your nerves.'

I initially bit my lip but was still bursting with rage so that I had to let it out:

'Lord Marshal, a young man has just been murdered in front of your eyes and you seem oblivious.'

'What would you have me do about it?'

'Arrest her!'

'Eleanor is already in Lady Nicola's custody. She's not going anywhere. Besides, she was right. What the boy did amounts to high treason for which the penalty is, and has always been, death. Surely you wouldn't argue with that?'

'After due process of law!'

'Eleanor is a princess of the blood royal – the earl of Salisbury confirmed as much. Who here is qualified to judge her? My lords Salisbury and Chester are two of the most senior noblemen in the land. If they can't do it, who can? In any case, the boy tried to escape. Eleanor stopped him.'

'Only once she knew no-one was falling for her tricks. And to stop him saying anything to expose her own greater treachery!'

'You think she was behind the deception?'

'Don't you?'

He shrugged. 'Possibly. But she claimed to have been duped by him. A difficult claim to refute.'

'No, not with Gelyn dead and unable to defend himself - which I strongly suspect was her intention all along.'

'True or not, her schemes will avail her nothing. You heard my lords Salisbury and Chester. She will not supplant Henry. Her actions today only confirmed their decision. If she thought it would change their minds it had the opposite effect. They are more for Henry now than ever.'

'Forgive me, my lord, but all this talk of kings and princes is beyond me. I'm less bothered about who sits on the throne than seeing justice done for an innocent young man.'

'Yes I know, and that's really why I wanted to speak to you.'

I frowned. 'I don't follow.'

He poured himself another cup of wine before continuing.

'Let me see if I've got this right. You are Master Walter, the same Master Walter who was physician to the abbey some eighteen years ago?'

'For my sins.'

'And for everybody else's I hope,' he smiled. 'You were there, I think, when King John fell ill and cured him.'

'I am honoured you remember.'

'What I remember, Master Walter, is that there was a murder of a child – a miller's son I believe. You solved it.'

'I was instrumental in obtaining the solution, yes.'

He nodded. 'I want you to do it again.'

I frowned. 'Solve a child murder?'

'Not a child. Sir Reginald Croc.'

I had to think for a moment who he meant. 'The knight who killed the leader of the French forces? But I understood that was a revenge killing by one of the rebels. The bishop of Winchester said so.'

He pouted. 'Bishop Peter doesn't always get things right.'

'You're not convinced?'

'Let's just say I'd like it confirmed.'

'I'm flattered you think me capable, my lord. But I don't even know the man. I know nothing about him.'

'All the better. You can't be accused of prejudice.'

'But -'

'Brother, you wanted explanations for all those dead. Here's your chance to account for one at least.'

'I meant the ordinary soldiers. Sir Reginald was a knight.'

'Does that make him less worthy of your skills?'

'It's not that. I'm just not sure I'm capable.'

'I'll be the judge of that.' He looked at me seriously. 'I'm relying on you, Master Walter. I want this matter cleared up. Trust me, it's important. Now, I must get to Nottingham to inform the king – the real king - of his great victory here in Lincoln.'

'What about Lady Maude – I mean Princess Eleanor?'

'She will remain in the care of Lady Nicola for now.'

He started to leave, but before he did I couldn't resist asking one more thing:

'My lord, that business about the birthmark. Was it true?'

He replied without turning round. 'Do I look like the kind of man who looks under the armpits of princes?'

'And Sicily?'

'I wasn't even there.'

Chapter Ten
GROUND RULES

It's at times like this that I really do wish I could learn to keep my big mouth shut. If I hadn't spoken out at the meeting the Marshal might not have noticed me and I wouldn't now be saddled with this new task. After all the horrors I'd witnessed in Lincoln over the previous few hours the last thing I wanted was to have to investigate a murder. In any case, what is murder in time of war? As far as I could see it was all murder.

I wanted to tell Jocelin about what had happened in the Lucy Tower and the Marshal's request but I couldn't find him anywhere. He seemed to have vanished. It wasn't until mid-afternoon that he finally reappeared.

'Where have you been? I've been going frantic!'

'I've been d-down in the archives,' he replied cheerfully. 'They have a very impressive library down there. A-and the archivist here, Brother Emmanuel, is a remarkable f-fellow. Did you kn-know he was once a clerk in the household of Archbishop S-Stephen?'

'You don't say?'

'Yes, I d-do. And he was v-very helpful. Once I told him of my f-failing eyesight he was only t-too happy to decipher f-for me. My Emanuensis I call him,' he beamed at his own pun. 'It's all Lady N-Nicola's archive of course. She has an amazing collection of old m-manuscripts.'

'Well I'm glad you enjoyed yourself, because while you've been indulging your passion for old books I've been busy with other things.'

'Yes, I s-saw you leave with B-Bishop P-Peter. I tried to f-follow but the soldiers wouldn't let me. Still, you don't s-seem to have s-suffered much.'

'If only everybody was so lucky.'

'What do you m-mean?'

I didn't know any other way to tell him except to come straight out with it:

'Maude killed Gelyn.'

He looked aghast. 'What? How?'

'She slit his throat right there in front of everybody. Practically took his head off.'

Jocelin gasped. 'B-but why?'

'In order to get the throne for herself.'

I gave him a quick résumé of what had taken place at the meeting.

'S-so she really is who she claims? The P-Princess Eleanor?' he said when I'd finished.

'According to Earl Ranulf, her stepfather. He should know.'

'Unless he's p-party to the f-fraud as well.'

I shook my head. 'I doubt that. He was Arthur's stepfather too, remember, yet he made no attempt to defend Gelyn. No, I think the whole scheme was Eleanor's from start to finish. I'm guessing that was why she came to Lincoln, to confront the Marshal and stake her claim to the throne.'

'But I th-thought she wanted the throne for Gelyn – I m-mean Arthur?'

'She did, when everybody thought Gelyn really was Arthur. But once the Marshal exposed him as an imposter she "executed" him – her word for it, by the way. Now no-one can doubt Arthur really is dead and Eleanor is next in line for the crown.'

'What about Henry?'

I shrugged. 'Her claim is as good as his – better in fact. Her father was the older brother. That was always Arthur's argument when John took the throne, of course. But I think the Marshal has already made up his mind about that. I mean, if the choice is between a compliant nine-year-old Henry or Eleanor, who would you choose?'

Jocelin nodded. 'Henry. One thing still p-puzzles me, though. H-how did she know the M-Marshal would be here?'

'The French army is here – half of them at least. Where else would the Marshal be?'

He cringed. 'Dear God, what a b-bloody game of ch-chess this trip is turning out to be. Everywhere kings and queens, b-bishops and castles, but only one pawn: Gelyn. And as usual the p-pawn is the first piece on the b-board to be s-sacrificed.'

'Not necessarily in this case. There's also a knight.'

He shook his head. 'I d-don't f-follow.'

'The Marshal has asked me to investigate the death of Sir Reginald Croc. He's the knight who killed the French commander – count somebody-or-other.'

'Do you th-think it's connected? With Maude – I mean, E-Eleanor.'

'I don't know. But the Marshal is very keen to have us investigate it.'

'Us? I th-thought you s-said he asked you?'

'You'll want to help, won't you?'

He frowned. 'I-I'm n-not sure.'

'Why, what else have you got to do? Dig around some dusty old archive in candle-light? If you're not blind now you will be after that. Wouldn't you prefer to do some real digging out in the open?'

'And g-get myself k-killed in the process?'

'Don't be so dramatic. Who's going to want to kill you? Except me perhaps, for being obstructive,' I grinned.

He pouted. 'De la Perche.'

'What?'

'The name of the F-French commander. It was C-Count Th-Thomas de la Perche.'

'Well there you are, then. You know more about it than I do.'

'Only because B-Brother Emmanuel was t-talking about him. He s-said he was a high-ranking F-French n-nobleman, c-close to the d-dauphin.'

'Huh! No wonder their lordships were so put out. He was one of them.' I shook my head. 'Samson used to say the nobility stick together like dog-shit sticks to fur. And he was right. I wouldn't be surprised if our noble lords Salisbury and Chester and this count weren't all related in some way. So, what do you say? Will you help me or not?'

'Do I have a ch-choice?'

'Good man.' I rubbed my hands together. 'Right then. First things first. We'll have to find someone who knew this knight. We can start by asking around among the common soldiery. You take the cathedral -'

'The c-cathedral? Why there?'

'Didn't you see that lot going in there with hammers and knives earlier? I don't think they were going to arrange the flowers. They were after the silver and gold.'

'What? Th-then we must s-stop them!' he said jumping up.

'How?'

'B-by threatening them will divine r-retribution. Remind them that ch-church p-property is sacrosanct.'

'That's just the point. At the moment they don't think it is. Since Legate Guala excommunicated all Lincoln's citizens for harbouring the rebels everything's up for grabs. Church property, church buildings.'

'Th-then I will remind them that God s-sees all and there will be a p-price to p-pay later.'

'Do that and they probably will kill you.'

He frowned and sat down again. 'They'll hand them back, surely, once they sober up and r-realise what they've done? I m-mean, the holy vessels…'

'Hardly. They'll be cut up and melted down before the day is out. Anyway, while they're in the cathedral they're not in the alehouses getting drunk and doing worse.'

'What could be worse than d-desecrating ch-church property? Oh this is m-monstrous! I h-hate this place. Can't we just g-go home? We've achieved what we set out to do, delivered the Lady Maude - I mean P-Princess Eleanor. I'm s-sure no-one will notice our going.'

'The Marshal will. Besides,' I added wryly, 'you haven't had a chance to visit your cousins yet. Where in Lincoln did you say they lived again?'

'I d-didn't.' He pouted. 'All right. But what will you be d-doing while I'm in the cathedral?'

'I'll go to the inns - more my sort of level. Someone there must know Sir Reginald.'

Jocelin got to his feet again, a little unsteadily this time. I put out a hand to steady him.

'Are you all right, old thing? You don't look very well.'

'Do you w-wonder? We've j-just witnessed a tragedy of monumental proportions. Men dying in grotesque c-circumstances. Yet here we are f-fussing about the d-death of one knight. It's ... perverse.'

'That's the world we live in I'm afraid, my friend. Not all men are equally valued. Others think this one is worth the trouble.'

'I just h-hope we survive long enough t-to achieve it.'

Prophetic words indeed.

Chapter Eleven
THE HORRORS THAT MEN DO

And so to our allotted tasks: Jocelin to the cathedral to try to glean something useful about Sir Reginald from the marauding bands of royalist soldiery despoiling God's house – good luck with that. Me to the alehouses to do the same. We'd meet up later to compare notes. I have to say, though, it felt good to be doing something useful and not just sitting around wringing our hands and bemoaning the state of the world.

For Jocelin this was relatively easy. The cathedral is bang opposite the castle in the main square of the town, you can hardly miss it. In any case, the doors had been flung open and people were coming and going as they pleased smashing treasured icons and prising brass inscriptions off tombs as well as breaking into the vestry and stealing the gold and silver. It is just a pity Lincoln's own bishop wasn't here to stop these profanities for I doubt whether Bishop Peter would. He probably thought it the just spoils of war. This cathedral is a new one, by the way. The old one was demolished some thirty years ago by a huge earth tremor that shook the building to its foundations. An ominous portent for the future perhaps?

The alehouses were a different matter. There were plenty of them to choose from and all filled with royalist troops toasting their victory. But which should I try first? I didn't know the town and I didn't want to engage in a lengthy and ultimately fruitless search for anyone who might have known our murdered knight. I needed to get my bearings first.

As I've already mentioned, Lincoln is built on a steep incline – absurdly steep. I used to think the slope up from Bury abbey to the marketplace was steep but that's nothing compared to this. The castle and cathedral sit at the top of this precipice with the rest of the town falling – and I use the word advisedly - down to the River Witham several hundred feet below. Whose idea it was to site a town in such a place is anybody's guess - someone with no sense of balance. Between the castle and the river and falling rapidly away is a warren of winding alleys where the majority of the population live and work mostly in the weaving trade, the cloth they produce being dyed the town's eponymous colour. Everyone's heard of Lincoln Green. We even wear it in Bury, much to the annoyance of our own cloth merchants. The colour is a mixture of two dyes – blue woad and yellow weld. Originally Lincolnites used just the weld which gave rise to their other sobriquet, "yellowbellies". Good job they added the woad.

And fine cloth is not all that Lincoln has to offer. Despite being more than thirty miles from the sea the town has a substantial harbour known as the Brayford Pool. Indeed, the name Lincoln derives from the old British meaning a colony on the lake. Why do I mention this now? Because from what I know of waterside towns the best alehouses are always down by the shoreline. With this thought in mind I headed there first, although as things turned out I rather wished I hadn't.

By now the fighting was well and truly over, but the aftermath had only just begun which for some of the town's residents was even worse. Our troops were determined to enjoy themselves at the expense of the local population - their payment for backing the wrong side. All along the route I came across atrocities perpetrated by our heroes, so many in fact that I wondered why I'd bothered speaking up for them. Anyone foolish enough to be out on the streets was beaten up and robbed; houses were ransacked, the houses of Jews in particular. That's the other thing Lincoln is famous for, by the way, its Jewish population. Some of the wealthiest Jews in England live here many of whom probably helped finance the royalist army. The thanks they got was to be fleeced mercilessly by troops of that same army. Any refusing to pay up were having their teeth pulled out one by one until they did.

But that was only money. Worst of all to suffer were the town's womenfolk. You can imagine what was happening to them without my having to describe it. And I didn't even need to imagine because it was all done quite openly with no attempt at concealment. All along the route I had to shut my ears to their screams since there was little I or anybody else could do about it. Having said that I did manage to interrupt one incident, though through no gallantry of mine. The man in question had the good grace once he'd seen my monk's robe to stop what he was doing and pull up his breeches. I didn't expect gratitude from the girl either, but nor did I expect her to snarl at me as she deposited the silver coin the man had given her inside her cleavage. However, it was a different story down at Brayford Pool.

As I've already explained, this is a lake where boats could be tied up and goods loaded and unloaded. When I arrived there was little evidence of trade going on. Many of the town's womenfolk were trying to escape their tormentors by sailing across the water to sanctuary on the other side. But that was their mistake. By the time I arrived a large crowd had gathered on the shore to watch as dozens of women were frantically loading onto a few flimsy boats along with their children, their servants and as many of their possessions as they could carry. The atmosphere was near hysterical: children were crying, their mothers distraught and anxious. There was nothing anyone could do to dissuade them from boarding or to deter the men who were pursuing them. But it was obvious to everyone that the boats were too few in number and would soon became overloaded. And so it turned out to be. Once fully loaded the vessels managed to leave shore all right but half way out all the boats capsized and everyone on board was drowned.

'Wh-what *everyone?*' gasped Jocelin when I told him later.

I nodded. 'As far as I could tell.'

He sat down and wiped his brow with a cloth.

'There were attempts to rescue some,' I went on, 'but none I saw succeeded. At least it finally brought the men to their senses and put an end to the violence, which was something I suppose.'

'T-too late for those w-women and ch-children!' he said indignantly.

I nodded. 'Indeed.'

I should point out that all this took place while the Marshal was away in Nottingham with the king. Would he have stopped it had he been here? I like to think he would. There was no attempt to do so by our two earls or Bishop Peter - too busy enjoying the fruits of victory themselves.

And what in all this horror of my errand to discover something of Sir Reginald Croc? With all that was going on I didn't really get the chance to ask anyone about him so I came away empty-handed. However, Jocelin seemed to have had more luck.

'B-by all accounts he wasn't the most p-pleasant of men,' he said once he'd recovered. 'A v-violent man of l-low origins and even l-lower morals. He was one of the knights who ch-chased the r-rebels down the slope and out of the town.'

'Isn't that what you'd expect of one of our knights? Chase and capture the enemy?'

'Chase and c-capture, yes. But th-that's not all he did.'

'Go on.'

'At one of the bridges a f-fleeing French knight stopped to help his wife m-mount his horse so she could cross the river b-but Sir Reginald told him to leave her behind.'

'For what purpose?'

'C-can't you guess? Anyway, the m-man refused and charged at Sir Reginald with his lance unseating him.'

'Good for him! Is that how Croc died? By a lance blow?'

Jocelin shook his head. 'Apparently he was only w-winded. He got back up on his f-feet but by then the other knight had already r-ridden off.'

'Well at least that tells us that Sir Reginald was still alive after the incident with the French commander.' I frowned. 'You know, I find that whole business a little odd. I mean, why didn't the count surrender? He was surrounded. He must have known the game was up. If he'd surrendered then he would have been taken alive. Yet he chose to carry on fighting. It was a suicidal thing to do.'

'Th-that's one interpretation.'

'You have another?'

He pouted. 'What if the count th-thought his life was in danger and he w-wouldn't be t-taken alive? Even I would c-carry on f-fighting in that c-case.'

'You mean Croc killed him deliberately? But that would go completely against all the rules of chivalry.'

'As I say, he was a man of l-low m-morals.'

'He was still a knight, and a knight in the Marshal's service. No, I prefer Earl Ranulf's version, that the count was killed accidentally - a lucky strike.'

'Through the *oiliére* of his helmet? It would h-have needed to be inc-credibly lucky if it was.'

'Well what else could it have been? Killing the count made no sense. As leader of the French as well as being a senior member of their nobility, capturing him alive should have been a foregone conclusion – and a valuable prize. If anyone was worth a king's ransom it surely should have been him. Like the Marshal said, a dead knight is no value to anyone.'

'N-not to the c-country, perhaps.'

'What's that supposed to mean?'

He looked hesitant. 'Something I d-didn't t-tell you earlier. You remember you supposed the Earls Salisbury and Chester m-might be related to the dead count?'

'What of it?'

He shook his head. 'Not them. The Marshal.'

I reeled. 'What?'

'S-something else Emmanuel t-told me. One of the Marshal's aunts was m-married to a de la Perche. With the c-count dead the M-Marshal is in line to inherit his estates.'

I looked at him aghast. 'What are you saying? That the Marshal had Croc kill the count in order to get his hands on his money? That's an outrageous suggestion!'

'Nevertheless a r-reasonable one – g-given the circumstances.'

I put my hand on Jocelin's shoulder – something that's always guaranteed to make him wince.

'Jocelin, my dear friend. William Marshal has estates all over England, Ireland and Normandy. He's the earl of Pembroke. He's already wealthy beyond the dreams of avarice. Why would he want more?'

'The Marshal is also an old man with m-many s-sons. They will all want to inherit when he d-dies. A house divided is a house halved, thirded, quartered...'

'But you forget who we're talking about. William Marshal is no ordinary knight. He's a man of impeccable honour. Even the king of France said so. You're making him out to be a common thief!'

'When m-money is involved honour quickly goes out the w-window.'

I frowned. 'You're seriously suggesting that the Marshal had Croc kill the count in order to inherit a few acres of farmland?'

He snorted. 'Hardly a f-few.'

'Next you'll be suggesting he killed Croc in order to cover it up.'

Jocelin didn't reply.

'My God, you are suggesting it!' I pointed a finger at him. 'You think he's the murderer!'

'All I'm suggesting is that as a hypothesis it f-fits all the f-facts: The c-count's death; why he refused to surrender; Sir Reginald's d-death so soon afterwards.'

'If that's your theory then answer me this: Why did he ask us – me - to investigate? Surely it would make better sense to let one of the rebels take the blame, as Bishop Peter suggested.'

He shrugged. 'M-maybe the Marshal h-had no choice. He h-had to order an investigation or risk looking as though he had s-something to hide.'

I shook my head. 'No, I'm sorry. If I'm to accuse someone like William Marshal of murder I need better proof than that. And I guarantee that when I get it it'll show the opposite, that he is completely innocent.'

'How will you d-do that?'

'By speaking to those knights who were present when the count was killed. They'll be able to clear this matter up once and for all.'

'That may be d-difficult.'

'Oh? Why?'

'All the knights who were in the Marshal's r-retinue went with him to N-Nottingham.'

'Then I'll speak to them when they get back.'

'If he l-let's them c-come back.'

'Why wouldn't he? No, don't answer that, I can guess what you'd say.' I frowned. 'There must be someone we can talk to who saw what happened.'

Jocelin looked sheepish. 'There is one man.'

'Who? Another knight?'

'N-not a knight.'

'You mean a common soldier?'

'Not a s-soldier either.'

'Well who then?'

He grimaced uncomfortably. 'A hermit.'

I looked at him. 'A hermit? In the middle of a battle? Now I know you're joking.'

'He wasn't *in* the battle so much as on the sidelines – as a s-sort of onlooker offering spiritual support. N-not even a hermit really. M-more like a m-mystic. He confirmed how Sir Reginald stabbed the c-count through his visor – that much he saw for himself. B-but the count didn't die immediately. He managed to strike three more b-blows on the Marshal's helmet b-before falling off his horse.'

'Is that it?'

'N-not quite. The hermit also s-said that Sir Reginald…' He hesitated.

'Well go on.'

'He said Sir Reginald … v-vanished in a p-puff of smoke. Even that's n-not the end of it. Apparently a storm blew up afterwards and the H-Holy M-Mother was seen hovering over the site where the count died.'

'Oh, this is becoming more and more bizarre!'

Jocelin frowned. 'Walter, you shouldn't be so s-sceptical about these things. It could be that by appearing thus Our L-Lady was g-giving her blessing to our v-victory over the French. Or m-maybe she wants his m-murder solved.'

'Is that why you agreed to help me? Because the Holy Mother ordained it? Well I don't remember any storm yesterday nor hearing of anyone else seeing visions of the Virgin Mary. Do you?'

Jocelin grimaced awkwardly.

I nodded. 'Thought not. However, your mystic friend has confirmed one thing at least.'

'What's that?'

'That the count attacked the Marshal *after* he was stabbed. Which gives the lie to the notion that Sir Reginald had to kill him in order to save the Marshal's life.'

'So you agree it m-might have been deliberate?'

'I agree that it muddies the water.'

'So wh-what next?'

'Well if we can't talk to the people who went to Nottingham with the Marshal we'll have to talk to the one person who didn't.'

'And wh-who might that be?'

'Sir Reginald himself.'

Jocelin gave a nervous laugh. 'H-how do you propose to d-do that?'

'By examining his body.'

'That may be easier s-said than done. N-nobody knows where he was b-buried.'

'I thought you said just now he disappeared in a puff of smoke?'

He looked diffident. 'Th-that's what the hermit s-said.'

'Then we'll just have to find out won't we? And by the way, how did you get that black eye?'

Jocelin's hand shot to his left eye. 'One of the m-men in the cathedral. He was p-prising a jewel off the coffin of the b-blessèd Hugh of Avalon.'

I grinned. 'I warned you not to preach at them.'

Chapter Twelve
DIGGING FOR CLUES

Here I have a confession to make. I may have told Jocelin that I didn't get any anywhere with my searches among the poolside alehouses but that wasn't entirely true. I did manage to speak to one man, the leader of the royalist *routiers* as it turned out, the same one who nearly got himself captured at the start of the battle and had to be rescued. As things turned out, I rather wished he hadn't. It wasn't the most enjoyable of encounters, certainly not one I would want to share with Jocelin. In any case, he didn't tell me anything that was of any use to our investigation, although he did confirm Jocelin's portrayal of Sir Reginald Croc as a deeply unpleasant man. It made me wonder why we were bothering to investigate his murder since the world was clearly a better place without him. Mind you, the same could be said for most of his former mercenary colleagues - and this one not least.

There's no other way to put it: Fawkes de Bréauté is a brute of a man. To be fair, I suppose a man who earns his living by fighting has to be so in order to be effective, but that didn't make him any the more attractive. He also had a particular penchant for terrorizing abbots. Apparently he would demand money from them and threaten to burn down their abbey if they didn't pay up. Usually they did. So you can see he's not going to get a very good report from me - or from any other monk for that matter. His ruthless efficiency did, however, endear him to King John who employed his services in helping him recover his lost lands in Normandy, and more recently in this war against the barons. In this he was as pitiless and self-serving as he was in all his other endeavours. The only positive thing I can say about the man is that he remained loyal to his royalist masters throughout never once being tempted to join the rebel side, and thus continues to enjoy their patronage now.

I found him in one of the least reputable drinking establishments on the banks of the Brayford Pool. He was surrounded by his cronies and had a young girl sitting on his knee. The girl could not have been more than fourteen summers old. She was stripped to the waist while Fawkes was … how can I put this delicately? … fondling her. The girl looked terrified. How I managed to sit still and not drag her away from him I don't know. Well yes, actually I do know: for self-preservation. Had I made one move towards their man his brutish lieutenants would have slit my throat without a second thought. For his part Fawkes was happy to talk to me. I think he enjoyed my discomfort at being in his company as much as I detested it.

What he told me was that Croc had been one of his more successful protégés adopting many of his mentor's techniques. Like Fawkes he'd been noticed by King John who had put him in charge of various hostages of which there were many. Once King John died Croc rejoined his old mercenary master to fight on the side of the royalist cause which is how he came to be with the Marshal when they captured the comte de la Perche. None of this made my task of identifying his killer any easier for

Croc would have made many enemies among the families and friends of his charges any one of whom could have been responsible for his death. It was a question I put to Fawkes:

'Do you have any idea of who might have wanted to kill Sir Reginald?'

'*Mais oui, bien sûr.*'

My eyes widened. 'You do? Who?'

He pointed to one of his men. 'Jules here would like to kill Croc, would you not Jules?'

The man was bleary-eyed with booze and had half his nose missing. He snarled his agreement. Indeed, he would dearly like to kill Croc. He would like to tear out his black heart – like this, and demonstrated the manoeuvre to the cheers of his colleagues. But was he our killer? Surely it couldn't be that simple? Fawkes soon answered that question. He pointed to another man:

'Louis also would like to kill him.'

'Louis?'

He nodded. 'Louis, tell the brother what you would like to do to Croc.'

'What would I do to Croc? I would sink my teeth into his throat and drink his blood! Slurp! Slurp!'

And Jean would do the same – only worse. And Alexandre too. And Vincent. And Jean Marie. And Pierre. Fawkes went around the room pointing to each man in turn. They all would like to kill Croc.

'*Et moi aussi*,' grinned Fawkes finally pointing to himself. 'I too would like to kill Croc.' He then roared with laughter. His men roared too enjoying the jest and thumped each other - and me - heartily on the back.

I left the alehouse feeling more depressed than ever.

It was evident that neither Jocelin nor I had got anywhere with our enquiries, the whole process had been a waste of time. We were never going to find Croc's killer that way. We had to go back to basics and eliminate those suspects we could definitely identify first. So far these amounted to four:

- An anonymous rebel or French soldier in revenge for Croc killing the comte de la Perche, their commander-in-chief.

- An equally anonymous baron from either camp also for revenge but for a different reason. Barons don't like their fellow nobles of whichever side killed in battle. It sets a bad precedent.

- Thirdly, the French knight at the Bargate whose wife Croc had tried to abduct for his own purposes.

- And finally, reluctantly, but to keep Jocelin happy, the Marshal, though I thought that was a complete non-starter.

'This notion of a rebel soldier. Whose idea was that?'

'You said it was Bishop P-Peter's.'

'Did I? In that case we can strike him from the list straight away.'

Jocelin tutted. 'You don't like Bishop Peter so th-therefore you disregard his suggestion. Is that l-l-logical?'

'I've no objection to Bishop Peter,' I said airily. 'Other than the fact he's a cleric who wears armour; he's a bully and a drunkard; and if it wasn't for him we wouldn't have this accursed war that has left so many dead and the country in ruins. Apart from that, I quite like the man.'

'Wh-why do you say he s-started the war?'

'Didn't you know? I thought you were the one up to your armpits in the archives. It was Bishop Peter who suspended Stephen Langton from his position as archbishop and then excommunicated anyone who opposed King John. That set the whole miserable ball rolling.'

'I d-don't think you should dismiss his suggestion just for that. It seems perfectly l-logical to me that Croc's death was a revenge k-killing.'

'Really? I thought you were convinced it was the Marshal?'

'I am t-trying to be objective – which is something you're not.'

'I am being objective. I've accepted your hypothesis about the Marshal haven't I? however ludicrous and utterly preposterous it is.'

Jocelin sighed. 'It's all a bit airy-fairy. Anonymous rebels and nobles. There's no r-real evidence that such p-persons even exist. We could be ch-chasing sh-shadows.'

'What about this French knight at the Bargate? He's real enough. I take it he managed to recover his wife before taking flight?'

'I b-believe so, yes.'

'And Croc was still alive then?'

'Yes.'

'Then we'll have to discount him too. He'd have been half way to London by the time Croc was killed.'

'He m-might have returned to avenge his w-wife's honour.'

'And risk his own life in the process? Not very likely.'

'I w-wouldn't be so s-sure. The French take their w-wives' honour very s-seriously.'

'Their wives' or their own?'

'Is there a d-difference?'

I pouted. 'All right. We'll keep him on the list - for now. Who's left?'

'The M-Marshal.'

I scowled. 'Can't we discount him too? You're disparaging the man who just saved his country from a fate worse than death – a Frenchman on the throne of England, for heaven's sake! Who ever heard of such a thing?'

'We've had F-French k-kings before.'

'Name one.'

'William of Normandy.'

I shook my head. 'William of Normandy *spoke* French. His ancestors were Vikings. North-men. Men from the north – see? Anyway, that was a long time ago. Times have changed. We don't have French kings anymore.'

'We m-may do again if the dauphin w-wins this war.'

'He won't.'

Jocelin sighed. 'You've become very patriotic all of a s-sudden, Walter. Was it meeting this man Fawkes that h-hardened you against our G-Gallic neighbours?'

'Not at all. I've nothing against the French. Some of my best friends are French. I just don't like the idea of one of them sitting on *our* throne, that's all.'

'T-try telling that to Bishop Peter. He th-thinks you're in league with them.'

'Bishop Peter is a -'

'Frenchman?' said Jocelin.

I pouted. 'Anyway, we're getting off the point. We've got this French knight with the wife – at your insistence.'

'A-and the Marshal.'

'Also at your insistence. What about this other idea of yours about the murderer being one of our barons. Another one of your objective deductions?'

He shrugged. 'The count was no ordinary nobleman. He was m-married to a niece of the old king and so c-cousin to this new one. A m-man of such high standing being k-killed by a c-common routier?' He shook his head. 'Our b-barons wouldn't like that. They could g-get very angry about s-something like that.'

'Angry enough to want to kill Croc?'

Jocelin shrugged. 'Why n-not?'

'All right. Leaving aside half the population of England who have a grudge against the man we are left with with *four* possible suspects: An anonymous rebel soldier; a disgruntled French knight; some unknown irate baron…'

'And?' he prompted.

I frowned. 'The Marshal.'

'N-not much whittling done there. We've ended up with the s-same number as we started with.'

'Then we'll have to try another way.'

'How?'

'Well, we can start by examining the body. Have you managed to find out what happened to it yet?'

'It was discovered in a d-ditch beside the wall of the c-castle.'

'Good. So where is it now? We need to see it before it gets interred.'

'T-too late. He's already been buried.'

'What? Where?'

'In the g-grounds of Saint Paul's church.'

'And you let them?'

'I d-didn't have any s-say in it.'

'Then we'll have to dig him up.'

Jocelin looked horrified. 'D-dig up a b-body lying in c-consecrated g-ground? You c-can't! It would be s-sacrilege!'

'It isn't consecrated ground - not at the moment at any rate. Don't you remember? Legate Guala placed the whole of Lincoln under interdict. The church has abandoned it.'

He was still looking unhappy.

'Oh don't look so miserable. Tell you what, I'll do the digging and afterwards you can give me absolution.'

'Walter you -!'

Saint Paul's church stands opposite the castle's northeast corner which is close to where Croc's body was apparently discovered. And that raised some interesting questions for it was a long way from where he was last seen alive, nearly half a mile away at the Bargate. How did it get here and when? Was he killed here or somewhere else and the body dumped here? And how exactly did he die? I was hoping an examination of the body might throw up some answers.

By now the streets of Lincoln were largely deserted. The worst of the violence had subsided and the clearing up was slowly getting under way. We discovered one old boy trundling up the street with his cart laden with naked corpses. These were all young men most likely soldiers killed in battle, although without their clothes it was impossible to be certain.

'Why have you s-stripped them?' Jocelin asked the man.

'That worn't me, brother. They all be nekkid where I found them. Clothes is money, see? Specially boots. Ye can get a good dinner for a pair of strong lee-ther boots.'

Jocelin asked him if he knew anything about the man found in the ditch next to the castle.

'One I missed,' he sighed regretfully. 'But I aren't surprised.'

'Why's that?'

He nodded towards the castle. 'See that wall? What do ye notice 'bout it?'

We both looked up at the intimidating edifice that rose stark and sheer before us. It looked exactly like every other part of the castle to me and I said as much to the man.

He smiled with satisfaction. 'Ah, but it en't. That be the castle's blind side. No tower, see? No turrets neither. No-one inside can see out 'cept through them loops.'

'L-loops?' frowned Jocelin.

'*Arrow* loops, brother. For shooting arrows through acourse.' He shook his head at Jocelin's amazing ignorance. 'But they only looks out, not down.'

'S-so what are you s-saying? If I wanted somewhere to hide a body th-this is where I'd d-do it?'

'Which suggests someone who knew the castle well enough,' I nodded.

The man merely smiled. 'Now, if it wor me doing the killin' – which it worn't; and me doin' the hidin' – which it ain't; that's where I'd be puttin' it. At the foot o' that wall.'

Which is precisely where the body was hidden.

'Well, thank you for your advice, my man. We won't keep you.'

The man tutted and started on his way.

Jocelin nodded at the cart. 'It's a very Christian thing you d-do, brother, to be c-caring for the dead like this. I c-commend you.'

'Aye,' he agreed. 'An' it's a very Christian penny I gets for each one I teks to the churchyard.' He chuckled and trundled off.

'We have f-fallen into the depths of Hades,' sighed Jocelin watching him go. 'When will we be able to c-climb out? Murder, dumping b-bodies like they were dogs. Where will it end?'

We went into the churchyard and looked around for a fresh grave. The place was a mess. Grave markers knocked over. Earth disturbed. It looked like a battlefield – which of course it was.

'This looks promising,' I said pointing to one loose pile. 'Look, a fresh mound. Not much earth disturbed either, so it must post-date the battle.'

'H-how will we know if it's Croc?'

I thought for a moment. 'I've got an idea. Wait here.'

I found a couple of boozed-up soldiers and tempted them into the churchyard with the promise of buried treasure. They were too sozzled to realize that no-one buries treasure in a churchyard. We found the grave-digger's shovel in a nearby wooden shed.

'Is this strictly legal?' asked one stopping after a few minutes digging to wipe his brow. 'This is sacred ground isn't it?'

Jocelin opened his mouth to speak but I put my hand on his arm before he had a chance.

'The pope himself has declared the churches of Lincoln defiled,' I told the man seriously. 'On account of all the inhabitants being excommunicate for backing the wrong side in the war.'

The man still wasn't sure. Words like "defiled" and "excomm…" What was it?

'I didn't see no pope here today.'

I smiled. 'Trust us. We're monks. We know about these things.'

The man sniffed and handed the shovel to his mate. 'Your turn.'

After a few more minutes he too paused. 'How far down is this buried treasure, brother?'

The question caught me off-guard. 'I'm not sure. Erm, Brother Jocelin?'

'He was b-buried in a h-hurry,' said Jocelin. 'N-not very deep. He c-can't be very much f-further down n-now.'

'He?' asked the man.

'*It,*' I corrected, smiling encouragement. 'Carry on my friend. You're doing a grand job.'

The man gave me a suspicious look but continued digging. After a few more spadefuls he hit something soft.

'What's this? Doesn't feel like silver to me.'

'Oh, cloth of gold I expect,' I said quickly getting to my feet. 'Fetch the barrow,' I whispered to Jocelin.

The man dug again. A hand appeared. He leapt back.

'Urrgh!'

I jumped into the hole and scraped around the protruding appendage. It was a hand all right. The right one. And it was fresh. It had to be Sir Reginald.

"Ere,' said the man, recovering his composure. 'I thought you said it was treasure.'

But his friend tapped him on the shoulder and pointed into the hole. The hand had fingers and on one of the fingers was a ruby ring. Squatting down, the man stared up at me as he started easing the ring off the finger daring me to stop him. I didn't. I couldn't if I'd wanted to. Both men were gone before Jocelin came round the corner trundling the barrow.

He looked about him. 'Where…? How...?'

'The art of gentle persuasion, my friend,' I grinned. 'Logic and objectivity. Now, let's get Sir Reginald onto the barrow before we lose him again.'

Chapter Thirteen
EXAMINING THE BODY

'You can't bring that in here!'

Jocelin and I halted. We were in the entrance to the Lucy Tower with the body of Sir Reginald suspended between us: I had the head end, Jocelin the feet. We'd had to remove him from the barrow, the entrance to the tower having been barricaded against rebel attack so that it was no wider than a single man to get through. The stairs to the tower, which was where we were headed, were on my right but these were being guarded by one of Lady Nicola's guards. The lady herself stood by an open window a few feet above us glowering down.

I should perhaps take a moment to describe this lady. Nicola de la Haye was a formidable-looking woman despite her size. Now in her late sixties, she stood less than fifteen hands high but was even more impressive in the flesh than her reputation. I'd already witnessed what she was capable of up on the bulwarks of the castle at the start of the battle. One of our crossbowmen had been taking too long to reload his arbalest in Lady Nicola's opinion. She had snatched the machine from him, fired down at the rebels, reloaded and fired again three times to the bowman's two.

'And if you don't do the same,' she warned him handing it back. 'Next time it'll be you I'll be aiming at!'

Now she had me in her sights.

'Dear lady,' I called up to her and giving her my most obsequious smile. 'This is the body of Sir Reginald Croc the valiant knight who killed the leader of the rebel forces, the comte de la Perche. He was himself viciously cut down by assailants unknown.'

'So?'

'I am a physician by training and have been tasked by my lord Marshal to carry out an investigation into Sir Reginald's death to try to establish the cause and perpetrator of this dreadful crime.'

'I repeat. So?'

'In order to fulfil my duty I need to examine the body.'

'Not in here you don't. Take him into Saint Paul's.'

'Saint Paul's is not suitable, my lady. The place has been ransacked, there's nowhere to lay the body. And it's dark inside the church. I may miss something.'

'Not my problem.'

'But what will the Marshal say if I fail to carry out my task?'

'He'll say you failed to carry out your task.'

'But my lady!'

I looked for help at Jocelin but he was starting to look desperate. Sir Reginald's body was growing heavier and had begun to sag between us. We were also causing a blockage in the gateway with pedestrian traffic being held up on either side of us unable to get through and growing more and more impatient by the minute. Pretty soon no-one was going to be able to move either in or out. The only obvious exit was up the stairs to the tower.

'My lady, I beg you!'

Seeing the situation was hopeless the guard looked up at his mistress. 'He's right, my lady.'

At last she relented. 'All right. Bring him up.'

A trestle table was set up in a room on the first floor of the tower and we laid Sir Reginald's body out on top. It was a relief to get him off our hands. In life he had not been a particularly tall man but he must have been stocky and was very heavy.

Lady Nicola insisted on being there to keep a watch on what we were doing. She stood a few feet away between two sturdy guards with her arms folded across her ample bosom while I performed. She was an intimidating presence. I'd have preferred to carry out my inspection without an audience but I had to get on with it. I began by carefully examining the body.

'What exactly are you looking for?' she asked after a few minutes.

'Evidence of how Sir Reginald met his end, my lady.'

'He was a soldier. How do soldiers usually meet their end in a battle?'

'This death didn't occur in battle. It happened after the fighting was over.'

'How do you know that?'

I explained that he was seen well after the rebel army was routed although I didn't go into details. Also that his body had been deliberately hidden from view, not taken away by colleagues or left lying exposed on the battlefield.

She grunted her acceptance of that. 'You said he was a knight?'

'Indeed he was.'

'He's practically naked. What happened to his armour?'

A good question.

'P-probably r-removed when he was b-buried, m-my l-lady,' stammered Jocelin.

'Well you won't be able to tell much with him in his undergarments. You'll have to strip him to the flesh.'

She was right of course. I took out my knife from inside my robe, but hesitated.

She gave a wry smile. 'Don't worry about me, brother, I've had two husbands and borne four children. I know what to expect. I promise I won't faint with shock.'

Sir Reginald's body had already begun to swell under the clothing, but I was able to cut him loose without too much trouble. The naked body of a once proud warrior now lay bloated and discoloured before me. Shorn of his military veneer he looked utterly ordinary and I couldn't but reflect, as I had on similar occasions in the past, how death levels us all.

The lady came over. 'I see he's missing a ring.'

I looked up with interest. 'Well now, how would you know that?'

'Because the finger it sat upon is also missing. I presume that's the reason.'

I looked. She was right. The middle finger of the right hand had been ripped off. Those damned grave-diggers!

'Well I never!'

'Really brother?' she smirked. 'Never?'

I jerked upright. 'What? You think that I...?' I threw my arms out. 'My lady, search us. Please. I insist!'

'Thank you. I will.' She nodded to her two guards who marched across and patted us both down – intimately. Jocelin's face went puce with embarrassment. When they'd finished, both guards shook their heads.

Lady Nicola grunted. 'Carry on.'

There was nothing else for it. Without further ado I thrust my knife deep into the man's groin and sliced him all the way to his gullet in a single stroke. Sir Reginald's body belched, wobbled and with all the gas that had built up inside, yards of intestine came worming their way out of the gaping wound like a nest of slippery eels wriggling to escape. What had moments earlier been a robust human being was now split in two and rapidly spreading out over the bench. I removed even more of Croc making as much squelching noise as I could and piled it up in handfuls on the bench.

Seeing and smelling this, first one guard fainted then the other. Lady Nicola looked at her two heroes lying sprawled on the floor and snorted her contempt.

'Let me know when you are done,' she said and marched out of the room.

Slowly the two guards recovered their senses and staggered out of the room leaving us alone. I quickly closed the door after them and went straight back to studying Sir Reginald's corpse.

'Right,' I said to Jocelin scooping up Croc's innards and plopping them back inside the body. 'Let's get him sewn up.'

'Aren't you g-going to examine him?'

'And discover what? That his last meal was porridge? No, that was for Lady N's benefit. There's nothing inside the man that's of interest to us. It's the outside I want to look at.'

I imagine Jocelin was grateful to be purblind while I roughly stitched Sir Reginald back together, though that wouldn't have helped his nose.

'Don't you faint on me as well or we shall never get this done.'

'W-what are we looking for?' he asked.

'As I told Lady Nicola, signs of foul play.'

'You said evidence.'

'Same thing.'

I examined Sir Reginald's head and neck. There was a very obvious knife cut right round the throat.

'Th-that's what k-killed him,' said Jocelin with confidence.

I shook my head. 'I don't think so. It's barely a scratch. It might have given him a sore throat but that's about all. It certainly wouldn't have killed him. No, something else did for our friend here. That wound is merely cosmetic.'

'You m-mean someone wanted to conceal the r-real cause of death?'

'It certainly looks that way.' I sniffed his breath. 'Can you smell anything?'

'I'd r-rather not.'

'Almonds. And you know what that means.'

'Th-that his last meal wasn't p-porridge?'

'*Kyanos* - cyanide. Sir Reginald was poisoned.'

I carefully inspected the rest of his body but found nothing of interest. As an afterthought I examined his clothes. Something caught my eye.

'Well now, will you look at that!'

He squinted. 'What am I l-looking at?'

I shook my head. 'Never mind. Fetch me some parchment.'

'P-parchment? Are we t-taking n-notes now?'

'Don't be ridiculous. Can't you see?'

'You know I c-can't,' he said indignantly.

We paused while I waited.

'Parchment brother?' I prompted. 'And not for writing.'

He reluctantly left the room and came back a few minutes later with a square of white linen.

'I c-couldn't find any p-parchment. Will this d-do?'

'It'll have to.'

I carefully placed what I had found onto the linen cloth and held it up to the light.

'Now can you see?'

He squinted harder, then gasped. 'Goodness!'
'Getting closer, wouldn't you say?' I grinned.

Lady Nicola was waiting downstairs for us when we finished. She wasn't going to let us leave before showing her what we'd found.

'So brother, what did you discover?'

'Alas, nothing my lady.'

'What, nothing at all? You mean I let you make a mess of my solar for nothing? Show me your hands.'

Anticipating her curiosity, I'd already hidden the square of linen beneath the folds of my robe so I could truthfully hold up my hands revealing nothing. She surely wasn't going to get her guards to frisk us again.

She frowned. 'Have you at least worked out how he died?'

'His throat appears to have been cut.'

'Appears to have been - or was?'

'Is there a difference?'

'You tell me. You're the physician.'

I gave her one of my apothecary brother Joseph's most Jewish of Jewish shrugs.

Clearly frustrated, she pursed her lips. 'Where are you going now?'

'To continue our investigation elsewhere.'

'And leave me with the body? What do expect me to do with it?'

'My apologies, my lady. We will return to remove it - in a day or two when our work is complete.'

'And in the meantime he rots and I'm to put up with the smell?' I was about to reply but she waved me away. 'Oh never mind. I'll deal with it.'

'You are most kind, my lady,' I bowed and started to leave – but then had a thought. 'Erm, do you happen to know if the Marshal is due to return soon?'

'The Regent has more important things to worry about than the death of one knight. He's with the king in Nottingham. Nottingham, in case you don't know, is more than a day's ride away. I doubt he'll be back until the middle of next week if he returns at all. Whatever you wish to say to him will have to wait till then.'

In fact, the Marshal was back in Lincoln that very evening.

Chapter Fourteen
TWISTING THE TIGER'S TALE

Nottingham is indeed more than a day's ride away - Lady Nicola was right about that. At forty miles distance it's twice as far as most people would normally expect to travel in a single day, and that's assuming good conditions of ground and weather. The Marshal managed to get there and back in just two days, something that would have exhausted a man half his age. For someone in his eighth decade of life, and one who had just fought and won the greatest land battle in living memory, it was nothing short of miraculous. And his work is not yet finished. As I write, the dauphin is still in England, still vowing to be king, still with his army albeit halved as a result of his defeat in Lincoln. But unlike the Marshal he can easily replenish his losses from France - something his wife, Blanche, is actively pursuing on the other side of the Channel, so I'm told. I foresee further struggles ahead.

But none of this is really my concern. Having waited overnight for the Marshal to rest and recover from his journey I made my application to speak with him early next morning.

He was eating his breakfast when Jocelin and I were ushered in, examining documents and receiving reports, men coming and going all whilst interrogating me.

'How are you getting on with your investigation, brother?' he asked as soon as we entered. 'Have you managed to make any progress yet?'

'We have narrowed the field down to three suspects, my lord.'

'We?'

'Oh, erm, Brother Jocelin has agreed to assist me – I didn't think you'd object.'

He gave Jocelin a cursory glance.

'Who are these three suspects and what are their motives for killing Sir Reginald?'

I listed them in order: a rebel soldier; a French knight; and – possibly – a royalist baron.

His eyebrows went up at the third suggestion. 'An English baron, you mean? Have you anyone in mind?'

'Not yet, my lord. The idea is mere conjecture so far.'

'Based on what?'

'It is thought that such a noble, if he exists, would resent a commoner like Sir Reginald killing so highly esteemed a magnate as the comte de la Perche.'

He nodded. 'That makes sense. But before you start bandying names about you'd better be sure of your facts. The baronage of England are a jittery lot. They wouldn't take kindly to the suggestion that one of their number could be capable of committing anything so shaming as murder.'

Slaughtering thousands – yes; taxing to the point of starvation – yes; trampling crops under foot, pillage, rape - yes. But murder – no.

'As I say, it's just a theory.'

'All right. Who else?'

'There's Bishop Peter's suggestion that the killer could be a rebel soldier taking revenge on Sir Reginald for killing the comte.'

'What does the man say?'

'We haven't actually apprehended him yet, or even know if he exists. Once again, it's a theory.'

'Have you any suspect who isn't a theory?'

'One, my lord.' I described the incident with the French knight at the Bargate and the suggestion that he might have wanted revenge for Sir Reginald dishonouring his wife.

'Where is this French knight now?'

'On his way back to join his compatriots, I imagine.'

'So you've not managed to speak to him either?'

'Not yet, my lord.'

'So to sum up: you have a theoretical rebel soldier, a fanciful baron, and a vanished French knight. Not very good is it, Master Walter? I thought you'd be better at it than this.'

That, I admit, rattled me a bit. After all, I didn't ask for this job. It made me say next what perhaps I shouldn't have done:

'There is a fourth possibility.'

'Another theory?'

'Not exactly.'

'I'm listening.'

I hesitated. Beside me I could feel Jocelin tense up. He knew what was coming.

I took a breath. 'The fourth suspect, my lord, is someone who would gain personal profit from the death of the comte de la Perche. Someone who might have enticed Sir Reginald to kill the count in order to secure that wealth. He would then have Sir Reginald killed in order to conceal his own guilt.'

I had come as close as I dare to implicating the Marshal without actually naming him. I held my breath waiting for his reaction. Would he recognize himself as the unnamed suspect? Would I be clapped in irons and thrown in a dungeon? Have my tongue ripped out so that I was unable to repeat the slander? Or would I simply be dispatched to the gallows as the traitor Bishop Peter had already accused me of being? Any would silence me.

As it turned out none of these things happened. He remained completely impassive.

'Have you anyone specific in mind?' he asked quietly.

'At this stage, my lord, I'd rather not name names before I am sure of the facts. If I am wrong it could damage reputations. If I'm right then we are confident the truth will out in the fullness of time.'

'So what is your next step?'

'With your permission, my lord, I would like to continue my enquiries further afield. In which regard may we request letters patent - or some form of written authority to continue our work?'

He thought about that before answering.

'I will instruct my clerks to draw up a note authorizing you to speak to whoever you wish.'

'Thank you, my lord.'

'Anything else?'

'No, my lord.'

'Then I bid you good day, brother - and success in your endeavours.'

As soon as we were back in our room Jocelin made straight for the drinks table and poured two full cups of wine. He swallowed one straight down and immediately started on the second.

'I should watch that. You'll be turning into an alcoholic.'

He glared at me. 'My G-God, Walter de Ixworth, you've some spit! H-how can you b-be so c-calm? D-didn't you s-see what you j-just did? You just p-practically accused William Marshal, the m-most p-powerful m-man in all England, of committing m-m-murder!'

'I thought that's what you wanted.'

'I d-didn't mean for you to accuse him to his f-face!'

'I did nothing of the sort. I deliberately didn't mention names. I was very specific about that.'

'B-but it was obvious who you were t-talking about. The w-way he was l-looking at you. I thought he was going to c-cleave you on the spot!' He took another gulp of wine.

'Really? I thought he was a bit of a pussy-cat.'

'Oh, he's f-feline all right. One with sharp t-teeth and c-claws that can r-rip a man's th-throat out.'

'Ah, but the question is, did he rip Sir Reginald's throat out?'

'I th-thought you said Sir Reginald was k-killed by p-poison.'

'Exactly, which is one reason I'm hesitant to accuse the Marshal. Poison is a woman's weapon. A real man like the Marshal would use the blade.'

'N-not if he had an accomplice - a f-female accomplice.'

'Like who? Lady Nicola you mean?' I shook my head. 'You saw her reaction at the autopsy. She had no idea about Sir Reginald. I'm not sure she even knew who he was. She'd have to be a good actress to put on a show like that. But I agree, that doesn't entirely rule the Marshal out.'

'So you're beginning to agree with me?'

'I'll admit that after what I'd seen of our leaders over the past couple of days nothing would surprise me. But the Marshal's different. I'm disinclined to believe him capable of such duplicity.'

'Give him the b-benefit of the doubt you mean?'

'Precisely.'

'Well I hope it's not a f-foolhardy j-judgement. A man is known not j-just by his own actions but by the c-company he k-keeps.'

'You mean men like Bishop Peter and the earls Salisbury and Chester?'

'I m-mean men l-like Sir Reginald. He was one of the Marshal's l-lieutenants. O-on his payroll at l-least.'

I have to agree he was right about that. Sir Reginald was in the Marshal's retinue at the time the comte de la Perche's death. He must have known what sort of man he was. And not forgetting Fawkes de Bréauté – another man of dubious morality still in his employ. Did that mean they were all cut from the same cloth?

'You don't g-get to be as r-rich and powerful as the Marshal without b-bending a f-few rules,' said Jocelin.

'Like what exactly?'

'Like that b-business about s-selling knights for r-ransom. You know that's how he m-made his first fortune, by winning ransoms in the t-tournament?'

'That was just skill. He was better at it than the rest, that's all.'

'Perhaps. B-but there's m-more.'

I sighed. 'All great men have stories told about them. Go on. What's the Marshal's?'

'It's said that in his youth he once chased after a r-runaway m-monk who was eloping with the daughter of a friend of his. He c-caught them and c-confiscated the money they were hoping to live on.'

'What's wrong with that? Monks eloping should be punished and not left to enjoy the fruit of their nefarious acts.'

'M-maybe, but it's what the Marshal d-did with the m-money after he caught the m-monk and his paramour.'

'What did he do with it?'

'He k-kept it for himself – although he d-did allow the couple to k-keep their horse.'

'Well, there you are then. Others would have been less generous. Anyway,' I frowned. 'Where do you get these stories from? They sound apocryphal to me.'

'You kn-know how these r-rumours spread. It's c-common knowledge among the troops. And you've just warned him that we suspect him of b-being a m-murderer.'

'He let us go didn't he?'

'F-for now.'

I pouted. 'If he was going to arrest us he'd have done so already and no-one would be any the wiser. Instead he has given us free range to interview whomsoever we please.'

'There's still t-time to change all that.'

'What, you think the Marshal's going to have us assassinated? Ambushed on the road?'

'I'm j-just s-saying, watch your back from now on.'

'Prrrf! Stuff and nonsense!'

'So what now? What do you intend d-doing with those l-letters patent?'

'Now I want to try to find that French knight.'

'I th-thought you wanted to dismiss him as a p-possibility.'

'I've changed my mind. It's like the Marshal said, he's our only really tangible suspect. We should try to find him if only to eliminate him.'

'How? We know n-nothing about him - his name, where he's f-from, where he was g-going or anything.'

'That's why we need to move further afield. He can't be that difficult to find. He's a rebel in enemy territory.

He should stick out like a sore thumb. And a retreating army will want to stick together for safety which means there's only one trail to follow. Even we should be able to do that.'

Jocelin pulled a face.

'You don't seem too keen, brother. What's bothering you now?'

He hesitated before saying: 'You remember that hermit I was t-telling you about?'

I nodded. 'The one who saw visions of the Virgin? What about him?'

'His b-body was found in the B-Brayford P-Pool this morning. D-drowned.'

'Deliberately?'

He shrugged.

'You think he was murdered too? By the same killer perhaps as killed Sir Reginald I suppose?'

'He was there when Sir Reginald k-killed the c-count. He s-saw what happened. M-maybe he had a story to tell which we will now n-never know.'

'I suppose you think the Marshal had a hand in that too?'

'One by one those who w-were there at the time of the c-count's death are being eliminated. The last man s-standing...'

I nodded. 'Is the Marshal.'

I didn't believe it was William Marshal doing these things. But just to be on the safe side I didn't tell him where we were going.

Chapter Fifteen
CHASING SOUTH

It was a relief to be getting out of Lincoln for a while. The worst of the reprisals had ended but collaborators were still being winkled out and dealt with. All the usual punishments were being meted out: ears cut off, noses split, eyes gauged out. Not that Lincolnites had much choice about which side they supported I suppose. They'd have been condemned whichever side they'd been on.

What was left of the defeated Franco-rebel army and managed to escape were now in full retreat most of them heading south towards London which was still in the hands of the dauphin. I reasoned that since our man was on horseback he was probably in the vanguard and must be well away by now so if we were to catch up with him we'd better not hang about.

'We could do with s-some decent horses,' said Jocelin. 'Can we g-get any do you th-think?'

'Are there any left? So many were killed in the battle.'

It took us a while but by using the letters patent from the Marshal we were able to commandeer two nags of dubious quality that had somehow managed to survive the slaughter and set off the following day as soon as it was light.

We took the same route out of Lincoln as we'd used to come in: Ermine Street, that great road that runs the whole length of England. We knew we were on the right track as we came across a number of rebel stragglers along the way, mostly the injured unable to keep up with the main group. I'm ashamed to say they received no mercy from any villagers they encountered. You may remember that shepherd who helped us at the Bargate. We came across him again. This time he wasn't alone but had a few of his fellow villagers with him. He still had his stick but this time he wasn't using it to herd sheep. They'd captured a fleeing French soldier and bound his arms and legs in such a way that he was being forced to run around on his elbows and knees like a dog. Modesty forbids me to tell you where the shepherd had thrust his stick, but suffice to say every dog needs a tail. All this for the amusement of his fellow villagers.

I can't say I was entirely surprised by all this. The common perception of a farmer being a sweet little ol' boy, leaning on a gate, chewing on a stalk of straw, is not my experience. I've always found them to be violent and aggressive men willing to fight at the drop of a hat. I suppose they have to be. They have a lot of crops and animals to protect – not so much from marauding foreign armies as from each other. So it didn't altogether surprise me to see this one taking out his spleen on this unfortunate Frenchman.

We couldn't pass by without trying to help this poor wretch. At great risk to ourselves Jocelin and I unbound him, covered his nakedness as best we could and sent him on his way. He ran as fast as he could though how far he'd get before someone else accosted him was anyone's guess. But at least we'd given him a fighting chance. As for the villagers – they'd had their fun for the day and didn't try to stop us.

However distressing it was, he was one of the fortunate ones losing only his dignity and the skin from his elbows and knees. Others were less lucky. We came across men buried up to their necks in the ground and were being used for target practice by boys whose aim after years of scaring birds off the village crops was excellent. Others had their noses or ears nailed to church doors. The only way to free these poor wretches was to chop off the affixed appendage. Nasty, but the alternative was to leave them to starve to death. I suppose we shouldn't be too judgemental. The French had done as much if not worse to these very same villagers when they thought they were winning. It just gives the truth to the old adage that you should be careful on whose fingers you tread on the way up for you may meet them again on the way down. However, all this diversion was slowing us down and we really needed to get a move on or the day would be gone and we'd hardly have made any progress.

At midday, having made our way some distance from Lincoln town, we found a small isolated farmstead that looked relatively unscathed by the war and we stopped to refill our water bottles. The farmer was a kindly rustic who was only too pleased to replenish our water and offered to share his midday meal with us. It was a warm sunny day and we ate al fresco in his yard joined by his two sons, a couple of strapping Lincolnshire lads.

'Are you all men here?' I asked tucking into a fine spiced sausage.

The man seemed a little hesitant to answer at first but then admitted he also had a wife and three daughters.

'You have to understand, brother, with so many fo'ners about we have to be careful.'

'S-so you k-keep your wife and daughters hidden away,' nodded Jocelin with approval. 'Very w-wise.'

'You've heard about the battle in Lincoln town?' I asked him.

'We knowed summat wor afoot on account of all them Frenchies fleeing past hereabouts.'

'Ah, so I'd be right in thinking the bulk of them came this way?'

'Aye, a few.'

'You're f-fortunate to be away from the r-road,' said Jocelin. 'Unlikely to be p-pestered.'

The man didn't reply.

I have to say I felt a little uneasy though I couldn't say exactly why. We chatted amiably about this and that, nothing of any consequence. There was a question forming in my mind which I was hesitant to ask, but eventually my curiosity got the better of me:

'I couldn't help noticing, you seem to have a newly-dug grave.' I nodded to where there was a small mound of freshly-turned earth a few yards away. 'Not a family member I hope?'

The farmer shook his head. 'One of them Frenchies.'

'So you haven't managed to avoid the war entirely?'

Again, the man didn't reply.

I nodded again at the grave. 'I must say it's very decent of you to give a Christian burial to an enemy soldier. How did he die, may I ask?'

'Oh he en't dead,' said the farmer. 'Least ways not yet.'

I stopped chewing and looked at the man. It took me a moment to fully comprehend the meaning of his words.

'Not *yet?* But you don't mean…? You're surely not saying that he's… *still alive?*'

'Like I say, brother. Not for much longer.'

I stared around the table at each of the three men in turn and then at Jocelin who was looking back at me with a mixture of horror and disbelief on his face. A moment later our bench went one way and we went the other as we dived for the grave and started frantically digging with our hands. Fortunately the soil was only inches deep and I quickly uncovered a foot. Jocelin scrabbled at the other end of the grave and a face appeared. As soon as the light hit the man he started spluttering and gasping for air. God be thanked he was still alive!

We dragged him out of the grave. His hands and feet were bound so that he couldn't have dug himself out. I splashed water over his face to clear the worst of the soil and released his bonds. He was whimpering, clasping his hands together in supplication and thanking us and God over and over for his deliverance.

The farmer and his sons stood a few feet away while we performed this resurrection. I scowled silently up at them unable to find the words to express what I was feeling.

'They stole our crops, raped our women, murdered our chil'en,' the man kept repeating. 'It's what they deserve!'

He then stomped off back into the house followed by his two sons and slammed the door shut.

We settled the Frenchman down on the bench and gave him water to drink and the remainder of our food which he ate with ravenous gusto. He was still shaking from his ordeal. Eventually he had recovered enough to tell us his story.

It seemed he was indeed one of the Franco-rebel soldiers who'd been at the battle in Lincoln. Just as we thought, he along with many of his comrades had fled south heading for London, and like us he had stopped at the farm to beg for some water. Instead, the farmer and his sons had over-powered him, bound him and dug a shallow grave intending to bury him alive. All this must have happened just a short while before we arrived. Any longer and he wouldn't be alive to tell the tale.

'*Je te dois ma vie!*' he kept repeating, tears of gratitude running down his cheeks. 'I owe you my life!'

I shook my head. 'You owe us nothing, my son. It is we who must beg your forgiveness for the way you've been treated by our fellow countrymen. I am ashamed to call myself an Englishman. Rest assured, this will not go unpunished.'

I was sure the Marshal would condemn all such acts of barbarism however much provoked. But the man's only concern was to get away and rejoin his comrades before anything worse befell him. He thanked us again and started to leave saying if there was anything he could do for us we were only to ask.

'Actually there is one thing. We are looking for a colleague of yours. A knight. We don't know his name or anything about him other than he was at the battle in Lincoln.'

The man was reluctant to answer. 'You wish me to betray one of my own countrymen?'

'I think you can see we are not in the business of handing out retribution. It is purely for information that we seek this man. I assure you he will come to no harm from us.'

'What information?' he asked cautiously.

'He was in an altercation with another man - at the bridge at Lincoln. The man we seek unseated an English knight. That's all we know about him. We're not even sure if he's French or English.'

The man hesitated before answering. Finally he said: 'He is French.'

'How do you know?'

'I was there. I saw.'

Jocelin and I exchanged glances. 'You w-witnessed the altercation?' said Jocelin. 'C-can you describe what happened?'

He hesitated again. 'Why you wish to know this?'

'Because the English knight is now dead,' I said.

'Not by our hand. But I am glad of it.'

'Why?'

'This man. *C'était un animal.*'

Jocelin shot me a look. 'In what w-way an animal?' he asked. 'Wh-what do you m-mean?'

The man sat down again and raised his chin towards the house. 'This farmer accuses me of rape.' He shook his head. 'I do not rape. I do not murder innocent children either. I steal food, yes, but that is because I am hungry. But this man you speak of…'

'Sir R-Reginald C-Croc - yes?'

He sighed. 'The fighting is over – you understand?'

We both nodded.

'We are running. All is confusion. So many men. Too many to cross the bridge at once. Some try to jump the water. A woman falls. Her husband …' He sighed shaking his head.

'*Son mari,*' prompted Jocelin.

'*Il s'est arrêté pour la récupérer.*'

'Her husband stopped to p-pick her up,' Jocelin translated. 'Th-this is what I heard, Walter – remember?'

'Then what happened?' I asked. 'The English knight told him to leave her?'

'*Oui. Mais il ne comprenait pas le sens de la chevalerie française.*'

'Yes, b-but he underestimated F-French ch-chivalry,' said Jocelin.

'*Le chevalier récupéra sa lance.*'

'The knight p-picked up his l-lance.'

'*Il a chargé.*'

139

'He charged.'

'Il l'a frappé à la poitrine et l'a renversé.'

'He hit Croc in the ch-chest unseating him,' said Jocelin with satisfaction.

'And that's all he did?' I asked. 'The French knight didn't try to finish him off?'

'Pas assez de temps. Il a récupéré sa femme et est parti.'

'N-no time for that. He p-picked up his wife and rode off.'

'But what of Croc? What happened to him?'

The man gave a wry smile. 'He was *en colère. Il se leva en secouant son poing*.'

'He got up shaking his fist in anger.'

'*Mais il était impuissant!*'

'B-but he was p-powerless to do anything,' concluded Jocelin.

'You are certain of that?' I said. 'Listen to me, my friend. The English knight was still alive when the French knight rode away – yes? It's important that we know.'

He shrugged a negligent shoulder. 'Yes. He was still alive.'

'And the French knight? Do you know where he is now?'

The man frowned defensively. 'Why do you wish to know this? I have told you all.'

'We need to be sure. I'm not doubting your word but my masters in Lincoln won't be satisfied unless we hear it from the man himself.'

The man demurred. 'I will not tell you where he is.'

No. I suppose that was too much to ask.

'All right. But we are heading in the right direction?'

'France is that way. Why should we wish to go another? And now, my friends, I must go there too.' He started to leave.

'You haven't yet given us your name,' I called after him.

He paused without turning round. 'Pascal. Pascal du Bûr.'

'Thank you Pascal du Bûr.'

The man grunted and went on his way.

We sat for a moment going over what we had heard. Then I glared at the farmhouse door shut aggressively against us.

'Come,' I said. 'Let us leave this place too before I do something I regret.'

Chapter Sixteen
IN UP TO OUR NECKS

I was still feeling wretched about what happened at the farm. I'd heard of such things before of course but never thought to have to witness them. What devil possesses a man to commit such atrocities? That farmer wasn't a monster. Tomorrow he will probably go out into the fields, find one of his sheep fallen into a ditch and move heaven and earth to end its suffering. Yet he could do that to a fellow human being. It was beyond comprehension. The only thing I can say is that it convinces me all the more that war is evil.

I could tell by the way Jocelin was behaving that he felt the same way. He'd gone quiet for a long time as we rode on gazing into empty space.

'The w-world is out of k-kilter,' he said morosely.

'It's the war, my friend. Once the fighting is over things will get back to normal. You'll see.'

'I'm not sure what normal is any m-more. A d-dozen centuries after Christ's P-Passion and we are still b-barbarians. The v-vision of that man in the grave will h-haunt me for the rest of my d-days. Oh, why did I let you persuade me to c-come on this awful j-journey?'

My jaw dropped open. '*Me* persuade *you*? As I remember it, it was *you* persuaded *me*!'

'But I d-didn't know you were g-going to l-lead me into the m-mouth of Hell!'

I bit my lip. There was no point in arguing. We had more important things to do than indulge in self-analysis.

Apart from a few stragglers we'd not come across any more rebels either nailed to church doors or buried alive, thank God. I guessed the bulk of them must be further ahead, among them our man, though just how much further was anybody's guess. But there was no point killing the horses trying to catch up. They needed to rest and so did we. Finding somewhere for the night had to be our next priority.

We were now approaching Sleaford. This is quite a busy little market town and when we got there the marketplace was still buzzing - you'd hardly know there was a war on. But I suppose for most people, unless they are directly caught up in it, life simply carries on as normal. I couldn't believe that fleeing rebels would be so foolish as to try to enter the town. The townsfolk would pretty soon swap their bells and clappers for cudgels and pikes. They'd most likely have gone a long way round which would be to our advantage. As a couple of elderly monks we could easily pass directly through the town without being challenged thereby stealing a march on our quarry.

Since there is no Benedictine house in Sleaford we decided to try the church of Saint Denys and crave a barn floor for the night. It was a decision we were to regret.

The prebendary of Saint Denys, Father Quennel, was a most welcoming fellow. He was happy - nay, *eager* to offer us a warm bed for the night, not a cold barn floor. He also fed us and our horses all of which did much to revive my belief in the basic goodness of mankind after it had been so severely dented earlier in the day. I should have realised such generosity never comes without a price.

'Where did you say you've come from?' Quennel asked pouring us each a cup of ale.

'Lincoln. And much relieved we are to be out of it. No doubt you will have heard what happened there?'

'I believe I did hear something. A battle of some sort, wasn't it?'

'Of s-some s-sort?' scoffed Jocelin accepting his ale. 'It was a-p-pocalyptic!'

Quennel nodded. 'Yes, I heard it was something of a rout. And you are monks of the cathedral there?'

'No no,' I said. 'We're from the abbey of Saint Edmundsbury in Suffolk.'

Quennel's eyebrows went up. 'Suffolk? You are a long way from home. What brings you all the way up here, I wonder?'

I opened my hands in despair. 'It's a long story.'

'And Sleaford?'

'An even longer one.'

There followed an awkward silence while we sat sipping our ale.

'A-actually we're on the hunt!' blustered Jocelin at last.

'A hunt?' said Quennel. 'You'll find little game in Sleaford, I fear.'

Jocelin grinned stupidly. 'Ours is a h-human quarry.'

'What Brother Jocelin means,' I said glaring at him - I could see the ale was getting to him already. 'What he means is we are trying to find someone who may help us solve a riddle.'

'Intriguing. Something to do with the battle?'

'Only tangentially.'

'An interesting choice of word. It does indeed sound like a riddle.'

'Oh it's that all r-right,' snickered Jocelin. 'A F-French r-riddle.'

'Curiouser and curiouser.'

'It's not that we don't wish to tell you, father,' I said giving Jocelin another admonishing look. 'But we are under oath to the bishop of Winchester not to discuss.'

'Ah well, if it's the bishop of Winchester ...'

'You know of Bishop Peter?'

'I know he is the second most senior advisor to King Henry,' smiled our host. 'Second only to the Earl Marshal.'

I was impressed. 'You are well informed. Even we didn't know that.'

He smiled. 'One likes to keep abreast of these things. You've no idea how long the bishop will remain in Lincoln? Or what he intends doing next?'

'I'm afraid I don't.'

Do you ever get that feeling that you've said something you shouldn't ought to have? Like somebody is watching you, listening. I had it then. I don't think Jocelin did. He was too far gone on Father Quennel's ale to notice anything much. I was uncomfortable about discussing the battle in Lincoln with the prebendary but I couldn't have explained why. We spoke no more on the subject but went in to supper which we ate in silence. Afterwards we said our goodnights and Jocelin and I retired to our room.

'Oath to B-Bishop P-Peter!' snorted Jocelin once we were alone.

'I had to say something. You were about to give away everything.'

'W-would it have m-mattered if I had? Our mission is not a s-secret.'

'Father Quennel is a stranger to us. We don't know him. Better we keep our purpose to ourselves.'

'L-like you did with Brother Magnus?'

'That was different.'

'How d-different?'

'I don't know. It just was.'

He pouted. 'Well I r-rather like our host. He's very g-generous with his ale.'

'Yes, a bit too generous. And a bit too curious.'

Our room was on the upper floor of the house. A single bed of course. Jocelin was already snoring on his side as I lay down and closed my eyes. I had barely begun to drift off when the shock came. In the darkness I felt a hand grip my shoulder and the unmistakable touch of cold steel on my windpipe. I heard Jocelin gasp indicating the same thing was happening to him. The hand holding me did so so tightly that I couldn't move an inch. Not that I wanted to. One slip and the knife would have sliced my head off.

'What do you want?' I gulped. 'We are poor monks, we have no valuables.'

I could feel the man's breath on my neck. 'I hear you have been looking for me, *mon frère.*'

The accent was French. He could only be one person: the knight at the Bargate. Pascal must have told him we were looking for him. He patted me down. Once he'd found my knife he released me so that I could at least turn around and look at him. The man holding Jocelin was Father Quennel.

'I thought your questions were a little too probing,' I said to him angrily. 'Are you really the prebendary here? Or have you done away with him?'

'You should have answered, brother. It might have saved all this.'

'Quennel is the priest of Saint Deny,' said the Frenchman. 'He also happens to be my wife's brother.'

'Ah yes, the wife who fell from her horse. I thought I detected a slight accent. So you are French too?' I said to Quennel.

He shook his head. 'Norman. I had an English nurse.'

'Like Janus.'

He frowned. 'Who?'

'Janus, the Roman god of duality. He had two faces as well.'

Quennel's eyes narrowed.

'You have not answered my question,' said the knight.

'What was it again?'

'I asked why you are looking for me? Two monks alone. You have no soldiers so you have not come to arrest me.'

'We haven't come to arrest anyone. We are after information, that's all.'

'Concerning this knight I downed. You have already had your answer to that question.'

I nodded. 'From your other compatriot, Pascal. But I need to hear it from you.'

'Then you have come a long way for nothing. There is no more I can tell you. I did not kill this knight. He was still alive when I left him.'

'Maybe you returned later to finish the job.'

He snorted. '*Mon frère*, I had him on his back on the ground. If I had wanted him dead I could have done it there and then.'

'So why didn't you?'

'I had more important things to worry about. It may have escaped your notice but at the time we were being pursued by your army. The man was down, he could do me no more harm.'

I shook my head. 'That wouldn't have prevented you. He was the enemy. One quick flick of your knife. It would have taken but a moment. I can tell you that had it been the other way round you wouldn't be alive now. Well now he is dead. And I need to find out why.'

'For what reason? Hundreds died in Lincoln. What is so important about this knight?'

'That I couldn't tell you. All I know is that it is my commission.'

'I have told you all there is to know.'

'But can I believe you?'

'Whether or not you do is of little interest to me. I will soon be in France and out of this accursed land for ever. But since you insist, I'll admit it. I slit his cowardly throat for the dog he was just as you suggest. There. Are you satisfied? And now I will do the same to you.'

He suddenly grabbed me, spun me round and put his knife against my gullet again. He held my arms back with his hand on my throat. The man was bigger, younger and stronger than me. Opposite, I could see Jocelin, his eyes as wide as saucers with fear. Was he the last person I would see in this life? Was I his? I didn't know for my head began to swim and the world went black.

Chapter Seventeen
AND OVER OUR HEADS

When I awoke the next morning I found I was still lying on the floor exactly where I'd collapsed the night before. Jocelin was already awake and sitting on a stool holding his head in his hands. I sat up with a jolt and immediately wished I hadn't. My head spun wildly and started pounding and I felt nauseas as soon as I moved.

'I t-tried to lift you onto the bed,' Jocelin explained. 'B-but you were t-too heavy. S-sorry.'

'We're both still alive - at least I think we are. I'll let you know when I get the feeling back in my teeth. What was in that ale Quennel gave us?'

'I d-don't kn-know. But if I ever s-see him again I'll…!'

'You've changed your tune. Last night you thought he was a splendid fellow.'

'Th-that was before he held a kn-knife at my throat and n-nearly t-twisted my arm off.'

'I did try to warn you.'

'I guess I'm just n-not a v-very good judge of men.'

'I'll remind you of that sometime.'

I held my hand out in front of me. It was shaking, I'd like to think from the effects of the drug but it could simply be fear. I staggered to the door and hesitantly looked out.

'H-have they g-gone?' Jocelin asked.

'I think so.'

He breathed a sigh of relief. 'I r-really th-thought we were d-done for this time.'

'We very nearly were.'

I found another stool and sat down on it to try to stop the world from spinning.

'What time of day do you think it is?'

Jocelin squinted through a crack in the shutters. 'Past noon I'd say.'

'Well, if they wanted time to get away they've certainly had that. Even if we called the guard out now we'd never catch them. And I don't much feel like running around at the moment. Let's go downstairs and see what we can find.'

There was plenty of food and drink left behind in the kitchen but neither of us wanted to eat.

'I d-don't think I w-will ever eat again,' frowned Jocelin. 'Whatever it was Quennel put in our ale has sickened my stomach.' He clenched his fists. 'Ooh, if I ever c-come across that p-priest again…'

'I doubt you will. He'll have joined the other rebels by now. He was obviously their spy.'

'Why do you think they l-let us live? With us out of the way he c-could have c-carried on s-spying for them.'

'If it wasn't for our meeting with Pascal I think they might have done.'

'You th-think that's what s-saved us?'

'Well, they say one good turn deserves another. We resurrected Pascal from one hole and he's just dug us out of another. Anyway, after Lincoln I don't suppose there is much use for Quennel's services anymore.'

'At least now we kn-know who killed Sir Reginald.'

I shook my head despondently. 'Oh, the knight didn't do it.'

'B-but he admitted it.'

'No he didn't. What he said was he slit Croc's throat whereas we know he was poisoned. And Croc's body was found up near the castle. When was he supposed to have done that? Besides, it's like he said, if he'd really wanted to kill Croc he could have done so far more easily at the Bargate.'

'Then why s-say he did?'

'Who knows? Out of devilment. It will hardly matter to him. He'll soon be in France or back with the dauphin.'

Jocelin grimaced. 'So w-what now?'

'Now we return to Lincoln and continue the investigation there.'

He groaned. 'D-do we have to? Can't we j-just g-go home? We're already half-way th-there. We d-did our b-best. We've r-ruled out the most likely s-suspect. What m-more can we do?'

'I gave my word to the Marshal.'

'To the real m-murderer you mean. With the F-French knight eliminated he's the only realistic s-suspect left. Once he realises that – once you t-tell him – the number of our d-days will be sh-short indeed.'

'There's still our rebel soldier – and don't forget the English baron.'

'Both of whom are c-conjectures. We d-don't know that either of them actually exists.'

I frowned. 'I simply cannot believe William Marshal, the Regent of England, is a murderer.'

'You j-just don't w-want to believe it. You'll still be protesting his innocence when we're both d-dangling from a rope.'

'Look, if you're that worried about it you can carry on to Bury and I'll go back alone. I release you from your obligation. There. You are free to do whatever you want.'

'My obligation!' he scoffed. 'The only obligation I had was to help f-ferry the Lady Maude to L-Lincoln. That s-seems like a l-lifetime ago.'

'Anyway,' I smiled, 'you still haven't visited your cousins in Lincoln yet. What will they say if you came all this way and didn't drop by to see them? I mean, this is your last chance before you die, remember?'

He looked at me shyly. 'I have a c-confession to m-make about th-that.'

'You don't have any cousins in Lincoln.'

He shook his head.

'Good job in that case that I never believed you did.'

I was putting on a brave face for Jocelin's sake but in reality I was as nervous about returning to Lincoln as he was. The fact remained that someone killed Croc and that someone was probably still in the town and knowing we were after him. By returning we might be placing our own lives at risk. Needless to say I didn't voice these fears to Jocelin. He was jittery enough as it was.

At least our journey back was less traumatic than the one down. We came across no more fleeing rebels. They would have long since passed by – at least, if they'd any sense they would. We took the journey slowly still feeling the effects of the drugged ale. Neither of us had any appetite and we needed to stop only the once to answer a call of nature. To cheer Jocelin up while we were occupied I decided to pose him a riddle.

'What is the cleanest leaf in Christendom?' I called out.

There was a pause. 'Is this another of your jokes, W-Walter?'

'Go on. What is it?'

I heard him sigh. 'I don't know. What is the c-cleanest l-leaf in Christendom?'

'The holly – because no-one will dare wipe their arse with it.'

I chuckled and expected Jocelin to do the same. But there was silence on the other side of the bush.

'Don't you get it? The holly leaf has prickles.'

'I g-get the joke Walter. I just d-don't think it's f-funny.'

'No sense of humour, Jocelin Brackland, that's your trouble.'

It was then that something swished past over my head. I thought at first it was a bird. If so it flew very fast and straight. I wondered what breed of bird it might be. But as I stood up to see another flew past only this time it didn't go over my head but nicked the top of my hand and embedded itself in a tree. I yelped in pain as I realised it wasn't a bird at all but a crossbow bolt. A moment earlier and it would have gone, not through my hand, but into my head – which I imagined was probably the intention.

I instantly dropped flat to the floor and yelled for Jocelin to do the same. 'Get down!'

'Wh-what? Why?'

'Just get down! We're under attack!'

He complied, and not a moment too soon as a third bolt flew between us this time at a different angle from the first two. The bowman was evidently working his way around to get a clearer shot. If we stayed where we were we'd be sitting ducks. We had to move – and fast.

'Jocelin!' I said in a loud whisper. 'We've got to hide!'

'H-hide w-where? We're in the m-middle of nowhere!'

He was right. We were at the edge of a small copse of trees. Our horses were hobbled out on the open road, there was no way we could get to them. We could hide among the trees but how long would it take for a bowman to work his way round and get a clear shot? We needed something else.

'Pigs!' whispered Jocelin.

'What?'

'Woodland p-pigs! Over there!' He jabbed a finger.

Sure enough in a clearing there was a small pig pen with a low flint wall surrounding it - abandoned by the look of it. The problem was getting to it across open ground.

'We'll have to make a d-dash for it! On a count of three! One -'

'No, wait!' I whispered. 'Let him release his next bolt first. It will take him time to reload. Then go.'

A moment later a fourth bolt flew between us. That was our cue.

'N-n-n-n-' stammered Jocelin. 'N-n-n-n-'

'Now?' I said.

I don't know if you've ever seen two elderly monks clutching their robes above their knees and high-tailing across a meadow, but it's not a pretty sight. It could only have taken us moments to cover the distance to the pen but it seemed like a lifetime. But somehow we made it unscathed. We dived down behind the wall just as another bolt slanted overhead and disappeared inside the pig-pen. But I was wrong about the pen being abandoned. It had a complement of about twenty piglets together with their sow. They had been lying quietly enjoying the afternoon sunshine until we interrupted their peace and sent them scattering in all directions. The pig-man – a lad of about twenty - must have been dozing too in his hut. When he heard the commotion he came out to see what was going on:

'Here, what…?'

'Get back inside!' I yelled.

He didn't need telling twice. Another bolt went flying over our heads and embedded itself in the door-jamb of the hut a few inches from his head. His eyes widened and he quickly retreated back inside the hut.

'I'm g-getting too old for this,' panted Jocelin.

'Why don't you stand up then? You won't have to worry about getting any older then!'

Actually that wasn't quite true. The bowman had had plenty of opportunity to drop Jocelin but he seemed to be aiming specifically at me.

'Who's d-doing this?' Jocelin gasped. 'And why?'

'I don't know! I'll ask him, shall I?'

'Where's it c-coming from?'

I pointed. 'Over that way.'

By now my injured hand was starting to throb and blood was oozing from the wound. And it was extremely painful.

'Here, l-let me see,' said Jocelin examining the wound. He then pulled off his shirt, tore it into strips and wrapped these around the wound. I was impressed. No greater love hath any man than he should rip up his undershirt for a friend.

We hadn't heard from the bowman for a few minutes so Jocelin poked his head tentatively over the wall.

'Do you think he's s-still there?'

Another bolt came whizzing over the top of us but fell harmlessly in the mud. That answered that question. A few moments later another went into the wall beside us. The bowman was getting closer.

'We can't stay here,' I whispered.

'And g-go where?'

'If I knew that we'd have already done it!'

Just then as luck - or Providence - would have it, a haywain came trundling around the edge of the wood. If we could make it to him we might stand a chance. But once again we'd have to risk being out in the open and I didn't think our trick of waiting for him to reload would work a second time. Besides, we couldn't wait. With each passing moment the haywain was getting further away. The same thought must have occurred to Jocelin for he reached up and gently eased the latch of the pigsty and pushed open the gate.

'What are you doing?'

'I once h-helped Brother Owen in the abbey p-piggery. W-watch me and do what I do!'

Once the gate was fully open he suddenly leapt up and started waving his arms about like a demented windmill yelling Ha! Ha! Ha! at the top of his voice. I thought for a moment he'd gone mad, but then I realised what he was doing. The pigs were already in a state of agitation and didn't need much encouragement to start squealing and bolt through the opening.

'C-come on!' shouted Jocelin.

Taking my courage, and my robe, in my one good hand and keeping my head as low as possible, I followed Jocelin as fast as I could as we ran towards the haywain. The pigs were no cover but they created just enough confusion to allow us the few seconds we needed. Once behind the wain we were able to get round to the side furthest from the bowman and by walking slowly alongside it were hidden by the load of hay. To gain sight of us again the bowman would now have to go in a huge arc around the cart. For the moment at least we were safe.

We managed to make it to a nearby inn, but I still felt vulnerable. We had to assume my would-be assassin was still outside somewhere waiting for us. And I say *my* assassin advisedly for it seemed it was me he was after though I couldn't begin to imagine why. We'd also lost the horses and couldn't risk going back for them. We were on foot, exposed with no idea when the next attack might come. Meanwhile I still had my injured hand.

Jocelin went down to the kitchen and came back with a bowl of hot water and some towels. He also made an oily black liquid and immersed my hand in it.

I frowned. 'What do you think you're doing?'

'Treating your w-wound. I'm the ph-physician now and you're the p-patient. So sh-shut up and d-do as you're told for once.'

'You've become very masterful all of a sudden. What happened to the mouse who wanted to go home?'

'I d-don't like being shot at. It m-makes me angry.'

'It wasn't you he was aiming at.' I sniffed the bowl. 'What's in it? It smells like fish.'

'It's s-seaweed.'

'It's what?' I said withdrawing my hand fast.

He pushed it back down again. 'It's my own concoction. It will c-clean the wound and prevent m-mortification. You're n-not the only one who experiments with h-herbs.'

'But it stings.'

'Good. That means it's d-doing you good.'

'Then why is my hand turning blue?'

'P-purple. And it's s-supposed to.'

He dried my hand and then re-bandaged it with strips of clean linen. I had to admit once the stinging had worn off it felt a whole lot better even if it didn't look it.

Once he'd finished he sat down heavily and sighed. 'Who's d-doing this, Walter?'

'Someone who doesn't like me, that's obvious.'

'M-maybe it's our Frenchman friend. Maybe he ch-changed his mind about l-letting us go. O-or F-Father Quennel n-now that he knows you kn-know he's a c-collaborator.'

'You know it too. No, there has to be a simpler explanation.'

'S-something to do with the m-murder then?'

'It has to be. It's the only other explanation.'

'Even so, wh-why just you? I'm as much involved now as you.'

'The Marshal gave the commission to me. Maybe whoever is doing this sees me as the threat. But I shouldn't look too smug. It may be your turn next. The question now is how we are going to get out of here and back to Lincoln without one or other of us ending up looking like Saint Sebastian.'

'I've been th-thinking about that. What you n-need is a d-disguise.'

I looked at him uncertainly. 'What sort of disguise?'

'S-something no-one would suspect.'

'You mean like a Russian with snow on his boots? Or an Arab maybe, with a turban?' I rather liked that idea.

'I was th-thinking of something a l-little less exotic.'

'Like what?'

He grimaced. 'P-promise you won't j-jump down my th-throat?'

Chapter Eighteen
A DRESSING UP

'A *woman?* You want me to dress up like a woman? You must be mad!'

But I could see he was being serious.

'Why n-not?'

'Because it'll never work, that's why not. I mean, no-one's ever going to believe I'm a woman. I'm much too tall for a start.'

'You've d-done it b-before.'

'When?'

'One Easter – d-don't you remember? The abbey put on a performance of N-Noah and the F-Flood. Your r-rendition of Noah's wife was very convincing. You were quite a sh-shrew as I r-remember,' he grinned.

'That was thirty years ago. And I only had to convince an audience of gullible townsfolk, not a lunatic bowman intent on killing me.'

'It worked for William L-Longchamp.'

'Who?'

'King Richard's ch-chancellor. When he fell out of f-favour with King John and was t-trying to escape to France, he dressed as a w-woman and tried to board a ship. He'd have made it too if a f-fisherman hadn't mistaken him for a p-prostitute and offered him a groat for his f-favours.'

'Well there you are then. It didn't work for him either.'

'The f-fisherman was convinced.'

'He must have been at sea too long. As I remember it Lord Longchamp resembled nothing so much as a deformed ape.'

'B-better than his other d-disguise.'

'Which was?'

'As a m-monk.'

I pouted. 'Well I won't do it. A man dressing as a woman indeed! There must be a dozen laws against it. I'd end up in the stocks.'

'R-rather there than in your g-grave.'

'In any case,' I went on, 'if you're with me the bowman is bound to know it's me. No-one's that stupid.'

'I'll k-keep my d-distance when we're in p-public. No-one will even kn-know we're together.'

I frowned. 'No I'm sorry, the whole thing's impractical. For a start, where am I going to find women's clothing? And any that fit me? No no, it's a hopeless idea.'

'Is that your f-final word?'

'It is.'

'Ssh! Keep your voice down or she'll hear us!'

The woman was a few yards away hanging out washing on a gorse bush next to a small brook, her kirtle tucked up under her belt and her sleeves rolled up. We were a few yards away hiding behind another bush and watching her. She had just finished pummelling a robe that looked as though it might just possibly fit me and was hanging it out to dry.

'When she g-goes b-back to f-fetch another article,' whispered Jocelin, 'I'll step out and eng-gage her in c-conversation while you g-grab the d-d-d-dress.'

'In that case you'd better stop stuttering or we shall be here all night.'

'I c-can't h-help it,' he frowned. 'When I g-get n-nervous I s-s-stutter.'

'Then I'll go and talk to her while you grab the dress.'

He shook his head emphatically. 'No, you're s-stealthier than me. I'd only m-mess it up. I'll k-keep her t-talking. You g-get the dress.'

Before I could stop him he was already on his feet and making his way over to the woman who was now standing in the middle of the stream pummelling another piece of linen. It looked like heavy work. She seemed happy to stop for a breather. I couldn't hear what he was saying to her but soon she was smiling and nodding.

'Oh Mary, Jesus and all the saints preserve me!' I prayed and crossed myself several times.

I waited until Jocelin had her full attention and then I sneaked forward to grab the dress. But gorse being a prickly plant would not give up ownership easily. The dress snagged. I tugged, but it would not come. I tugged again and in my clumsiness it tore. The woman heard the rip and turned to catch me in mid-action.

If we thought running from the bowman was dangerous enough, getting away from this harridan brandishing a pummelling dolly was positively homicidal. In the end she threw the thing at me and her aim was better than the bowman's. It hit me on the back of my head making me momentarily lose my footing. But we made it to a pair of waiting nags we'd stolen earlier and just managed to waddle off in the nick of time closely pursued by curses and much waving of fists.

'Why did I let you talk me into this?' I growled.

'It w-worked, didn't it? Anyway, the dress f-fits, which is the m-main thing.'

'Only just. It only comes half-way down my legs.'

'Then you'd b-better roll up your r-robe.'

'And expose my hairy calves? Very feminine I'm sure!'

We were in a small copse just outside a village a few miles south of Lincoln. We'd managed to get away from the woman whose dress I was trying on although there was probably a hue and cry out for us already. The trouble was the dress wasn't completely dry and to make matters worse my monk's robe was bunched up underneath which made me look like a badly-stuffed rag-doll.

'How do women wear these things?' I said despondently. 'It only fits where it touches.'

'B-be patient. It feels s-strange because you're not used to it. Give it a ch-chance. Here.'

He handed me a woman's coif to hide my tonsure. There was nothing I could do about my beard. Luckily I'd been shaved at the abbey just before we came away so there was only a few days worth of growth.

'K-keep your head down and n-no-one will n-notice. Now, try walking up and down a b-bit.'

I marched away from him and then back. But he was frowning again.

'You c-can't stride about like that. People will g-guess you're a m-man straight away.'

'How should I stride?'

'L-like a woman, with d-dainty little feminine steps. Like this.' He demonstrated by tottering a few steps on his toes. Then tottered back again.

'If I walk like that I'll be crippled before we get half way back to Lincoln – if I'm not arrested first.'

I had another go making him guffaw with laughter.

'Now what are you laughing at?'

'I've j-just realised who you remind me of. M-Mother Han.'

'Thank you very much. I've achieved my life's ambition at last.'

'You'll be all right. J-just k-keep your injured hand hidden. In fact, b-better to hide the arm entirely. That should p-put off too much attention.'

'What sort of attention?'

'Hopefully n-none - now that you're officially a wanted f-felon,' he grinned.

'I see, that's why you wanted it to be me to steal the dress. Well I'm sorry to disappoint you but I will expunge my sinful act by repaying the woman once we've returned to Bury.'

'I n-never th-thought you'd do anything else.'

The rest of our journey back to Lincoln was tortuous. We took a circuitous route to avoid any settlements and hopefully our bowman as well. Fortunately sunset is late this time of the year which meant we had plenty of daylight hours in which to travel, but it also meant we had a long and tiring day. We could have camped out under the stars but the way things were that would have been very hazardous – and cold. A fire would have been completely out of the question. We really needed somewhere to rest for the night.

As luck would have it just as twilight was descending we came to a crossroads and the inevitable inn. With candle-light showing at the windows and smoke from a fire within, it looked warm and inviting. We decided to take the risk and ventured inside.

Jocelin went off to speak to the innkeeper about some food and the possibility of sleeping in their barn - we daren't risk taking a room in case there were other lodgers with whom we'd probably have to share beds. That was all right for Jocelin, but I'd have to share with a woman which would have given the game away straight away. While he was negotiating our accommodation I waited nervously in a dark corner trying not to draw attention to myself.

Fortunately there were few other customers in the place. No-one took much notice of me – except one man. He was sitting a few feet away drinking alone. He was a big, gruff-looking fellow and kept staring at me with quizzical eyes. Had he guessed my secret? Could he perhaps even be my archer assassin? He certainly looked vicious enough. I tried my best to ignore him hoping Jocelin would hurry back, but he was still in deep conversation with the landlord and had his back to us. Meanwhile the man kept staring at me between sups of his ale. Eventually he came over and sat on Jocelin's stool.

'You, er, with that monk?' he asked.

I just giggled in what I'd hoped was a feminine manner and put my hand over my mouth. I kept my head down praying the man would go away and that Jocelin would hurry up, or at least turn round and see the impending danger.

'You his servant?'

I giggled again and nodded coyly. I could feel my heart beginning to pound.

'Servant, eh?' he frowned. 'Bit unusual that, ennit? A woman serving a monk?'

I didn't reply but tried to turn further away. Where the devil was Jocelin?

The man leaned closer and lowered his voice. 'Do we mean "serving" or do we mean "*serving*"?' He winked lasciviously.

The situation was becoming serious. If Jocelin didn't hurry back soon it could end in disaster.

At last Jocelin returned – and not a moment too soon.

'What's g-going on here?' he demanded sternly.

'Jes' making polite conversation, brother, tha's all,' said the man.

'Well k-kindly desist!'

The man put up two placatory palms and moved back. But he hadn't quite finished yet:

'Mind you, it's a good disguise.'

I felt the blood drain from my face. Jocelin stared at me wide-eyed with alarm.

'Wh-what do you m-mean?'

'This.' He tugged on Jocelin's robe. 'You're not a real monk, are you?'

'I'll have you know -' Jocelin began, but the man shook a dismissive head.

'No need to get defensive, brother. We all have a living to make. But I do like your friend. She has a nice fruity voice. I like a woman with a fruity voice. It's very sexy.' He winked at me again.

'You d-don't want to m-mess with this l-lady,' Jocelin cautioned seriously. 'Apart f-from anything else, she only h-has one arm.'

'That's all right,' said the man. 'My late wife only had one eye. I en't fussy.' He leaned forward and pinched my cheek between two gnarled fingers. 'How much, missy? A groat?'

By now I'd had enough and shot to my feet. 'How dare you!' I said in my normal manly voice. 'I'll have you know I am no harlot - or any other kind of woman for that matter. I am a man!' And to prove it I pulled off my coif to reveal my monk's tonsure. 'There, what do you say now?'

I was aware that all conversation in the place had stopped as every head turned towards us. The man stared too. He frowned. His eyes narrowed dangerously. Then they widened. Finally he shrugged.

'Two groats then.'

We only just managed to get out of the building before we were grabbed. Fortunately our horses hadn't yet been unsaddled and we were able to leap onto them and ride off with only a handful of the younger men chasing us and shouting abuse. In our haste neither of us noticed the shadowy figure that had been sitting in another corner of the room and who had slunk out after us.

We galloped until we were sure no-one was following us and then we stopped, exhausted. It was no good. We had to rest. It was very late and dark. The horses handn't been fed or watered. We managed to find a small brook and let them drink while Jocelin and I collapsed onto the bank.

'Any more bright ideas?' I asked him.

'H-how was I to know you'd f-find the only man in England who's attracted to m-masculine women?'

'Believe me, he's not alone.'

'At least we kn-know the disguise w-works. Everyone else in the inn t-took you for a woman. All except the innkeeper. I th-think he guessed j-judging by what he was asking for the use of his b-barn.'

'Well I hope you didn't pay him because we're going to have to camp out in the open - again.'

He groaned. 'I'm g-getting too old for this. D-dragged half way across L-Lincolnshire. Attacked by r-rebels. P-poisoned -'

I sat up. 'Shush!'

He shook his head. 'No, it's n-no good Walter, I'm s-sick of all this. I -'

I put my hand over his mouth. 'Shut up Jocelin for heaven's sake and listen!'

We waited. There was the sound of a twig snapping.

'What was that?' I whispered.

'I d-didn't hear anything,' he whispered back.

'Are you deaf as well as blind?'

Another twig snapped.

'Over there!'

'S-someone from the inn?'

'No!' I hissed. 'It's him! The bowman!'

'Oh dear G-God!' said Jocelin crossing himself furiously.

I wasn't having this. After what happened at the inn my blood was still up.

'I'm going to put a stop to this!'

'Wh-what are you going to do?'

'You carry on talking as though I'm still here,' I whispered. 'I'll sneak round and surprise him.'

'Wh-what if he thinks I'm you?'

'You don't look anything like me.'

'It's p-pitch b-black! He won't kn-know the d-difference!'

'I'm wearing a dress remember? I'll be quick. I promise.'

Before he could offer any more objections I slunk away.

I've always prided myself on being able to see in the dark but in this case my assailant wasn't difficult to locate. My little ruse seemed to have worked. He clearly thought we were both still together - I could hear Jocelin chattering to himself a few feet away. I saw no sign of the crossbow but I did see the flash of a blade.

He had a knife!

I quickly felt for my own small dagger. It wasn't there! Damn! I'd forgotten, that French knight took it from me. No time to worry about that now. I had to act before he could pounce on poor Jocelin. It was now or never. I lunged forward and caught the swine around the neck.

'Aha! Got you my friend!'

I spun him round, knocked the knife out of his hand and doubled him over onto his back with me on top, my knee on his chest.

'Run out of bolts, have you? Not so clever now, are we? Right! Let's see who you are!'

I pulled back his hood and clenched a fist ready to knock a few teeth out – but stopped.

'Maude? I mean, Eleanor?'

'Get off me you brute!' she said punching my arm.

Jocelin had heard the commotion and by now had joined us just as two more riders rode up. I couldn't believe my eyes. It was the same captain of horse we'd first met a few days earlier on the road to Lincoln. As soon as he saw us he groaned.

'Not you three again. The innkeeper said there some dangerous bandits about. If I'd have known it was you …' He shook his head in despair.

Eleanor and I both scrambled to our feet.

'Captain,' she said before I had a chance to speak, 'I demand you arrest this man. He just attacked me.'

My jaw fell to the floor. '*I* attacked *you*? You just tried to slit my throat!'

'With what? I have no knife.'

'Yes you do. I saw it!'

'Search me!'

She held up her hands which of course were now empty, the knife having been lost in the undergrowth.

No chance of finding it in the darkness. I pouted my annoyance.

'Captain,' Eleanor went on, 'you saw what was happening. It was *his* knee on *my* throat. *I* am the victim here!'

My jaw fell even further if that were possible. '*She's* not the victim. *I* am. Look, I'll prove it to you.' I struggled to roll up the sleeve of the dress to reveal my bandaged hand. 'There! What do you think of that?'

The captain leaned down from his saddle to see. 'Very neat. Bandaged it as well, did she?'

'Yes,' I nodded. 'True, it is an old wound. But she did it. Yesterday. With a crossbow.'

Eleanor snorted. 'Do I look as though I could handle a crossbow? I am but a weak and feeble woman.'

'Weak and feeble? Her? Ask her what she was doing out here alone if not to attack me? Go on, ask her!'

The captain raised quizzical eyebrows.

'I was out for a ride,' explained Eleanor indignantly.

I nearly choked. 'Out for a ride? In the middle of the night?'

'I often ride out after sunset. I find the darkness - comforting.'

'A likely story! So what were you doing hiding in the bushes? In fact, how did you manage to get out at all? You were supposed to be locked up in Lincoln Castle!'

'Tch! The castle doesn't stand that can hold me!'

'A moment ago you were weak and feeble,' reminded the captain.

'Ha! Well said, captain!'

She gave him her most seductive feminine smile. 'Captain - *cher capitaine*,' she mooed, fluttering her eyelids at him. 'You cannot believe a word this man says. *He's* the criminal here. It's obvious, can't you see?

Look, he's even wearing a disguise. I ask you, is that the sign of an innocent man?'

'You were in disguise the last time we met I seem to remember.'

Plus you've conveniently forgotten about your jewels, I could have added, although perhaps this was not quite the right moment to accuse the captain of theft.

'That was different,' she sniffed.

The captain turned back to me. 'Well brother?'

I wriggled uncomfortably in the dress now torn and muddied from the scuffle. 'I-I know how it looks. B-but I can explain.'

'Stammer back too, I see.'

I pouted. 'Captain, you have to believe me. I really am the victim here. I was attacked by this woman and her crossbow and had to don this female garb in order to escape. Ask my colleague here.'

Jocelin took a breath and raised a finger. 'W-w-w -' he stammered.

'Where is this crossbow anyway?' asked the captain. 'I don't see it anywhere.'

'Precisely!' trumpeted Eleanor. 'Where is it? Show us! You can't.'

'Well not now, obviously. But everything I've been saying is true. Ask Brother Jocelin. Jocelin, for heaven's sake, tell the captain!'

'D-d-d-d -' said Jocelin.

'Well of course he'd agree,' said Eleanor. 'The pair of them are in it together. They shit through the same arsehole.'

'N-n-n-n -' frowned Jocelin.

The captain scratched his head. He clearly didn't know what to believe. But I wasn't about to flutter my eyelids in order to persuade him. I drew myself erect and tried to look as dignified as a man can in a woman's dress.

'Captain, I am Brother Walter de Ixworth, physician to the abbot of Saint Edmund's. I request that you arrest this woman and take her to Lincoln Castle - at once!'

Eleanor stepped forward, equally erect. 'And I am Eleanor, Queen of England, and I *demand* that you arrest *him* and take him to Lincoln Castle – immediately!'

We both glared at each other.

The captain looked from one to the other. 'You, brother, want me to take this woman to Lincoln Castle?'

I nodded. 'I do!'

'And you, madam, want me to take him to Lincoln Castle?'

'*Certainement!*'

He shrugged. 'Well then, I suppose I'd better take you both to Lincoln Castle.' He signalled to his sergeant who now rode forward.

'Your Highness, if you wouldn't mind,' he said to Eleanor giving her an over-elaborate bow from his saddle. 'And you, brother,' he said to Jocelin. Then he turned to me: 'You too,' he sniggered. 'Sister.'

Chapter Nineteen
A DRESSING DOWN

By the time we got back to Lincoln the sun was coming up. I was dead on my feet not having slept for twenty-four hours. Jocelin was in an even worse state, poor old thing, but then he has a decade on me. Eleanor, needless to say, was as alert as ever, chattering non-stop to – or rather *at* – the captain who bore it with all the resignation of a seasoned soldier used to suffering. I could only admire his forbearance.

We were taken to the half-finished bishop's palace next to the cathedral. It seemed our captain was Bishop Peter's man which explained why we were brought here rather than to the castle. With Lincoln's own bishop still absent, Bishop Peter had temporarily occupied his throne. I believe he had once been the precentor here so no doubt he felt a certain proprietorial right. For once he even looked a little like a real bishop, no longer adorned in breastplate and gauntlets but wearing a chasuble and stole.

The three of us - Jocelin, Eleanor and I - were lined up before his excellency who was eyeing us all with undisguised contempt – and me in particular. But then I was still wearing the woman's dress not yet having had a chance to remove it. Still, I was determined this time to get my side of the story across first before Eleanor had a chance to contradict me:

'My lord bishop,' I began, 'I really must protest at the way Brother Jocelin and I have been treated. We were on official business having been delegated by the lord Regent to investigate the murder of Sir Reginald Croc. This document will explain everything if you would care to look at it.' I proffered the letters patent given me by Earl Marshal.

Bishop Peter didn't even bother to glance at it. He just continued to stare at me with a look of pure disgust on his face. 'What are you? Some kind of pervert?'

I never realised before how much venom could be injected into that one word. I looked down at the dress. Filthy and bedraggled as it was, it did look a mess I have to admit. Hardly surprising after what it had been through.

'I know how this looks,' I said. 'But it was a necessary diversion -'

'Necessary diversion?' Eleanor sneered. 'Lord bishop, this man – this *dégénéré* - has been going around the country dressed as you see him, meeting with rebels, relishing their company and indulging in God alone knows what depravity with them. You cannot believe a word he says. I suggest – nay, I *demand* that you throw him into the dungeon forthwith!'

Give him his due, Bishop Peter couldn't be accused of favouritism. He disliked Lady Eleanor every bit as much as he disliked me.

'This is a house of God, madam,' he said wearily. 'We don't have dungeons here.'

'Fine. Then execute him.'

'For wearing women's clothing?'

'For treason! He has betrayed his country as well as his sex. He does not deserve to live.'

The bishop sighed. 'You're very keen on that word, if you don't mind my saying.'

'That is because I see it going on around me all the time.' She curled her lip. 'Oh, you English. You are all the same. As perfidious as you are weak.'

'For your information, madam, I am not English either. I was born in Touraine. I am as French as you.'

Ha! Bravo, monsieur l'évêque! I was beginning to like him.

'Then you should be ashamed of yourself!'

The bishop extended an episcopal finger towards her. 'You, madam, have nothing to reprimand anybody about. You left your lawful custody without authorization and rode abroad. In deference to your rank you had been left unshackled but you have abused that privilege. Rest assured, you will not get that opportunity again! As for you, monk. Is she right? Have you been helping the king's enemies – again?'

I looked at him seriously. 'When I find a man with his hands and feet cut off, yes my lord, I give him aid. I believe it is my Christian duty. Even to a rebel.'

'Then can you think of any reason why I should not do as the lady suggests and hang you here and now?'

'One reason. I believe she murdered Sir Reginald Croc. That is the real reason she's been following me. That is why she tried to kill me and why she is trying to silence me now.'

Next to me I heard Jocelin gasp. I don't know why I said it. I hadn't intended to. I certainly hadn't planned it. It just sort of slipped out. But when I thought about it, it did make sense, though evidently not to the lady:

'This is absurd!' Eleanor reeled. 'What possible reason would I have for murdering Croc? You can see what he's doing. He's trying to save his own skin by accusing me.'

'My lord, if you would just allow me to explain -' I tried again.

But the bishop threw up a hand. 'No. I don't want to hear any more of your explanations.'

'But I do.'

The voice had come from the back of the room. We all turned to see William Marshal standing there. I cannot tell you what a relief it was to see him.

'My lord regent,' said Bishop Peter. 'We thought you were in Nottingham.'

'And so I shall be – later. For the moment I want to hear what Brother Walter has to say.'

'Whatever it is will be lies!' insisted the lady.

'In that case he will be found out. But until I've heard him I cannot judge.'

'And will I be extended the same privilege?'

'Of course. You will have every opportunity to refute his word.'

'His word!' she sneered. 'The word of a Judas. You shouldn't be listening to him. He shouldn't be speaking at all. He should be hanged for treason!'

Bishop Peter rolled his eyes. 'There she goes again.'

Eleanor rounded on him. 'Are you going to take the word of a lowly monk above that of the Queen of England?'

'There is no Queen of England, madam,' said the Marshal equably.

'Only because I haven't been crowned yet.'

'Nor will you be. No woman has ever sat on the throne of England.'

'Not in her own right, perhaps. But as the wife of a king?'

Next to me Jocelin gasped again. My God, I thought. The woman will stop at nothing to get her hands on the levers of power. Bishop Peter looked confused:

'Wife of a king? What's she talking about?'

'Henry and Eleanor,' she said. 'It has a certain ring to it, don't you think?' She raised speculative eyebrows.

She was alluding to her grandparents, that more famous duo of the same name, King Henry and Queen Eleanor of Aquitaine. But Eleanor wasn't just hinting. She was in deadly earnest:

'Think about it, my lords. It would secure the throne and solve the succession question once and for all. I am single. I presume Henry is too.'

'But he is also your cousin,' said the Marshal. 'And I believe the church has some opinion on the subject of consanguinity?' He raised questioning eyes at the bishop who shrugged non-committally.

'I'm sure an arrangement could be made with the pope,' said Eleanor.

'I'm sure it could. However, Henry is but nine years old. He has a few years yet before he has to decide whom he wishes to marry, though I doubt it will be you.'

'Oh? Why not?'

'Because by the time he is old enough to father a child you will be beyond the age of being able to give him an heir. And that above all is the prime function of a queen consort. It will be your own body, madam, not my words that will deny you the throne.'

It had been her last desperate shot. Her quiver was finally empty. She frowned; she scowled and then she went red in the face. She looked like a volcano about to erupt. And then she did:

'*But I am your queeeen!!!*'

For a moment all we could do was stare at her. She looked wild. Her eyes were rolling and her mouth was distorted. It was an extraordinary display, but it settled one thing: if I doubted her heritage before I did so no longer. The Plantagenets are famous for their fiery temperaments - her grandfather was supposed to have chewed the carpet when in one of his rages. Eleanor didn't quite go that far but she certainly had his flaming temper along with his flaming red hair. No wonder they are called the Devil's brood.

While she was in that state there was no reasoning with her so that was where the meeting ended, which suited me as I needed time to sort out what I was going to say to the Marshal. I managed to scuttle out before the bishop could stop me, no doubt thinking I'd thwarted him again. I could foresee further trouble ahead from him in the future, but I couldn't worry about that now.

Once back in our own room Jocelin was looking deathly pale. 'I c-can't take m-much m-more of this,' he said wiping his brow. 'Marriage? To Henry? Was she s-serious?'

'Deadly. And I can't say I'm entirely surprised. When you think about it, it was the obvious next step.'

'Then what were you th-thinking of, accusing her like that?'

'I had to say something or Bishop Peter would have lynched me. At least now the Marshal's back we should start to get some sensible answers.'

'I'm g-glad you think so. M-my guess is he'll actually do what Bishop Peter only th-threatened - hang you and me too I sh-shouldn't w-wonder.'

'Why would he do that? You heard him. He wants to know what we have to say. Once he hears our argument he'll see the logic of it.'

'Well of c-course he's going to agree it was Eleanor! He'd agree to anything that w-will divert attention away from himself.'

'We'll see. But first I need is get out of this female garb. If I'm to impress the Marshal with reasoned argument I can't do it dressed like a pantomime dame.'

I began untying the top of the dress but was finding it difficult with my wounded hand.

'Here, l-let me see that.' He turned the bandaged hand over in his own and tutted. 'It's filthy. It n-needs redressing. Wait here.'

He went off and came back with some clean water and a bowl. He then unwrapped the soiled bandage and delicately washed the wound. It was actually looking not too bad – no puss or redness, just a bit sore. Whatever was in that seaweed concoction he'd used seemed to have done the trick. He then dried it and wrapped some fresh linen strips round it. When he finished I examined his handiwork with my trained physician's eye.

'Hm, not bad. I might even give you a job when we get back to Bury.'

'If we ever m-manage to g-get back.'

He collected up his equipment while I finished getting out of the dress.

'That's better,' I said scratching myself. 'But please, don't ever suggest I do anything like that again.'

'It w-worked, didn't it? You s-succeeded in avoiding the b-bowman's bolts.'

'The only thing I succeeded in doing was to convince Bishop Peter that I'm some kind of deviant collaborator. As for our bowman – bow-*woman* I should say - it didn't put Eleanor off. She wasn't fooled by my disguise.'

'Without the c-crossbow you've no way of p-proving it was Eleanor who attacked you.'

'She had a knife, didn't she?'

'You've no p-proof of that either.'

I frowned. 'No-one can doubt she's capable. You saw that exhibition just now. She's as mad as a nest of wasps – and just as dangerous.'

'S-so would you be if you'd been incarcerated for m-most of your l-life.'

He went off to empty his bowl.

'What did you just say?' I asked when he came back.

'I said -'

'Yes, I heard you.' I tapped my chin thoughtfully. 'D'you know, old friend, I think you may just have cracked it.'

'C-cracked what?'

'The case.'

He shook his head. 'I d-don't f-follow.'

'Never mind. At least now I've got something solid to put to the Marshal.'

Chapter Twenty
A CLOSE SHAVE

At this point I should mention something about Jocelin that I haven't spoken of before. In addition to all his other debilities he suffers from an unfortunate malady that sometimes afflicts devout men, namely "martyrdom tendency". Such people joyfully embrace suffering as a demonstration of their faith, and the more intense their agony the greater their joy. When the early Christians were thrown into the arena to be mauled by wild beasts they often went willingly, singing psalms, knowing they would soon be rewarded in Heaven. Of course, these people were saints and would have had their pain removed by God. We ordinary mortals may not be so fortunate. In Jocelin's case the symptoms don't appear very often but when they do they can have devastating consequences. Why do I mention this now? Because he was about to do something that was likely to get him strung up, or racked, or at the very least flung into a dark hole somewhere and left to rot. Not as messy as having one's liver ripped out by lions perhaps, but just as terminal. Fair enough if he was the only person affected. The trouble was he might be taking me with him.

As we followed the guard across the yard from the cathedral I noticed he was starting to drag his feet.

'What's the matter, brother? Nervous about meeting the Marshal again?'

'It's n-not that.'

'Well what then?'

He grimaced. 'The M-Marshal will be asking about the investigation - yes?'

'That's the general idea.'

'And he'll be c-curious to know who your s-suspects are?'

'Of course.'

Finally he sighed: 'It's n-no g-good, Walter. I am g-going to have to t-tell him.'

'Tell him what?'

'That I believe he is the murderer.'

I stopped dead in my tracks. Up ahead the guard did the same and turned to see what the hold-up was. I pulled Jocelin to one side.

'Are you mad?' I whispered urgently. 'A few minutes ago you said you were afraid the Marshal might clap us in irons. He certainly will if you start accusing him of murder.'

'I d-don't see why. You practically did the same.'

'When?'

'At our l-last m-meeting with him. You m-mentioned about the fourth suspect g-gaining from the comte's death. He would n-need to be v-very stupid not to r-realise who you were t-talking about.'

'That was different. I deliberately didn't mention names. It was ambiguous. He could choose not to understand if he wished. You accuse him directly to his face and he won't be able to ignore it.'

'I c-cannot help it, Walter, my c-conscience won't allow me to remain silent.'

'Very laudable – and very suicidal. Jocelin, this isn't just any old suspect we're talking about. This is the Earl

Regent, the most powerful man in England. He has priorities that supersede those of little people like you and me. He can't allow his important work to be jeopardised for the sake of one man's murder.'

'Are you s-saying that Sir Reginald's l-life is worth l-less than that of the Regent?'

'I most certainly am.'

'Then wh-where is your Ch-Christian notion of all men being equal before God?'

'I'll worry about that later. For now my only concern is staying alive until supper.'

'If you're g-going to accuse the L-Lady Eleanor I must d-do the s-same for the Marshal. I've said all along th-that he's our m-man. You told me I had c-cracked the case. *Ergo,* I must be right.'

'That's not what I meant.'

'Then what did you m-mean?'

I looked across at the waiting guard who was beginning to grow impatient.

'There isn't time now to explain.'

'Then you l-leave me no choice. I m-must speak out.'

'Do so and we are both dead.'

'If that is God's w-will,' he said piously lowering his eyes.

'Jocelin!'

But it was too late. The guard was beckoning us again. We were committed.

We found the Marshal in the stable block getting ready to ride. He was alone except for his groom who was helping him on with his boots.

'I can't be long. I have to get back to Nottingham to the king. Tell me quickly what you've got.'

He listened while I went through everything that had happened since our last meeting: The journey down to

Sleaford; what happened on the way and why I found it necessary to put on a disguise.

'So let's see,' he said when I'd finished. 'You've been here five days. In that time you've been shot at, nearly got yourself decapitated, managed to upset the local villagers, turned a princess of the blood royal against you and made an enemy of the bishop of Winchester. Quite an achievement.'

'I'm sorry to have been such an embarrassment, my lord.'

'Oh, don't be. Anyone who can stir up that much trouble in a single week must be doing something right. But this murder. You now believe the Lady Eleanor to be the culprit?'

'I believe so, yes.'

'Why?'

'Well for a start she's more than capable of killing a man – she proved that with the unfortunate Gelyn. She's also ambitious and will stop at nothing to get what she wants. And she thinks God is on her side.'

He snorted. 'We all think that, brother.'

'She also attacked me, I think because she knows I'm onto her. She denies it of course, but there's no disputing she was following us and I was injured by a bolt that she fired. You don't do that without good reason.'

'Still not proof.'

'And she managed to get out of Lincoln castle. That can't have been easy. She went to great trouble just to silence me.'

'Don't be too sure about that. She's done it before. Lady Eleanor has been incarcerated in various supposedly secure locations all round the country only to escape each time. She's good at it. And she often has help. She may never be queen but there are many supporters who think she should.' He looked at me. 'Is that it?'

'That's all.'

'Well you'll have to do better than that if you wish to indict the lady.'

He looked at Jocelin who so far had said nothing but was hopping from one foot to the other.

'Brother you look agitated. Have you some thoughts on the matter?'

'I think you'll find Brother Jocelin and I are in full agreement,' I said quickly before he had a chance to speak.

'Is that so, brother?'

Jocelin took a breath – but I interrupted him again:

'Brother Jocelin's contribution to this investigation has been invaluable, simply invaluable. But as I say, we are in complete agreement over this.'

'I'm sure, but if you don't mind, I'd like to hear it from him.' He turned back to Jocelin. 'So, brother, have you anything to say - and before Brother Walter interrupts you again?'

I knew when I was defeated. Inwardly I groaned. I'd done everything I could think of to avert the coming disaster that now looked inevitable. Just as we were doing so well, too. Was he really going to ruin everything? Surely he couldn't be that foolish.

'Yes my lord, as a m-matter of f-fact I do have s-something to say. What I th-think is -'

I slapped my forehead. 'Oh, what an idiot I am! I nearly forgot.'

The Marshal sighed. 'Yes, Master Walter?'

'My lord, I was meaning to ask: In light of what we were saying about the princess, may I have your permission to interview the lady?'

'You wish to speak to the princess in person?'

'I do.'

'After what she tried to do to you in the woods yesterday?'

'If you wouldn't mind.'

He shrugged. 'If you think it will help. But you should wear some stout body armour when you do.'

'Indeed so, my lord! Ha ha! Ha ha ha ha!' I laughed – rather too hysterically I fear.

The Marshal turned back to Jocelin once more. 'Well brother? You were about to say?'

Jocelin opened his mouth - but then closed it again.

The Marshal frowned. 'What? Nothing?'

Jocelin shook his head.

'In that case you'll forgive me, brothers, but I must away. If I am to get to Nottingham in daylight I must leave now. There is much still to do. The battle just won is a bonus but to secure the throne I must get Henry crowned in Westminster and unfortunately the dauphin still holds London. While I want this matter of Sir Reginald settled it cannot be allowed to drag on. I can give you twenty-four hours. After that I'm afraid we will have to draw a veil over it.'

'Thank you, my lord. We will do our best.'

'Good hunting.'

With that, he stomped out to his waiting steed and with a troop of twenty men-at-arms behind him rode swiftly away.

I heaved a huge sigh of relief and turned to Jocelin.

'Well? What happened? Why didn't you speak up? I thought you wanted to unburden your conscience.'

'You d-didn't give me m-much chance. Anyway, there's t-time enough for that once we've heard what the p-princess has to s-say.'

'Aha!' I nodded. 'So that's the reason. You're as curious as I am to hear what she has to say!'

'Let's just s-say I'm prepared to keep an open m-mind – unlike yours which is p-permanently c-closed. But don't think I've ch-changed mine. I still think the M-Marshal is the m-murderer and when your interview with Eleanor fails - as I'm sure it w-will - I will put my suspicions to him the v-very next time we meet.'

'But in the meantime we have twenty-four hours in order to prove I'm right. And if I succeed then it won't be necessary to implicate the Marshal at all.'

'And if we don't?'

'I'll plait the hangman's noose myself.'

Chapter Twenty-one
THE BUTTERFLY BISHOP

Twenty-four hours to solve the murder. Enough time, surely, to get a confession out of Eleanor. She will lie, she will prevaricate and wriggle like a worm to try to get out of it of course, but I am wise to her ways now. And the timing couldn't be better. She must have lost some of her confidence after the drubbing she received from the Marshal. She must be feeling wretched. Would I be so ungallant as to take advantage of a lady while she was down? Any other lady, perhaps not. This lady – absolutely!

Unfortunately things didn't quite work out as simply as I had hoped for other malign forces were at work. Early the next morning we were awoken by the sound of heavy footsteps on the stairs outside our room. The door was flung open and in marched four guards. In my semi-soporific state I thought this was an escort sent by the Marshal to take us to see Eleanor. I was soon disabused of that idea. The guards, two for each of us, marched us out into the courtyard where we were separated. Jocelin was led away towards the Observatory Tower while I was made to continue on to the cathedral. This, of course, was Bishop Peter territory.

St Mary's may not have a dungeon but it does have a strongroom into which I was unceremoniously thrust, the door slammed shut and I was left to ponder my fate.

What was Bishop Peter up to? Was he going to hang me after all as Eleanor had demanded and he had clearly preferred? With the Marshal absent who was there to stop him? I could get no explanation from the guards. I banged on the door and yelled till I was hoarse but got no response. I said twenty-four hours was enough time to interview Eleanor, but only just. If I didn't get out soon it would be too late to do anything.

I was left languishing for the entire morning growing more and more frustrated, but the door was eventually opened and I was led back to the bishop's palace. It appeared his excellency had been out hunting. A stag was laid out on a trestle table, still warm, with its head hanging over the edge of the table dripping blood onto the episcopal floor. The man himself was standing before it still in his hunting clothes, wine goblet in hand, with servants coming and going. At last we were left alone.

Bishop Peter didn't turn round but continued to study the stag. Whatever it was he wanted I needed to get it over with as quickly as possible.

'My lord bishop,' I began, 'if this is about the dress -'
'Magnificent beasts, aren't they?'
I frowned. 'What? Oh, the stag. Yes.'
'Worthy of the hunter's skill, wouldn't you say? This one carried on running even with three bolts in him. He must have known his time was up and yet he didn't stop. The life force, you see? It's unquenchable.'
'Indeed. My lord -' I tried again.
'I knew I'd seen you somewhere before,' he said turning round to face me. 'I just couldn't think where. It's taken me a while, but finally I've remembered.

Runnymede. It was after our business with the king had been concluded. You had an audience with him – a *private* audience from which we, his most trusted and senior advisers, were excluded. Why was that, I wonder?'

His words took me completely by surprise. I knew of course what he was referring to: Runnymede was the meadow on the banks of the Thames where the Great Charter – the *Magna Carta* - had been sealed. That seemed an age ago although it was only two years. But the bishop was right, I had been there. I'd gone with a small band of my brother monks that had accompanied Brother Hugh Northwold who was trying to get King John's approval for him to succeed as abbot of St Edmund's. The position had been vacant since the death of Abbot Samson three years earlier and King John had finally agreed to endorse him.

My presence, however, had nothing to do with either of these weighty matters. I was there purely in my capacity as abbey physician at the request of Prior Herbert who happened to be suffering from the toothache at the time. My audience with King John was also a matter of happenstance. At the time I had been investigating the murder of a young maid and the king wanted to hear my conclusions. It seemed, however, that Bishop Peter thought there was more to it than that.

'I'd often wondered what it was an insignificant monk had to say that commanded the attention of the king. And now here you are again doing the same thing with the Marshal.'

'My lord bishop, we both know the sanctity of the confessional -'

'Ah,' he smiled, 'the confessional. Now I know you're lying. King John never confessed to anything in his life and he certainly wouldn't to a mere monk.' He tapped his chest. 'That's what bishops are for.'

I cringed. 'Maybe confession is the wrong word. Taken into his confidence might be better. You wouldn't expect me to break faith with my sovereign, would you? Even a dead one. Or with the regent for that matter.'

'The regent isn't here and I have a duty to protect the realm in his absence.'

'I assure you I am no threat to the realm.'

'Aren't you? You consort with rebels. And all this trouble with the princess – that was you. You were the one brought her here along with her fake Arthur.'

'I had no idea who they were. I was simply told to bring them.'

'So you say.'

This was going badly. At this rate I was never going to get to interview Eleanor. I had to try another tack.

'My lord, may I take you into my confidence? As I was trying to explain yesterday, the Earl Marshal has given me a task to do.'

'The death of Sir Reginald – yes, I know.'

'Then you'll also know that the Marshal sets great store by resolving it. He is expecting an answer from me - today. If I am delayed …' I left the conclusion unspoken.

He gave a crooked smile and shook his head slowly. 'First lies now threats. Geoffrey de Saye warned me about you. He said you were a slippery customer and he was right.'

Geoffrey de Saye. Another icy blast from the past. I hadn't heard that name for a while and it sent shivers down my spine. Geoffrey de Saye had been my nemesis for most of the previous two decades and all because of a feud between our families that had nothing to do with me. He too had been at Runnymede and was now a leading rebel against the Marshal and King Henry.

But it seemed the bishop was already off on yet another tack. 'You claim not to have known that boy was an imposter. But I did.'

'Oh? How?'

'Because I've met Arthur - and I mean the real Arthur. *King* Arthur.'

My jaw fell open. Was he being serious? King Arthur was a myth. Or if he really did exist then it was hundreds of years ago. The monks of Glastonbury claimed to have found his bones but even they didn't go so far as to pretend he was still alive.

He smiled at my reaction. 'I can see that surprises you. But it's true. It was while I was out hunting in the woods around Winchester. He was dressed like an ordinary woodsman but I knew it was him straight away. He beckoned me to join him. I did so and we dined together, just the two of us, right there in the greenwood. What do you think of that?'

Yes he was being serious. I frowned. 'That must have been a great honour for your excellency.'

He nodded. 'It was. When we'd finished our meal I asked him for a token to commemorate the occasion whereupon he told me to close my fist.'

Bishop Peter held out his fist to me.

'He then blew on it.'

The bishop did the same.

'And when I opened it again, out flew… Guess what?'

'I cannot imagine.'

'A butterfly.'

He then opened his hand and sure enough a butterfly fluttered out. It was a good trick. I have to admit I was impressed.

He came up very close to me while I tried not to flinch. 'Take this as a warning my friend,' he breathed. 'I am wise to your games. You may have cast a spell over the regent but you cannot hoodwink me. If you try, I will know - and I will cut you down.'

'You see?' said Jocelin excitedly when I told him. 'You see? Bishop P-Peter suspects the M-Marshal too!'

'How on earth do you come to that conclusion?'

'"You c-cannot hoodwink me." B-Bishop P-Peter's own w-words! He knows about the Marshal. He's seen a s-spectre. Who knows what he told him.'

'Bishop Peter sees spectres everywhere, most of them in the bottom of a wine goblet.'

'Whatever the case, he's c-clearly heard the rumours about the M-Marshal.'

'Rumours aren't evidence. And anyway, the meeting wasn't about the Marshal. Bishop Peter was just taking advantage of his absence to throw his weight around, that's all. He's taken against me and wanted me to know it.'

Jocelin shook his head. 'Bishop Peter's a dangerous m-man to m-make an enemy of, Walter.'

'All the more reason to get this murder solved as soon as possible so we can leave this madhouse. The Marshal's given us twenty-four hours. Now thanks to Bishop Peter we have barely three left.'

'Then we must get to the L-Lady Eleanor as quickly as p-possible.'

'Indeed. But just before we do I'd like you to check on something for me with your friend, Brother Emmanuel.'

'The archivist? Why?'

'I think he may be able to give us another piece of the puzzle. And if I'm right the matter will soon be sewn up.'

Chapter Twenty-two
INTERVIEW WITH A VAMP

We hurried over to the Lucy Tower where Eleanor was being "entertained" by Lady Nicola - a slightly more comfortable confinement than the one I had just endured. Nevertheless, confinement it was and this time precautions had been taken against Eleanor's being able to abscond again. To this end she was given a room right at the top of the tower with one small window high up in the wall with a sheer drop the other side. Outside the room were posted two guards. Jocelin and I were frisked on our way in and our knives removed, though whether for Eleanor's benefit or ours I wasn't entirely sure.

Inside the room Eleanor was seated in regal splendour at the far end beneath the tiny window in a high-backed chair which had been provided by Lady Nicola, and flanked by three ladies-in-waiting, also courtesy of Nicola. She did not get up when Jocelin and I entered clearly expecting us to come to her. I could see we were in for some royal role-playing. I suppose if she couldn't truly be queen she could at least act the part. I was happy to go along with that if it helped get me some answers.

'My lady,' I began as we approached, but she immediately threw up her hand.

'Stop right there! Before we go any further: *Not* my lady. *Not* madam. From now on you will address me as Highness or this conversation ends here. I am a princess of the blood royal and will be addressed as such.'

Jocelin and I exchanged glances.

'I do apologise - your Highness,' I said bowing low.

'Hm!' she grunted. 'It's about time my rank was acknowledged. Oh, you wait till I'm queen, there'll be some changes around here I can tell you. And why are you so late? I understood from the Marshal you craved an audience in the fore-noon. It is now well past noon. I have been kept waiting for hours.'

'My apologies again, Highness. I ... overslept a little. But I hope you will honour me by answering a few questions now.'

'That depends on what they are. If you've come here to accuse me of crimes I have not committed then there is no point. So let us be clear from the start: I did *not* threaten you with a knife nor did I shoot a crossbow at you. Tch! The very idea! I wouldn't know one end of an arbalest from the other. As for the knife – where is it? Have you found it yet?'

'No, Highness.'

She smiled. 'Thought not.' She fluffed up her gown. 'Well, come on then. What is it you wish to ask me?'

'A simple question: How well did you know Sir Reginald Croc?'

The question clearly took her by surprise. She blinked hard. 'Who?'

'The knight who was killed in the battle. Have you forgotten?'

'Of course I haven't forgotten. Do you think I'm an idiot?'

'Well?'

She shrugged. 'I never met the man. How could I have done? He was English. I am Breton. I've been in this country for barely a few days and in Lincoln for just two.'

I pulled a face. 'That's not quite accurate, is it? You have in fact been a guest of King John ever since your brother's disappearance fourteen years ago. I believe that's right isn't it, Brother Jocelin?'

Jocelin nodded. 'B-Bristol, Yorkshire, Westmorland,' he read from the scroll he was carrying. 'S-strongholds all over England. L-Lady Nicola's archives are very c-comprehensive in such matters. Your l-last incarceration was in C-Corfe C-Castle, I believe.'

'From where you escaped in order to come here,' I added.

She blinked hard. 'Why should I be incarcerated anywhere?'

'For the same reason you have come to Lincoln now. Because you won't give up your claim to the throne. You've been trying ever since your late uncle, King John, was crowned.'

'*King* John!' she snorted. 'He was never king.'

'Well, now he's dead you finally got your opportunity to stake your claim. You must have been waiting for this moment for years.'

She glowered at me. 'The reason I came here was to put my brother on the throne, as I have been explaining over and over.'

'Gelyn wasn't your brother.'

'Well yes, I know that now. But I didn't at the time. Like everyone else I believed Gelyn was Arthur.'

'No you didn't. It was all a ruse. You coaxed Gelyn in the hope of convincing others. It had to be you. No-one else would have known those intimate details if Arthur's life.'

'And why would I do that – if, as you say, I wanted the throne for myself?'

'Quite simple really. You knew it wouldn't be easy to get accepted as queen – God knows you've been trying for long enough. As the Marshal said, there's never been a woman on the throne of England in her own right. The last one who tried – your great-grandmother Matilda as it happens – had to give up after nineteen years of civil war. So you had to find another way.'

'Which was?'

'You promoted Gelyn as Arthur. If he was accepted then all well and good. Gelyn would be king, but you would be the power behind the throne since he would be your puppet. On the other hand if he wasn't accepted, which was always going to be the most likely outcome, then you would denounce him as a fake, use that as proof that the real Arthur is indeed truly dead and you would become his rightful heir. Except it was all for nothing because your biggest obstacle was never Arthur – it was Henry.'

'Why?' she scoffed. 'Because he's my uncle's son? The barons have already said they will not accept any of John's lineage. They would rather a foreign king than a son of his.'

'That was before Lincoln. I think you'll find those barons who supported the dauphin before are now falling over themselves to return to the fold. Look out of the window. They're queuing up to get in.'

Of course she couldn't. The window was too high up. But it amused me to see her glance up at it.

'One battle doesn't win a war, *mon frère*. They will soon realise a child cannot rule this country. And when they do they will flock to my banner. You'll see.'

I inclined my head. 'Possibly. But in any case, these matters are beyond my competence. What I really came here to talk about is Sir Reginald Croc.'

'I keep telling you, I don't know him.'

'Well that's odd, because while you were in Corfe Castle he was your gaoler – that too is in the archives.'

Jocelin gave a nod of his head. 'It's a m-matter of r-record, Highness.' He held up his scroll for her to see.

Eleanor gave him a sneering smile. 'Well that's just where you're wrong, little man. My gaoler was Sir Peter Mauley.'

'That's t-true,' Jocelin agreed. 'B-but Sir Peter was hardly ever there, was he? Too b-busy looking after his other g-guest – someone even m-more august than yourself. King John's second son, the P-Prince Richard. Sir R-Reginald was his deputy.'

Eleanor contrived a negligent shrug of her shoulder. 'He might have been. I had so many gaolers. As you say, I have been confined for a decade and a half. I can't be expected to remember them all. Sir Reginald may have been one for a while. But so what? That's no reason for my wanting him dead, which I presume is where all this is leading.'

'So you do remember him?'

'What I remember is that he was killed by one of the rebel knights. Bishop Peter said as much.'

'That possibility has been ruled out.'

'Oh? By whom?'

'By me.'

She sneered. 'By you!'

'There is other evidence.'

'What other evidence?'

I nodded to Jocelin who now produced the piece of linen I had asked him to save after the autopsy. Inside, carefully preserved among the folds, were strands of hair - red hair.

Eleanor's eyes widened slightly when she saw them. She walked over and lightly touched the strands with her fingertips.

'Where did you get these?'

'Off Sir Reginald's body. It's the sort of thing murderers leave behind on their victims without realising it.'

'And because they are red they must be mine?'

'Are they?'

'I'm sure I am not the only redhead in Lincoln.'

'No, but there can't be many with hair over two feet long. A handful of women at most. We'll go and find them all shall we? It shouldn't take too long.'

Eleanor strolled around the room touching things, straightening cushions, moving chess pieces about. She then dismissed her three ladies who were only too pleased to scurry out. Once they'd gone Eleanor turned to face me again.

'Let me tell you about my life, brother. My father was Duke Geoffrey of Brittany, the fourth son of King Henry and Queen Eleanor of illustrious memory – but you know that already. Not that I ever knew my father. He died when I was two years old and I was brought up by my uncle, King Richard. That sounds generous doesn't it? The sort of thing a loving uncle would do. But don't be fooled. I was as much Richard's property as any other of his possessions – his castles, his jewels, his slippers. You see, princesses are not people. They are bargaining counters. Counties, provinces, sometimes whole realms can be exchanged for them. And not just land. At the age of nine I was betrothed to Frederick, the son of Duke Leopold of Austria, in exchange for Richard's release when he was captured on his way back from the Holy

Land. Then when that didn't happen I was promised to the dauphin – yes, this same Prince Louis who ravages the country even as we speak.' She smiled. 'Ironic isn't it? Had I married Louis I might already be queen of England. But that was not to be either. Richard was killed and my brother Arthur became heir to the throne. But as we know, my uncle John had other ideas. He stole the crown from my brother who then disappeared, many believe killed by John's own hand. Perhaps he should have done the same with me, but even John didn't scruple that far. Instead I was imprisoned - for the next fourteen years.'

She looked at me and for the first time I thought I saw true anguish in her eyes.

'Do you know what happens to royal princesses who are imprisoned and abandoned?'

'I can imagine.'

She shook her head. 'No need to imagine. I will tell you. They are the play things of any man who fancies his chances. I was eighteen years old when I was first incarcerated, alone and isolated in a foreign country whose language I could not speak, entirely dependent upon the goodwill of my gaolers.'

'Gaolers like Sir Reginald?'

She frowned. 'Yes all right, I admit he was one of them. There, are you satisfied?'

'Was he an easy host?' I asked delicately.

'He was, shall we say, more *attentive* than the rest. But time moves on, the wheel of fortune turns. When the present war erupted King John was forced to release all his hostages – all except me. I was deemed too dangerous to let loose.'

That I could believe.

'But with the help of some friends I managed to escape.'

'And came here,' I concluded for her. 'Tell me, did you know Sir Reginald was already in Lincoln when you decided to come here?'

'You mean did I take the opportunity to kill him in revenge for past indiscretions?'

'It would be understandable if you did.'

She started to chuckle, gently at first but gradually increasing until finally she threw back her head and roared with laughter. She was like a mad-woman again and quite terrifying. Given the life she had been forced to endure I would have been surprised if she weren't mad. But sympathy for her condition only went so far.

At last she stopped laughing and glared at me. 'Yes, I knew Sir Reginald was here. Yes, he was one of the reasons I came. But I didn't murder him in revenge for ravishing me. You fool, don't you see? Haven't you guessed it yet? *I was in love with him!*'

Next to me Jocelin gasped. I admit that I too was shocked. I truly hadn't expected that. Eleanor looked smug. She was clearly enjoying herself.

'As for these strands of hair,' she said picking them up in her fingers. 'You're right, they are mine. Evidence, yes. But not of murder. Of a lover's embrace.'

'Then if not you, who did kill him?'

She curled her lip. 'Why Gelyn of course.'

My jaw dropped further. 'Gelyn? Why?'

'Why do you think? Out of jealousy.'

I frowned trying to understand. 'You mean Gelyn was your lover too? But I thought -' I glanced at Jocelin.

She gave a coquettish shrug of her shoulder. 'You thought it was all a game? Not for Gelyn. Ask *him* if you don't believe me.' She thrust an accusative finger at Jocelin.

Jocelin's face went pale remembering, no doubt, her and Gelyn's intimacy on the back of the wagon.

She laughed again at his reaction. 'Of course Gelyn was in love with me! How do you imagine I got him to do what he did? He would have walked through fire for me. There's your murderer, brother. Not me. Gelyn.'

Back in our room Jocelin flopped down heavily onto the couch. 'D-do we believe her? I mean, Eleanor and Sir Reginald l-lovers? Is it p-possible?'

'I don't know. I have heard of such things before. A sort of bond builds between prisoner and gaoler. It sounds unlikely I know, but unless you've been in that situation it's hard to appreciate.'

Jocelin looked at me slyly. 'You were in that s-situation once. S-Samson locked you up on the b-bell tower.'

'Yes, but my gaoler was Mother Han's imbecilic husband. And it was only for a few days, not years like Eleanor. Although I have to admit,' I added coyly, 'by the end of it he was beginning to look rather appealing.'

Jocelin looked horrified. 'You're j-joking of course!'

'Hmm - maybe.'

He shook his head. 'S-so Eleanor may be right, then. Gelyn could have killed Croc in a f-fit of j-jealousy.'

'Gone off the idea of the Marshal have we?'

He frowned. 'I don't kn-know anything anymore. Everything is th-thrown up in the air.'

'Then let's think this through. The battle is over and Sir Reginald chases the rebels down to the Bargate where he has his encounter with the knight and his wife. He gets unseated then returns to the town where he is poisoned and his body is dumped outside the castle wall. Would Gelyn have had time to do all that? More importantly, would he have been intimate enough with Sir Reginald to be in a position to poison him? Lovers or not, Eleanor at least knew Croc – she's admitted as much. She's far more likely to have had such an opportunity.'

'The t-trouble is Gelyn is dead so we c-can't ask him.'

'Conveniently for Eleanor. What we really need to find out is where she was during the battle.'

'L-Lady N-Nicola would know. She had g-guardianship of her. But d-do you want to r-risk going to see her again? After what happened l-last time?

'We'll both go. But this time I'll do the talking.'

'Wh-what do you mean? You did the talking l-last time, and l-look where it g-got us.'

I stuck my tongue out at him.

Chapter Twenty-three
THAT WORTHY LADY

Lady Nicola was having her evening meal when we arrived at her chamber, but she agreed to see us anyway. The table set before her was groaning under the weight of mutton, pork, chicken, eggs, eels, herring, custards, pies. Seeing all that food reminded me that I hadn't eaten in twenty-four hours and from the look on Jocelin's face he must have been thinking the same.

Our pain must have been obvious for the lady stopped chewing for a moment and surveyed the feast before her:

'Forgive my extravagance, brothers, but you have to understand we've been under siege for nearly two years and victuals were getting low. We'd eaten all the horses and were even eyeing each other by the time the Marshal arrived, not that there was more than a mouthful of flesh on any one of us by that stage. This is the first decent meal I've had in months. But please, help yourselves -'

'Why thank you my lady,' I said starting forward.

'- to ale.'

I stopped. Ale on an empty stomach? Never a good idea at the best of times and we needed clear heads for what was to come.

'On second thoughts, perhaps not. But thank you.'

Lady Nicola shrugged. 'Suit yourself.' She took a bite out of a chicken wing and idly tossed the rest to her pet greyhound. I followed its elegant path through the air as it flew. It barely touched the sides of the animal's mouth before disappearing inside.

'Well? What can I do for you?'

I dragged my eyes back to the lady. 'We've come to ask you a few questions, if you will permit.'

'Concerning this knight who got himself murdered?'

'Er - yes.'

She shook her head. 'I can't tell you anything about that. I was up on the castle ramparts when it happened.'

'It's not so much where *you* were, my lady, as where Lady Eleanor was.'

'Why should I know where she was?'

'I thought the Marshal placed her into your care.'

'He did. But it was a busy time. You may have noticed, some Frenchmen were trying to knock down my castle walls at the time.'

'Er, m-may I ask?' interrupted Jocelin. 'Wh-what m-made you think it was Sir Reginald we wished to s-speak to you about?'

'I am chatelaine of Lincoln Castle, brother. It's my business to know everything. How else do you think I've managed to remain thus for so long?'

'By your great ability in defending it from marauding Frenchmen,' I smiled obsequiously. 'An ability, if I may say so, that I was privileged to witness for myself.'

'Ah!' she smiled. 'Flattery. That won't work with me, my friend. I've lived too long. No, the answer is far simpler: it's because of an absence of men.'

I frowned. 'I'm sorry, I'm not sure I follow.'

'Then allow me to explain. The office of constable of Lincoln has been in my family for generations. My father inherited it from his father and I inherited it from him. It should have gone to his son of course but he didn't have any, only daughters, of whom I was the eldest – d'you follow me so far?'

'I think so.'

'I too had a daughter and only one grandchild who was …' she smiled. 'Have a guess.'

'Another girl?'

She nodded. 'You're beginning to get the idea. So you see, with no men in the family I was stuck with the job. And if I say so myself, I made a half-decent fist of it. At least, that's what King John thought who insisted I remain in the post even though I was at the age when a woman should be doting on her grandchildren not shooting at besieging armies. But as I say -'

'You only had one granddaughter.'

'But now, as it happens, there is a man who is trying to take my title from me.'

'That man being...?'

'You've already met him. The earl of Salisbury.'

'Ah yes,' said Jocelin. 'The l-late king's half-brother. Isn't it his s-son who is betrothed to your g-granddaughter?'

Lady Nicola seemed impressed. 'I see you've been down in the archives, brother. Yes, the earl's son is indeed betrothed to my granddaughter. And in due course he may well inherit the title from her as both my husbands did from me when we married, though neither lived long enough to enjoy it. But the boy is barely out of nappies which is why his father is trying to claim the title for himself. But I have held this place for too long to give it up to the first man who fancies his chances just because I am a woman.'

'I think I am beginning to understand,' I said. 'Against all the odds you have made your way in a man's world highly successfully – and that's not flattery, by the way, merely observation.'

She acknowledged the compliment with a gracious incline of the head.

'Given all that, why should I help you destroy another woman who is trying to do the same thing?'

'You m-mean the P-Princess Eleanor?' frowned Jocelin trying to keep up.

'I don't like the woman,' said Nicola. 'She is a termagant and a trouble-maker. Maybe that's her fault, maybe not. But that doesn't mean I am going to help you thwart her.'

'So you cannot – or will not – explain how she managed to escape from the castle?'

'Oh, do you really need me to tell you? How does any vixen escape a trap? By cunning and guile of course. But exactly how you will not get out of me, even assuming I knew, which of course I don't.'

I nodded. There was clearly no point in continuing. I started to leave. But before I did I had one last question:

'Er, before I go, can you at least tell me one thing. Did the princess have any visitors while she was in your care?'

'Not visitors as such, no.'

'Meaning?'

'A holy man came to see her. But that was to hear her confession not to help her escape.'

'You're sure about that?'

'What other reason could there possibly be?' She popped a slice of mutton between her teeth and chewed aggressively.

'L-let you do the talking!' snorted Jocelin when we were alone again. 'F-f-fat lot of good that d-did!'

'Oh, I don't know. We learned a few things.'

'Like wh-what?'

'Well for a start, we now know that Lady Nicola thinks Eleanor is Sir Reginald's murderer.'

His jaw dropped open nearly as wide as mine. 'H-how on earth can you t-tell that?'

'The way she defended her. You heard her. The two of them have much in common. Both are women abused by unscrupulous men. Eleanor would have told Lady Nicola the same story she told us about the way Sir Reginald treated her only Nicola would have lent a much more sympathetic ear than ours.'

'You th-think Sir Reginald's murder was a conspiracy b-between these two women?'

'Not actively on the part of Lady Nicola perhaps. But she could have easily looked the other way while Eleanor escaped. If she could do it once, she could do it again.'

'That d-doesn't make her g-guilty.'

'In law it does.'

'Since when did you become a l-lawyer?'

'Samson used to quote it to me all the time,' I sniffed. 'Look, we agree it takes time to poison someone, yes?'

He nodded.

'Lady Nicola could have provided that time. In fact, she is the only person who could have provided it. And don't forget those strands of hair. Murderer or lover, Eleanor must have met up with Sir Reginald at some stage or else how did they get onto his body?'

'B-but what about d-dumping the b-body? She c-couldn't have done that on her own. She would have n-needed help.'

'Lady Nicola could have provided that too. She has plenty of man-power at her disposal. No, I think Eleanor is our murderer. She killed Sir Reginald for all the reasons we said – revenge for years of abuse at his hands.'

'Is that what you're going to t-tell the M-Marshal tomorrow?'

I frowned. 'I don't know what I'm going tell him yet.'

'I wouldn't mention L-Lady Nicola if I were you. She's one of the Marshal's c-closest allies.'

'I won't have to. The Marshal will draw his own conclusions.'

Jocelin went sullen.

'You still think it's him, don't you?'

'I d-didn't s-say that.'

'No, but you think it, which is why I can't take you with me when I speak to him. I'm sorry old friend but I am going to have to see him alone. I can't risk both our lives when we are so near the end.'

He looked relieved. I'm sure he didn't relish the thought of having to accuse the Marshal to his face. But he was still frowning.

'Don't look so glum. You know it's the right decision.'

'It's not that.'

'Well what then?'

He looked back at me in despair. 'A chicken wing, Walter.'

'What?'

'She g-gave her g-greyhound a whole ch-chicken w-wing.'

I grinned. 'Hard to credit isn't it?'

'I hope it ch-chokes her!'

'Lady Nicola?'

'The g-greyhound.'

Chapter Twenty-four
MARSHAL LORE

We eventually managed to grab some food for ourselves – just a plate of cold meat and some stale bread, nothing like the splendid array enjoyed by Lady Nicola. But I was so hungry I could have eaten the wax out of my ears. I then spent a restless night grappling with what I knew about the murder and what I was going to say to the Marshal the following morning.

I was certain in my own mind that Eleanor had done the deed. Naming Gelyn was cowardly since he was dead and couldn't defend himself. I didn't believe she and Sir Reginald were lovers. Quite the opposite: I was sure they'd been the deadliest of enemies. From what I'd heard about Sir Reginald I could quite believe he was the sort of man to take advantage of a defenceless young woman during her long detention. For his part King John wouldn't have interfered. On the contrary, he would probably have thought it a perk of the job as well as a way of demoralizing a potential trouble-maker. But if John did think that he didn't know Eleanor and had forgotten who her grandmother was. That other more celebrated Eleanor had been similarly locked away by her husband only to emerge decades later reinvigorated and ready to take over the regency for her favourite son Richard while he was away slaughtering Saracens in the

Holy Land. It might even have been her example that spurred her granddaughter to try something similar. Eleanor coming to Lincoln had always been for one reason: to stake her claim the throne. Finding Sir Reginald here was just a bonus. And what an opportunity, in the midst of the chaos and confusion of a battle, to be able to finally attain restitution for ancient injuries! It had all fallen so neatly into her lap: A ready culprit in the form of a jealous lover, Gelyn; a sympathetic collaborator in Lady Nicola; and the singular gift of one dishonourable act that diminished Sir Reginald in the eyes of his own comrades: the killing of the comte de la Perche. All together it added up to an opportunity not to be missed. And she grabbed it with both hands.

That, then, was my thesis. All I had to do now was convince the Marshal.

He must have arrived back from Nottingham some time during the night for he was waiting for me when I went to his rooms the next morning. I continued to marvel at his stamina and could only hope I would have half his energy at his advanced age.

'How fares the king, my lord?' I asked having made my salutations. 'Full of vigour and raring to get at the throat of the dauphin and his rebel allies?'

'When I left him the King of England was sitting on the floor playing with his toy soldiers.'

'While you play with real ones, my lord?'

I wasn't sure how he would take that, whether he might explode with anger. But I had judged the man correctly. He merely smiled.

'What have you got for me, brother? You've had your twenty-four hours. Now I want an answer. Who killed Sir Reginald Croc?'

'Before I answer that, may I ask why you are so keen to know? The battle of Lincoln was terrible. So many men died in the fighting. What's so special about this one?'

'You already know the answer to that. You were there when my lord Salisbury explained the rules of chivalry in time of war.'

'That no noblemen should be killed but rather taken hostage so as to ransom him later for profit,' I nodded. 'Yes, I remember. But Sir Reginald wasn't a member of a noble family. He was an ordinary soldier of fortune.'

'Oh, he was a little more than that, I think. Croc was one of King John's most loyal lieutenants. In a world of shifting allegiances that is worth more than a ransom.'

'And lately he served you in a similar capacity. Yet you must have known of his reputation. I'm a little surprised that you were happy to employ such a man.'

'In life, brother, we can't always choose our friends – at least, not in the circles I inhabit. Sometimes we have to accept what is available. If I dispensed with the services of every soldier of whose character I disapproved I wouldn't have much of an army left.'

'So you welcomed the service of an unsavoury knight in which capacity he killed the comte de la Perche, an act that flouted the very rule you just described.'

'That was indeed a great tragedy. But you heard what happened. The count refused to surrender. You would agree, I think, that in order to be taken alive a knight must first yield.'

'He could have been disabled. Was it really necessary for Sir Reginald to kill him?'

The Marshal frowned. 'You are not a soldier, brother, so I don't expect you to understand, but in the heat of battle men often have to make life and death decisions in the blink of an eye. There is little time for careful analysis of the consequences. Sir Reginald's job was to protect me and that's what he did. He acted on instinct – and, as it turned out good instinct. Even with a blade through his brain the count had enough left in him to strike me three times before dropping. If Croc hadn't killed him when he did he would almost certainly have done for me. Croc saved my life. So in answer to your question, that is one reason why I want to know his fate.'

'But not the only reason.'

'No, not the only reason. There's been a suggestion that I had Croc kill the count deliberately and then had Croc killed in order to conceal the fact.' He smiled. 'I can see by your lack of reaction that this is not news to you. These, of course, are just rumours and have no basis in fact, but rumours have a way of taking hold and I cannot afford to have my name besmirched in that way.'

'Why? Who would dare accuse the Regent of England?'

'Out loud, probably no-one. But the merest whisper would undermine my authority and thereby my ability to perform my duties.'

'After what you've achieved here? Surely no-one would dare challenge you. Your position is unassailable.'

'Is it? Brother, in my hands I have the care of two million souls - two million rebellious, wilful, stubborn English souls who need only the slightest excuse to bring down their rulers.'

'Good people all.'

'Agreed. But we are in uncharted waters. There has never been a regent before who was not a member of the royal family. My position is as precarious as it is novel. The slightest suspicion of impropriety on my part could end it.'

'You mean, like pointing out you have an aunt who is married to the la Perche family and as a consequence of his death are likely to inherit substantial wealth and property?'

The Marshal gave a wry smile. 'My, you have been working hard. But you're right, I am related to the de la Perche family and will likely inherit as a result of the count's death.'

'Which gives you a credible motive for wanting him dead.'

'And which is precisely why I need to know who really did kill Croc in order to dispel such suspicions. So, are you going to tell me or not?'

I took a deep breath in and held it. Finally I let it out: 'Gelyn killed Croc.'

The Marshal frowned. 'The boy who claimed to be Arthur?'

'According to Lady Eleanor.'

'But why? What possible reason would he have?'

I went through Eleanor's explanation: The fact that Sir Reginald was her gaoler, that she and he had become lovers and that Gelyn murdered him in a fit of jealous rage.

He listened in silence. When I finished he asked:

'Do you believe her?'

'I believe the boy was besotted with her. There's plenty of anecdotal evidence to support that.'

'Besotted enough to kill for her?'

'It's one possible explanation.'

'But you don't believe it's the right one?'

'Time and opportunity mitigate against it.'

He nodded. 'So what's your preference?'

'I believe Eleanor killed Sir Reginald in revenge for years of abuse at his hand. Not that I would blame her if she did. I've seen evidence of his behaviour towards women in distress. As for whether Eleanor is capable of killing a man - we've both seen evidence of that.'

He gave a wry smile. 'At least she can't claim it was for treason this time – Bishop Peter will be pleased to hear.'

'It really depends on whether you believe she could have been her gaoler's lover.'

'No brother, not whether *I* believe it but whether others believe it.'

He walked up and down weighing up what I'd said.

'I suppose it doesn't much matter which of them committed the crime, or whether neither of them did. Neither can be punished: Eleanor because of who she is, and Gelyn – well, he's beyond earthly punishment. The important thing is that there are now two other credible suspects.'

'To muddy the waters, my lord?'

'To create sufficient doubt. There will always be some who wish to believe the worst of me whatever the evidence. You may even believe it yourself.'

This would have been the perfect opening for Jocelin had he been here. I was glad I left him behind.

'There is something else you could do to allay those suspicions, my lord.'

'Oh? What's that?'

'You could renounce your inheritance of the Perche estate. While you benefit from the count's death the suspicion will always remain that you had a hand in his death and therefore in Croc's as well.'

He pulled a pained face. 'I'm not sure it would achieve much if I did. It's in the hands of the lawyers now. And these legal wranglings, you know – they can go on for years.'

'By which time the war will be over, King Henry will be crowned and you will be a national hero. No-one will be interested in the death of an insignificant knight in Lincoln or even remember his name.'

He smiled. 'You are beginning to understand the dirty world of politics, brother.'

'I hope not, my lord.'

A servant came in looking agitated. It seemed the Marshal had other pressing matters to attend to elsewhere.

'Well, thank you, Brother Walter. You have done well. I release you. You are free to return to your abbey. God safe you home.' He started to walk away.

'May I just ask, what will happen to the princess?'

'Eleanor? I'm afraid her fate was already sealed even before Croc's murder. You've seen her. She will never give up her claim to the throne. I will have to continue King John's policy of keeping her locked up and out of harm's way – for now at any rate. The new king is a child, he won't be of an age to rule in his own name for a decade at least. Until then he is vulnerable and England will have to be ruled by regents.'

'You mean by you?'

He shook his head. 'No, not by me. Believe it or not I don't want the job. Even if I did I am an old man and will be dead soon.'

'My lord Marshal, you have just won a heroic victory in battle. By all accounts you were right in the thick of the fighting. Men still tremble at the sight of your lance bearing down on them.'

'If only that were true,' he said sadly. 'In any case, it's beside the point. Winning battles is the easy part. Winning the peace is when the real work begins - to rebuild this country from the ravages of the past two years. That's a job for a younger man. I will start it but it will be for others to complete.'

'May I ask one last question – on a more personal note? Why me? Surely you have servants and officials with far greater resources than I have to carry out the investigation.'

'That is your greatest asset, my friend, the fact that you are a nobody. My officials might have investigated and come to the same conclusion but who would have believed them? They'd say anything I told them to say. Now, if someone like you, an outsider, a man of the cloth unable to be swayed by political pressure manages to find the murderer you are far more likely to be believed.'

'And if I hadn't?'

He shrugged. 'You'd have been packed off back to your abbey in Suffolk and no-one would have been the wiser. But for what it's worth, I wasn't lying when I said I remembered you. I remember that you solved the boy miller's murder. Not an easy task. At the time I was quite impressed. Take from that what you will.'

Down in the courtyard our old wagon was already waiting for us, freshly greased and laden with enough supplies to get us all the way to Bury. And harnessed to the front was not only Helios but also Hyperion, my wonderful Hyperion, who I last saw stuck in that accursed gate-bridge over the Sincil Dyke. I was so relieved to see him that I threw my arms around his neck and hugged him like a long-lost brother.

'Hyperion my boy! I thought you'd have been someone's supper by now!'

'After what he d-did to halt all those f-fleeing rebels?' said Jocelin. 'I should s-say not! He's a hero! Aren't you b-boy?'

He fondled the ox's ear affectionately. Needless to say Hyperion was utterly oblivious to his pivotal role in the defeat of the French invasion of England.

Once out of earshot Jocelin turned to me:

'Well? H-how did it go?'

'He seemed happy with my conclusions.'

'Which were?'

'That Sir Reginald Croc was most likely killed by either Princess Eleanor or her manservant.'

'You d-didn't implicate the Marshal?'

'He did that himself – only to deny it, of course. Although you still believe it to be true.'

'I'm c-certain of it.'

'And nothing I can say will change your mind?'

'N-nothing.'

There was no more to be said. Anyway, it hardly mattered anymore. As far as the Marshal was concerned the matter was settled and our services were at an end. He wanted us gone from the town as soon as possible so there could be no more awkward questions.

We clambered aboard the wagon. My injured hand was making it difficult for me to hold the reins properly so Jocelin had to take over. He sat next to me sullen and silent but I knew he'd come around if I left him alone. With one final look around and a flick of the whip our two beloved oxen started to move us slowly down the hill. We passed through streets where just a few days earlier there had been terrible slaughter, past the Brayford Pool where even more tragedy had occurred and at last we were out of the city. I can't say I was sorry to be leaving.

Part Three

THE JOURNEY BACK

Chapter Twenty-five
INTO DEEPER WATER

My intention was to take the same route back down as the one we had coming up. It was also the route the fleeing rebels had taken of course, at least as far as Sleaford although you can understand why we didn't want to stop there. At the ford over the Slea we veered off left taking the Boston road in the hope of spending the night at the priory again. By now the rebels and their French allies had long gone from the area and we came across no more unpleasant incidents - save one: At one river crossing the bridge was down and to get across the rebels had had to kill some of their horses to make a causeway. Half a dozen bloated corpses lay in the river bed swelling fast in the late spring sunshine and the stench could be smelt for miles around.

Jocelin groaned when he saw the carnage. 'When is all this k-killing g-going to stop?'

'They're only horses, brother.'

'Even so, they died because of m-man's ingratitude.' He frowned. 'Do you th-think horses have souls?'

'What a question! Of course they don't! But if they did they would go straight to heaven. They give and never grudge.'

'I d-don't suppose they have any choice,' he said gloomily. 'Everywhere there is s-suffering and m-misery.'

'Oh dear, you are in a bad way.'

'Not m-me, brother. The world.'

Poor old Jocelin. I think the emotional see-saw of the previous week had finally got to him.

It was late by the time we got to Boston. Prior Francis seemed no happier to see us this time than last. I assumed it was because he'd heard about the rebel débâcle at Lincoln and was fearful someone might remember the priory's previous history. He nevertheless welcomed us in curious to hear more about the battle in Lincoln.

'What I can't understand is how it came to take place at all. I thought the walls of Lincoln were supposed to be unassailable.'

'It w-wasn't the w-walls that gave way,' said Jocelin accepting a cup of ale. 'It was the g-gates. First the n-north gate, and then the west.'

'The *west* gate? I didn't know there was a west gate to Lincoln.'

'N-neither did the r-rebels. It was kept from them by the chatelaine of Lincoln.'

'Ah yes,' he nodded. 'Lady Nicola. An impressive lady.'

'Once inside the Marshal gave no quarter,' I told him. 'The rebels and their French allies were simply overwhelmed.'

'It was ch-chaos,' Jocelin continued. 'They stood no chance. Brother W-Walter and I w-watched it all from the castle ramparts.'

'It must have been exhilarating.'

'H-hardly that. M-more like a scene from the Apocalypse.'

'And their leaders?'

'All c-captured. All bar one.'

Francis nodded. 'The comte de la Perche. I heard he was murdered.'

I frowned. 'I'm not sure "murdered" is the right word, brother. Killed, certainly, by one of our knights who was then himself killed. As a matter of fact it was that which kept us in Lincoln for so long. We were tasked to find out how he died.'

'And did you?'

'Eventually. Although Brother Jocelin and I disagree on the identity of his killer.'

'Who do you say it was?' he asked pouring us more ale.

'I'd rather not go into it. It's all in the hands of the Marshal now. Best we leave it that way.'

He smiled. 'As you wish. Well, I must away and prepare your room. You're staying just the one night?'

'If that's all right.'

'I don't t-trust that man,' said Jocelin when he'd gone.

'You don't trust anybody.'

'Do you blame me after what we've s-seen? He's probably another s-spy - like Quennel.'

'He's just worried that's all. Remember where his sympathies once lay.'

'Aye. With the rebels. P-probably still do.'

'Well, after tomorrow we won't have to worry anymore. We'll be gone from here and then we can forget all about the whole sorry business.'

Hopeful words indeed.

We didn't join the other brothers in their chapel for compline as we should. I was so exhausted I'm not sure I could have stayed awake even if we had. Instead, we made our excuses to the prior and retired early. Even then I wasn't able to get much rest. Among his other complaints Jocelin has the usual problem associated with men of his age requiring frequent trips to the necessarium, especially at night, especially when he'd had too much ale. I think it fair to say that if he'd had better bladder control what happened next might never have occurred.

It was after I'd been asleep for an hour that I felt a hand shaking me violently.

'Walter, w-wake up!'

'Hm? What is it? What's happened?'

'We must g-go.'

'Go? Go where?'

'We have to l-leave. *Now!*'

I frowned. 'Are you mad? It's the middle of the night.'

'Never mind that. I've j-just been out to the n-necessarium. It was awful.'

I sighed. 'Jocelin, you can't expect a little priory like this to have the level of plumbing we have at Bury.'

'It's n-not the p-plumbing. There was a m-man standing in the d-doorway. He had no ears. And he c-cursed me - in French!'

'You're dreaming. Go back to sleep.' I turned over.

'Walter I'm s-serious. We –!'

Too late. I felt the now familiar sensation of cold steel on my neck and heard a soft voice in my ear:

'*Levez-vous, mon frère, s'il vous plaît. Doucement.*'

Oh, not again. This was becoming monotonous. I rose - slowly as instructed, the knife still at my throat. Another man was holding Jocelin in a similar manner. I was shocked to see half a dozen men in the room and they certainly weren't the priory monks. They all looked bedraggled and filthy. It didn't take much guessing who they were.

'What do you want?'

'You know who we are?'

'Of course we know who you are. The rebel army – or what's left of them.'

'*French* army, if you don't mind, *mon frère*. We are all French here. We had hoped you could pass the night in ignorance of our presence. But alas, your brother could not remain in his room.'

'An old man's weakness.'

'Indeed. But now you know we are here, which places us in a quandary.'

'You are worried we will tell? I assure you we won't.'

'Easy for you to say.'

'And even easier to do. Believe me, we will keep your presence a secret - at least until you have had time to escape.'

I wasn't lying. I was so tired I could have slept through the Exodus of the Israelites from Egypt.

'Ah well, here is our problem. Not all of us wish to leave. Our host, Brother Francis, for one. He has been kind enough to give us refuge, and others before us. But now his secret is out and he cannot stay either. So you see, it would be easier just to kill you.'

'Oh please,' I said lifting my chin. 'Be my guest, it would be a mercy. But if I might suggest, the knife is a messy instrument – all that blood.'

'What would you recommend?'

'Suffocation – or strangulation. Personally if I have the choice I would prefer strangulation. It's quicker.'

He tightened his grip on my throat and for a moment I thought he might even do it when I heard a familiar voice.

'Stop!'

The shout came from the doorway. It was Prior Francis. He pushed his way into the room and glared at the man holding the knife at my throat.

'What do you think you are you doing? This is a house of God. I give you sanctuary and this is how you repay it? With murder?'

'Do not blame us, brother. It was you let them in.'

'I had to let them in. If I hadn't they would have known something was wrong. It's your fault they saw you. It was your man who gave you away.'

'He is right.'

Another voice I recognised. Out of the corner of my eye I managed to glimpse Pascal, the man we rescued at the farm. He now stepped into the middle of the room and stood beside Brother Francis.

'I know these men. If they say they will not betray us they won't.'

'They are English,' said the knife-man. 'You cannot trust them.'

'These you can. They are the ones I told you about, the ones who rescued me. They are good men.'

'And when they call out the militia and we are slaughtered to a man, will you still defend them?'

'That won't happen.'

'You cannot be certain of that. You are gambling with the lives of your comrades, *mon ami*. It is too much to ask.'

'Then let us put it to the test.'

There then followed an animated discussion among all the men in rapid French – too rapid for me to follow. All the while the man with the knife kept it poised on my gullet awaiting the outcome. When it came he reluctantly removed the knife from my throat and let me go.

'It seems you have a guardian angel, *mon frère*.'

I gasped and quickly felt round my neck for damage. Apart from a few drops of blood it seemed intact.

Pascal came over. 'Thank you, my friend,' I said to him with all sincerity.

'I think that makes us even, don't you brother?'

It was then that Jocelin, silent until now, did something that I would never have thought possible. He turned to Prior Francis and said in a clear and steady voice:

'How many are you?'

'Why do you want to know?'

'Please, just answer.'

'These men here. More down below.'

'Show us.'

We were taken down a flight of steps and into the undercroft of the priory. There we found perhaps another twenty men. A good many of them were like Jocelin's man in the latrine: ear-less or worse. The half-dozen who had accosted us upstairs were evidently the fittest, the rest were in an even worse state. It was a dismal sight to see.

'What is it you want?' Jocelin asked them.

There was a pause.

'To live,' came a voice.

Jocelin looked at me. I shrugged. I knew what he was planning.

'We can take five,' he said. 'S-six at a p-pinch.'

It was still dark when we threw as much as we could out of the wagon to make room. We managed to squeeze nine of the sickest and most damaged men under the tarpaulin and laid empty flour sacks on top of them. Once on the open road they could come up for air but for the moment, until we got out of the town, they had to remain hidden and still. What happened to those left behind I don't know.

Just as were about to leave Prior Francis had one last thing to say:

'Brother Walter. Your investigation into the murder of Sir Reginald Croc. You have the wrong person.'

His words took me completely by surprise.

'Wha - what do you mean?'

'Simply that. The person you think murdered Sir Reginald, didn't.'

I wanted to stay and ask him more but there was no time. We couldn't stand about and risk someone from the town getting curious. The wagon was already moving and Prior Francis stepped back and disappeared into the darkness again.

'You s-see!' Jocelin whispered to me once we were moving. 'I t-told you so. *N-not* Gelyn. *N-not* Eleanor. There is only one p-person left!'

I pouted. 'Why would Prior Francis know anything? Lincoln is two days ride away. I doubt he's been out of Boston.'

'He d-didn't have to b-be. Any one of these m-men could have b-brought him the news. He's clearly been k-keeping abreast of what has been going on – as spies are w-wont to d-do.'

'But why would it matter to the rebel army who killed an obscure royalist knight?'

'Maybe he wasn't as obscure as we th-thought.'

He went quiet again. I looked at him.

'You're in one of your moods again. Come on, out with it. What's troubling you now?'

'You told that F-Frenchman with the knife to c-cut your th-throat. Th-that it would be a m-mercy.'

'Good God, you don't think I meant it, do you?'

'I hope not, because s-suicide is self-murder and against G-God's l-law.'

I put a reassuring hand on his shoulder. 'Jocelin, my dear, sweet old friend. Much as I look forward to seeing my maker in the face, I prefer to do so in his time rather than man's.'

He looked relieved. 'Good,' he smiled.

'Besides, I'm too much of a coward. I have an aversion to pain.'

My head was aching from thinking about it. Why Prior Francis chose that moment to tell me about the murder was a mystery. Maybe he was just mischief-making - he was, after all, still in the enemy camp. Whatever the truth, doubt had been cast which left the whole question of who really did kill Sir Reginald Croc wide open once again.

Chapter Twenty-six
AND DEEPER STILL

For those of you who do not know this part of Lincolnshire, Boston is about five miles from the coast and we made a small diversion to a fishing village on the shoreline. What the locals thought of two elderly monks trundling up to the shore in an ox-wagon and unloading nine bedraggled Frenchmen was anybody's guess. Fortunately nobody tried to challenge us. Once disgorged the men didn't hang about but piled into an upturned dinghy they found lying on the beach and started rowing out to sea for all they were worth. We didn't wait to see what happened to them but got away ourselves as fast as we could before some local fisherman took it into his head to start asking questions. I just prayed there were no soldiers nearby.

We were soon back on the road again and continuing south. I hadn't realised quite how exhausted I was both emotionally and physically. Neither of us had had much sleep for days and with everything else that had been going on I was utterly drained. Happily we made it to Lynn before curfew time and the town gates were locked against us and made our way to the priory of Saint Margaret in the hope of craving a bed for the night – and this time, dear God I beg of you, no interruptions.

Prior Magnus was as jolly and welcoming as on our first visit and eager to hear our news. All I wanted was to crawl into bed and sleep, but he would not let us go until we had satisfied at least part of his curiosity. He was particularly interested to hear about the true identity of Lady Maude.

'I knew there was something about her!' he said slapping his knee. 'But a princess! My word!' He chuckled making his voluminous belly wobble.

'A p-princess who wished to be q-queen,' said Jocelin. 'S-still wishes.'

'Do you think she ever will be?'

'Not if the Marshal has any say in it.'

'What a tale! This calls for a celebration! And with something a little more appropriate than sour ale!'

He snatched back our mugs, poured the ale away and came back with a whole flagon of Riesling.

'Good German wine from the Mosel valley,' he beamed. 'None of your French muck here!' He then offered up a toast: 'To King Harry! God save him and long may he prosper!'

'King Harry!' we said, raising our cups.

I only pretended to drink. After all that had happened recently I was reluctant to trust anybody, even another prior, even one as affable and apparently harmless as Magnus.

'But what about you?' I asked. 'Anything of interest happen since we were last here?'

What I really wanted to know was if anybody had seen our little diversion out of Boston. I know it was only hours earlier but news can travel faster than a speeding arrow in communities like this, especially bad news. I guessed if anyone was going to have heard what we were doing on the sea shore that morning it would be Magnus.

'Oh no, nothing much ever happens in Lynn, brother.'

'Ah well,' I smiled.

'Except maybe one thing. It was just before you arrived as a matter of fact. A dinghy was found washed up on the beach just up the coast from here.'

Jocelin and I glanced at each other.

'A d-dinghy?' stammered Jocelin.

'Is that so unusual?' I asked. 'Lynn is a seafaring port. I imagine a good many boats wash up without their crew. Fishing is a dangerous occupation.'

Magnus continued to smile. 'Did I say there was no crew?'

'Er, no. No you didn't.'

'S-so, was there any?' asked Jocelin. 'C-crew, I mean. O-or anyone else?'

'Like who?' Magnus raised questioning eyebrows.

'Oh, I r-really w-wouldn't kn-know, n-not being much of a s-sailor myself.'

'No, brother. The boat was empty. But still I thought you might be interested.'

'Why would we be interested in an empty dinghy?' I asked.

'Because a tarpaulin was found in it with your abbey's insignia stitched onto the lining.'

Jocelin nearly choked on his wine. I could feel my skin begin to prickle. Magnus looked from one of us to the other expecting a response. For once my mind went completely blank. I thrust out my cup.

'Er, do you think I could have another?'

'You haven't drunk your first yet, brother.'

'There was a lot of c-confusion after the b-battle,' said Jocelin. 'We lost s-sight of our wagon for a while. We very nearly l-lost one of our oxen, didn't we, Walter? Can you believe th-that? A whole ox!' He raised his eyes to heaven in dismay. 'P-perhaps the tarpaulin was s-stolen then. D-do you remember, brother? I think I m-may have m-mentioned it at the time.'

'A stolen tarpaulin,' I murmured. 'Yes.' I took a large swig of my wine.

Magnus nodded. 'That would explain it. But it's interesting you should mention your wagon because there was talk of another just like it on the beach on the Boston side of the Wash only this morning. Apparently the local fisher-folk saw it.'

I grinned idiotically. 'What, er, was this wagon doing on a beach? Did the fisher-folk say?'

'Oh, something about men jumping out and running down to the shore.' He laughed. 'If you can believe them. They were supposed to have stolen a dinghy – like the one I mentioned - and headed out to sea in it. It was all a bit confused. I wouldn't put too much credit in it. There was even a suggestion the men might be French. Can you believe that?'

'What, er, do Frenchmen look like, I wonder?'

'I've no idea. Garlic cloves around their necks perhaps?' he smiled. 'I doubt whether anyone in these parts will have ever seen one. These fishing communities are simple folk. They get some fanciful ideas.'

'Did they s-say what h-happened to these p-p-purported F-Frenchmen?' Jocelin asked.

Magnus shook his head. 'No. Although there have been reports of a cog in the vicinity flying the French colours. Maybe that's where the notion came from. But there are rumours like that all the time. In these nervous times people see spectres where there are none.'

'So it's possible they may heave been rescued?'

'*If* they were French. *If* there really was a French boat in the vicinity. *If* their dinghy didn't capsize and they didn't drown first - then yes, I suppose there is a chance they may have been picked up. But we shall never know shall we?' He smiled and picked up the flagon of Riesling. 'More wine, brothers?'

'He knows!' Jocelin rasped as soon as we were alone in our room.

'Of course he knows!' I whispered back. 'He's no fool. How many ox-drawn wagons driven by monks can there be on the shores of the Wash before dawn?'

'He d-didn't m-mention m-monks.'

'He didn't have to. We all knew what – and who - he was referring to.'

Jocelin bit a thumbnail nervously. 'It's that tarpaulin. How c-could you have been so c-careless?'

'I was doing the driving. You were the one sitting in the back.'

'I th-think we m-may have g-gotten away with it, though,' he nodded. 'He accepted my explanation of what happened to it.'

'You think so? Stolen, you said. Who the hell steals a tarpaulin from a wagon and leaves everything else?'

He frowned. 'You're right. It's v-very damning. Oh d-dear God! Do you th-think he'll h-have us arrested?'

I thought for a moment. 'No. If that was his intention then he's gone a funny way about it. I mean, why warn us first?'

Jocelin took a sharp intake of breath. 'M-maybe he's one of them! Maybe he's with the rebels, like Quennel and F-Francis! Maybe all the p-priors in this part of the world are in league with the d-dauphin?'

'I doubt that too. You heard him toast the king.'

'B-but the l-last time we were here he was ch-cheering for the dauphin.'

'Hardly cheering. He was merely pointing out that Prince Louis had more money and men than Henry, which at the time was true. That all changed after Lincoln.'

'In that case we are d-definitely s-sunk! He'll tell the town authorities and we'll be arrested!'

'Maybe not. All he's got is a lost, possibly stolen, tarpaulin and an empty dinghy. No proof of who was in it. Those fishermen never actually saw us. Magnus said they were vague. And where's the tarpaulin now? In the back of one of the fishermen's sheds under some lobster pots, I'll wager. It'll never see the light of day again. Without more evidence there's nothing to arrest us for.'

'You mean like d-dead F-Frenchmen w-washing up in L-Lynn harbour?'

'Exactly. And there haven't been any reports of that. We must just keep our nerve and pray there was indeed a French ship in the offing and all the men got picked up.'

'Th-that's not all I'll be p-praying for,' said Jocelin.

Neither of us slept very well that night in spite of our exhaustion. Every hoot of owl, every creak of rafter had us jumping out of bed. At any moment we were expecting the door to be kicked in and us being dragged off back to Lincoln in chains. To forestall them we even propped a chair against the door handle not that that would do much good. But in the event nothing untoward did happen and next morning Prior Magnus was as hale and hearty as ever despite the early hour – annoyingly so.

'Did you sleep well, brothers?'

'Excellently well, thank you, brother,' I yawned.

'Well, you don't look it. You have sacks under your eyes a pilgrim could sleep in,' he chuckled.

'It's been a tiring week.'

'Are you going to be able to stay awake long enough to get back to Bury? If not, you're welcome to stay another night.'

'N-n-no th-thank you, b-b-brother,' Jocelin put in hastily. 'I think Brother Walter and I would l-like to g-get back to the abbey as soon as p-possible – isn't that right, brother? In fact, if you d-don't m-mind, I th-think we'd best get under way right now. B-before b-breakfast. Bury is still a d-day's ride away.'

Magnus shrugged. 'As you wish.'

He came out into the yard with us.

'I've made you something to take on your journey.' He handed me a parcel.

'That's very generous brother,' I said taking it tentatively. 'What is it?'

'Pottage. Make up a fire and warm it up.'

'Thank you.' I started to climb onto the wagon.

'And don't worry. Your secret's safe with me.'

I stopped. 'Secret, brother?'

'About losing the abbey's tarpaulin. Valuable things, tarpaulins. Well, have a safe journey.'

He then made the sign of the Cross, turned on his heel and disappeared back inside the priory. We drove out of the priory yard in a daze.

Some might say it was a treasonable thing we did helping those Frenchmen escape – and they'd be right, it was. But nine sick and mutilated men, even if they were drafted back into the rebel army, were not going to make much of a difference to the outcome of the war. And after the way they had been shamefully mistreated by my fellow countrymen I thought we owed them a chance. Maybe Magnus had the same thought. Anyway it was too late to worry. What was done could not be undone. Time to think to the future.

Chapter Twenty-seven
A FRIENDLY FACE AT LAST - WELL, ALMOST

'Back again, brother? You just can't keep away!'

'Mother Benjamin,' I sighed. 'I have been to Saint George's thrice in the past fifteen years. I'd hardly call that excessive.'

'Maybe it just seems like more.' She glanced at Jocelin. 'Only two of you this time? No lady and her ... ahem ... manservant?'

'Not this time. Princess Eleanor has been unavoidably detained.'

Her eyebrows shot up. '*Princess* Eleanor! Now, isn't that interesting? Mind you, I can't say I'm surprised. She was just too, too…'

'Muscular?' I smiled. Her black-eye had almost entirely faded, I noted.

'I was going to say "imperious". What's her provenance, I wonder?'

'She's not a piece of *objet d'art*, Mother Superior.'

'Indeed not. Nothing so delicate - or decorative.'

'Ah well, others might disagree with you there. Alyenore la Brette, also known as the Fair Maid of Brittany, is regarded as one of Europe's great beauties.'

'Never married though, did she?' she smirked.

'Not for the want of suitors.'

'But none committed. Maybe they heard about her other talents. She's handy with a knife, I gather. A crossbow too?' Her lip curled sardonically.

'Oh, you heard about that?'

'We are not a complete backwater here at Saint George's, brother. She sounds quite a harpy. You did well to leave her behind.'

'As I say, she was detained.'

'Let's hope securely this time. And so having delivered your charge you are now expecting to find lodging here. Just for the one night, I presume?'

'If that's all right. And thank you. It's good of you to put us up like this at short notice.'

She shook her head. 'Goodness has nothing to do with it. It's my duty. Chapter sixty-one of the Rule, brother: "If a monk who is a stranger arriveth, let him be received for as long as he wishes."'

'That's very commendable.'

'"But if he is found to be troublesome he should be politely requested to leave,"' she added.

Yes, she would remember that bit.

'I've given you the same room as last time. I hope that's to your satisfaction.'

'Are you sure? I mean, two men sharing?'

'With a hand like that I doubt you can't get up to much mischief,' she said nodding at my injury. 'Supper at the usual time.'

'You know,' said Jocelin watching her go. 'I'm not usually a v-violent man, but Mother Benjamin…'

'She does have a way of bringing out the worst in one,' I smiled.

We both fell back exhausted on our beds. I lay with my eyes closed.

'I could sleep for a week,' I yawned.

'You were being v-very d-defensive of Eleanor. Anyone would th-think you l-liked her.'

'The honest truth is I pity her. Benjamin wasn't too far off the mark with that comment about her not marrying. I don't think they'll ever let her marry. Can you imagine if she did and had a child?'

'She'd p-probably eat it.'

'More importantly, we'd have all this over again. But the maternal instinct is natural for the female of any species – even Eleanor. I wonder how she copes.'

'I d-don't think women of Eleanor's rank th-think that way. Eleanor s-said princesses are bargaining counters. S-so are princes.'

Lurking in the shadows was my little friend, Sister Monica-Jerome. When the coast was clear she emerged into the daylight.

'I do like it when you come,' she grinned showing her prominent front teeth. 'Benjamin doesn't stop growling for days. Such fun!'

'She'll make all your lives a misery if she's in a bad temper.'

'I know!' she giggled. 'But it's worth it.'

'Monica-Jerome, you are a wicked woman!'

'If only,' she sighed. 'I'm a mouse, always will be.'

'Wouldn't you like to be mother superior? Make others' lives a misery?'

She thought about that for a moment.

'No.'

Supper was as plain this time as it was last. But at least there were no speeches time. For once we had a full night's rest and woke refreshed the following day. Having given our thanks and said our farewells, we were off again on the final leg of our odyssey. Just twelve miles to go now.

'I wonder what sort of reception we'll get from Prior Herbert?' I asked Jocelin.

'B-better than M-Mother B-Benjamin's,' he replied with confidence.

I wasn't so sure.

Chapter Twenty-eight
WELCOME HOME

'Ah! The wanderers returneth. Four days we said. What happened? Forget where you lived?'

Jocelin and I were standing in front of the prior's desk – no cushioned chairs this time.

'Four days up and four back I think it was, Brother Prior.'

'That's still only just over a week. You've been gone a fortnight.'

'We were r-rather preoccupied,' said Jocelin. 'One or two th-things c-cropped up.'

'Like the small matter of a siege by the rebels and their French allies.' I said. 'Maybe you heard about it?'

Herbert tutted and shook his head. 'Sarcasm was never your strongest suit, Walter. As a matter of fact we did hear something about your little to-do in Lincoln. It may interest you to know while you were swanning around the country at abbey expense we were visited by the real French army. They even tried to remove the body of the blessèd king-martyr. I soon put a stop to that.'

'H-how did you m-manage that?' asked Jocelin.

'By threatening them with the wrath of Saint Edmund of course. They soon saw sense and withdrew. It's a pity you two couldn't have done the same.'

'I'm n-not sure threats would have b-been enough, brother.'

He waved a dismissive hand in the air. 'In any case, that wasn't what you were sent there to do. Your mission was to deliver the Lady Maude and her manservant safely to her aunt. A simple enough task which I hope you managed without too many mishaps.'

I grimaced. 'Not entirely.'

Herbert rolled his eyes. 'What does that mean? You weren't rude to her, were you? I know you, Walter. When it comes to the ladies you sometimes forget your oath of constancy.'

'Nothing like that happened, brother.'

'Well then what? And why is your hand bandaged in that disgusting way?'

I looked down at the injured appendage. It was true the bandage had become a little soiled and frayed at the edges of late - hardly surprising given all it had been through. Jocelin had done well to provide me with any kind of dressing under the circumstances. I had meant to replace his improvised version with something a little more professional but hadn't quite gotten round to it yet.

'Actually I was shot with a crossbow bolt. By Lady Maude.'

'Really? Then perhaps I was right after all. Your dealings with her clearly weren't as innocent as you protest. A little over-familiar were you?'

I sighed. 'I assure you, brother, if I'd been at all familiar with that lady she wouldn't have stopped at a crossbow bolt. She'd have had me garotted, sliced into a dozen pieces and fried for breakfast.'

He snorted. 'That I can believe. Well if it wasn't to ward off your unwanted advances, why did she shoot you? You must have done something to upset her.'

'At the time I was in pursuit of a murderer at the request of the Marshal.'

He frowned. '*You* were? Why?'

'It seems the Marshal knew about my solving a previous murder here at the abbey some years ago. The miller-boy, Matthew. During Abbot Samson's time. Perhaps you remember the case?'

'Vaguely. But leaving aside the fact you shouldn't be accepting commissions without my approval, how did it lead to the Lady Maude shooting you?'

'She was the murderer.'

'Nonsense!' he snorted. 'Princesses of the blood royal don't commit murder.'

'S-so you already knew her t-true identity?' said Jocelin.

'I - may have done,' he said looking away.

'Then d-don't you th-think it might have been helpful to have t-told us before we went?'

'And what would you have done if I had? I'll tell you what you would have done. You'd have blurted it out thereby placing everybody's life at risk. No, better to travel in ignorance. That way you couldn't blather what you didn't know. Anyway, why did you think she was the murderer - in your expert opinion as master criminal investigators?'

'Well to begin with she's certainly capable of committing murder. She'd already killed her manservant, Gelyn.'

'That was an execution.'

'Oh, s-so you knew about that as well?' said Jocelin. 'If you don't mind my s-saying, brother, you seem know more about all this than you pretend.'

'What I know and what I don't know is none of your concern, Dom Jocelin. And you're getting off the point. Accusing the Princess Eleanor of such a heinous act is a serious matter. I only hope you had proof.'

'Unfortunately not enough.'

'Well then I was right not to tell you. Making wild accusations against a member of the royal family without evidence. You're lucky she didn't have you hanged.'

'Not for the want of trying. But the Marshal seemed happy enough with my conclusions.'

'In which case I hope you told him whose idea it was to send you. Or were you intending to take the credit yourself? Remember, your role was to represent the abbey not to win personal plaudits.'

'I'd like to know what our role really was. Why did you send us to Lincoln with the lady?'

Herbert shrugged. 'Convenience. Had she travelled alone her true identity would soon have been discovered. A couple of monks and a sick woman was excellent cover, if I do say so myself. Yes, it was my idea to pass the lady off as an invalid. I trust she gave a good performance?'

'Very convincing. She had us fooled – for a while at least.'

'When did you finally twig?'

'I'm not sure. Was it when she and Gelyn were cavorting in the back of the wagon together like a couple of love-sick adolescents? Or was it when she sliced through his neck with a dagger and sent the boy choking to his death?'

Herbert shook his head from side to side. 'Like I said, Walter, sarcasm not your forte. I had to come up with a cover that she would accept. You've seen what she's like. A difficult woman to please. So, what was the outcome?'

'The Marshal has her in custody. I doubt we shall hear from her again.'

He grunted. 'So long as it doesn't reflect badly on the abbey.'

'Meaning the abbey's reputation as fence-sitters survives intact.'

'Meaning we do God's will.'

'Which, naturally, is the same as your own, Brother Prior?'

One person who probably did know the prior's true plan was his clerk, Jephthet. Downstairs he was sitting at his desk with even more than his usual smug, self-satisfied look on his face.

'You go on,' I said to Jocelin. 'I just want a quick word with our friend here.'

He carried on outside while I went over to Jephthet's desk. I gave him my most benign smile.

'How have you been since I last saw you, my son?'

'Fine, thank you master.'

'No aches or pains? Bowels working properly are they?'

'Perfectly, thank you.'

'Good, good,' I smiled. 'How about your ankles?'

'My ankles, master?'

'Yes. I believe there has been an outbreak of bedbugs in the abbey in my absence. Nasty things bedbugs. Can drive a man mad at night.'

'Not that I've noticed.'

I frowned. 'What none at all?'

'No master.'

'You did get those blankets I sent over?'

'I did, and very warming they were.'

'I'm, erm, pleased to hear it.'

'Anything else I can help you with?'

'What? Er, no, thank you Jephthet.'

Everyone else in the abbey scratching for weeks, but not Jephthet. Why was I surprised? Even bedbugs wouldn't dare oppose him for fear of being consigned to the eternal flames. I swear the man has horns growing above his ears.

Out in the courtyard Jocelin was shaking his head.

'That went w-well.'

'Yes. Can't understand it. Most odd,' I said looking back at Jephthet.

'I meant B-Brother Prior.'

'Hm? Oh, you know Herbert. What's one murder here or a battle there so long as we get the job done?'

'How much do you think he r-really knew?'

'He certainly knew Eleanor's real identity and probably what her intention of going to Lincoln was, although I'm sure he'd have denied it if the whole thing had gone pear shaped. He just wanted to make sure he was keeping both sides happy as usual.'

'I wonder if we will ever know for c-certain who killed Sir Reginald?'

'Truthfully? I doubt it even matters. Just the suspicion will be enough to keep Eleanor locked up.'

'A-and the Marshal off the hook,' he nodded.

'There's one question that's been puzzling me, though. Why did you want to come with me? I mean really - and don't give me all that guff about distant cousins again.'

'It's very s-simple. I knew you were v-venturing into danger by g-going there. I couldn't l-let my old friend do that alone.'

'How did you know I was going into danger? Apart from the fact there was a war on and the roads were infested with cut-throats.'

'Fingernails.'

I frowned. 'Fingernails?'

Jocelin nodded. 'Gelyn ch-chewed his. No manservant d-does that. I knew there was s-something odd about him. And I was right, w-wasn't I?'

I looked at him admiringly. 'What an amazing fellow you are.'

He smiled modestly. 'One other th-thing has occurred t-to me.'

'Go on.'

'The d-day we arrived at Lincoln was the d-day of the b-battle – correct?'

I nodded. 'So?'

'We sh-should have arrived a day earlier. The r-reason we didn't was because we were delayed b-by that accident on the road.'

'Where is this leading?'

'Wh-what if the accident hadn't happened? Wh-what if we had arrived a d-day earlier? The M-Marshal's army wouldn't have arrived yet; Eleanor would have had the rebels to deal with. They m-might have accepted G-Gelyn as the real Arthur and …'

'We might now be cheering for a different king.'

He smiled. 'God m-moves in mysterious w-ways, Walter.'

'He does indeed.'

That, I hoped, was the final chapter in this sorry tale of mayhem, murder and megalomania. But it wasn't quite. As we were crossing the yard I heard a vaguely familiar voice behind us:

'That's them!'

I turned to see an angry-looking female marching towards us accompanied by a man who I knew to be one of the clerks in the sheriff's office.

'Oh G-God!' said Jocelin softly.

I frowned trying to recollect where I'd seen the woman before.

She stopped and thrust a podgy finger in my face. 'They stole my mother's robe!'

Of course! The washer-woman from outside Lincoln. I remembered I'd promised Jocelin I'd repay her - which I was quite happy to do. In fact, I was glad for the opportunity; one less sin to have on my conscience.

'You don't deny it?' said the clerk.

I shook my head. 'Not in the least.'

That took the wind out of their sail a little.

'How much?' I smiled reaching into my purse. 'Would seven pence cover it?' I was sure the robe wasn't worth more than six but I was prepared to be generous.

'Five,' she said.

My eyebrows shot up. 'Only five pence? Are you sure that's all you want?'

'Shillings.'

I gawped at the clerk but he wasn't batting an eyelid.

'I expect it had pearls sewn in the neck,' said Jocelin. 'A-and French lace trimmed the hem?'

I sighed. 'Of course it did.'

'Well?' said the clerk.

I pursed my lips. 'Two shillings.'

The woman folded her arms. 'Four.'

'Two and I'll forget the injury I incurred when you threw that dolly at me.'

We finally settled on three – thirty-six whole silver pennies. She went away happy. And so she should. For that she could clothe her entire family for a year.

Epilogue

So there you have it, the story of William Marshal and the Battle of Lincoln Fair, perhaps the most significant battle on English soil since Hastings. Battles like that don't happen very often: they're too risky. It's a case of Winner Takes All as King Harold saw - or would have seen if an arrow hadn't pierced his eye. The winners this time were the Marshal and King Harry but it could just as easily have gone the other way and we might now be shouting out "God Save the King" for Louis le Premier instead of Henry the Third.

The murder, too, was on a knife-edge. Was it Gelyn? Was it Eleanor? Or perhaps Jocelin was right and it was the Marshal after all. Or was it someone else entirely? That last minute intervention by Prior Francis threw me. Was he simply meddling or did he really know something? He seemed to be suggesting there was more to Sir Reginald's death than mere personalities, that other dark forces were at work. I had no way of knowing. However, that didn't stop me thinking about it, mostly when I should have been concentrating on others things, like during divine office. Fortunately it wasn't quite the end of the matter.

Towards the end of August late in the evening I was closing up my laboratorium ready for compline when I heard the door open quietly. I'd already extinguished all but one of my candles so it was dark in my hutch and I couldn't see much. Fearing it might be a robber, I armed myself with a cudgel and called out: 'Who's there?'

'You've no need to defend yourself, Master Walter. I mean you no harm.'

That voice. It could only belong to one person.

'My lord Marshal.'

He stepped out of the shadows. He was quite alone and dressed for riding so I knew this was not an official visit.

'I happened to be passing and thought I'd drop in and see how you were faring.'

That was a lie. Why would the Regent of England bother dropping by to offer salutations to me? I could guess the answer.

'This isn't about me, is it? It's about the murder.'

He inclined his head graciously. 'We couldn't leave things where they were. I owe you an explanation.'

'I thought it had been settled.'

'As far as I was concerned it had. But not for you, I think. Where we left it either the Princess Eleanor or her manservant were thought to be to blame. But I could see you weren't satisfied with that. So I've come to tell you the truth.'

'Which is?'

'That neither Eleanor nor Gelyn killed Sir Reginald Croc. It was me – or rather, it was I had him killed.'

'So Jocelin was right. He said all along you were the murderer.'

He smiled. 'Yes, I thought that was what he wanted to say when you stopped him. Although I dispute the word "murder".'

'What would you call it?'

He thought for a moment. 'A judicial execution.'

'You sound like Princess Eleanor. She said something similar of her killing of Gelyn. As far as I'm concerned murder is murder whoever is the perpetrator.'

He frowned. 'If you understood the circumstances you might be a little less judgemental.'

'Try me.'

'Very well.' He went over to my bench where I kept a flagon of ale. 'May I?'

I shrugged. He poured himself a cup and took a mouthful before continuing.

'What you have to realise is that Sir Reginald Croc was a routier – a mercenary.'

'Mercenaries made up half your army. He was still your man.'

He shook his head. 'Routiers are nobody's "men". They fight for money and will sell their services to whoever has the biggest purse. Back in May that was the dauphin.'

'But Croc remained loyal to you.'

'Only while we were winning. That's the other thing about mercenaries, they don't like to be on the losing side. It's bad for business. Lincoln was a pivotal point. Like everybody else Croc thought we would lose the Battle of Lincoln and was preparing to desert to the other side – and take quite a few of his fellows with him. That, incidentally, is the reason Count Thomas carried on fighting when he should have surrendered. Not from fear of losing his own life but confident that Croc would take mine.'

'But instead he took the count's.'

He nodded. 'In order to silence him before he could expose Croc's treachery. You once asked me why Croc didn't simply overpower him. There's your answer. Dead men cannot speak.'

'And that's the only reason? That was the price of a man's life?'

'Believe me, men have died for less.'

'All right. But it still doesn't explain why Croc had to die. You could have had him arrested and brought before the courts.'

'We were in the middle of a battle. There was no time for due process. A solution was needed before half my army deserted. The fate of England rested upon it.'

'My lord, you are Regent of England. If you cannot obey the law of the land what chance the rest of us?'

'Hm, I can see this is going to be more difficult than I thought. How can I explain it to you?' He took a sip of his ale and leaned back against my bench. 'Let me tell you a story.'

I snorted. 'Haven't we had enough of them?'

'This one is true. I grew up during the Anarchy, that great struggle between the present king's great-grandmother, the Empress Matilda, and King Stephen. My father was active during that struggle in support of the empress - to begin with at least. At one point he was defending a castle against Stephen who was trying to take it. Eventually my father agreed to surrender the castle offering me as hostage to guarantee his good faith. But then he changed his mind. So Stephen had me strapped to a trebuchet and threatened to catapult me into the castle if my father didn't surrender. I was six years old at the time.'

'So the father surrendered the castle to save his son.'

He shook his head. 'On the contrary. He told the king to do as he liked with me and that he had the hammer and anvil to make new sons.'

'Since you are still alive I take it the king didn't carry out his threat?'

'Clearly not. In fact the king and I became good friends and ended up playing conkers together under a chestnut tree.'

'So King Stephen valued the life of a child above that of a castle. The act of a true Christian man, I'd say.'

'A nice man, certainly,' he nodded. 'But nice men don't win many battles – which is the point of my story. You see, in this world you win by knowing what it is you want and letting no-one and nothing stand in your way. I've done it all my life. It is the only way to succeed.'

'That's a sad judgement on the state of humanity, my lord.'

'But an accurate one. Which is why I say Croc's death was unavoidable. We are at war fighting for our very survival. I had to put aside my personal feelings of justice for the greater good.'

'Fine words. I could even believe you - except for one thing. You tried to hide the fact by pretending Sir Reginald died by having his throat cut when in fact he was poisoned.'

He frowned. 'A diversionary tactic. I never expected the princess to be implicated.'

'But in fact by taking matters into your own hands you only raised old suspicions.'

'The important message would have gotten through to those who needed to know.'

'Which was?'

'That treachery comes at a price.'

'Those who needed to know,' I repeated. 'You mean men like Croc? Or Fawkes de Bréauté. Another one of your loyal henchmen.'

He looked up. 'You know of him?'

An image flashed through my mind again of Fawkes in that tavern with a half-naked and terrified girl seated on his lap.

'We met.'

'Then you'll know the sort of man he is. A useful man. A winner. Not the sort of man you want as an enemy.'

'Is that it then? Croc died so you could keep the loyalty of the likes of Fawkes de Bréauté?'

'Partly. There is the added complication of the princess.'

'What difficulty could she offer? She was locked up.'

'Not very securely, evidently, since she managed to get out and chase you across half the county,' he smiled. 'If, as she told you, Croc was indeed her lover, or even just one of her lovers…'

I nodded. 'Who's to say he wouldn't have tried to help her escape again to cause even more trouble. But if you knew all this right from the start why did you have me investigate Croc's death? I might have discovered the truth.'

'There was never any chance of that. As you admit yourself, you are a political innocent. And it achieved my aim.'

'In other words you used me.'

He smiled sadly. 'I'm afraid I did. And that is what I have come to apologize for. I hope in time you will come to see the necessity and forgive me. And if it's any consolation your contribution was a key element in keeping the army together and thereby securing our victory.'

'I'm glad to have been of service.'

The bell started ringing calling the brothers together to sing compline, the last office of the day.

'I have to go,' I said.

'And so must I. The dauphin is gathering a great fleet in the Channel ready to invade these islands again. We must stop him before he does or all that we have achieved so far will be as nought.' He started to leave.

'Just before you go, my lord, may I ask – what happened to Bishop Peter? When I saw him last he was asking me some awkward questions.'

'I cannot do all the things required of a regent. The bishop of Winchester has kindly agreed to take on the responsibility for the young king's education. It is a job that will keep him occupied for some years to come and one he will relish, so I don't think he will be resuming his conversation with you any time soon.'

'Thank you for that at least.'

He smiled. 'Don't mention it.'

So saying, he melted away as silently as he had come.

And now that I've told you all that, I have another confession to make: none of it actually happened. The Marshal did not come and visit me in my laboratorium to explain his actions – he's far too busy and important a personage to waste time apologizing to a lowly monk like me. What you just read is the conversation I imagined might have taken place had he done so. But the essentials are true, I am sure. It's the only explanation that adequately accounts for all that happened in Lincoln: the reason Count Thomas continued to fight when to do so was futile; the way Croc killed him so suddenly and unnecessarily; and why the other routiers did not abandon what they must have thought was a lost cause. Jocelin's instinct was spot on although I am loathe to think it was for the Marshal's personal gain. I prefer my version. But it's all conjecture. I doubt now if we shall ever know the truth. And then again, what is truth? As Abbot Samson once told me, truth is what those in power decide it to be. My meeting with the Marshal in my laboratorium was as real as Bishop Peter's was with King Arthur in the forest - though without the trick with the butterfly this time.

A few days later there was a tremendous sea battle off the coast of Kent. Among the combatants were indeed some of those routiers whose loyalty the Marshal was so keen to retain and without whom the battle might well have been lost. But the die had been cast at Lincoln. The French ships sunk by the English fleet that day were carrying the men and materials meant to replace those lost by the rebels at Lincoln. As a result the dauphin sued for peace, returned to France and was never again able to garner enough support to pursue his conquest of England.

Princess Eleanor likewise did not achieve her aim of becoming queen and is no doubt languishing in some cold northern edifice even as I write. Her grandmother, the legendary Eleanor of Aquitaine, did much the same and had to await the death of her husband before being released. But that Henry was already an old man when she went into captivity so her sojourn was a relatively short one. The princess will not be so lucky. This new Henry is still a child and will probably outlive his cousin. He will keep her locked out of harm's way I am sure. She will have her ladies about her of course and doubtless a suitor or two among her gaolers to ease the years of boredom, but she will never be in a position to cause any more trouble.

As for the rest: a year and a day after he was first declared king, Henry III was crowned at Westminster Abbey, and a few months after that William Marshal, earl of Pembroke, Regent of England, our latter-day King Arthur and saviour of his nation fell asleep for the last time, not on the fabled isle of Avalon, but peacefully in his own bed. How many of our other rulers can claim that?

HISTORICAL NOTE

THE BATTLE OF LINCOLN FAIR

The Second Battle of Lincoln, known as Lincoln Fair, was fought on Saturday 20th May 1217. It lasted approximately four hours which was a very long time for a land battle in Medieval times. It was between the forces of the English king, the nine-year-old Henry III, and Prince Louis of France, the dauphin. In the entire panoply of English warfare Lincoln Fair is one of the most important and decisive battles whose outcome would shape the future of England for generations to come. It is at least as important as the Battle of Hastings, the Battle of Britain and Waterloo. The English won. Had they lost Prince Louis would have become king of England, Magna Carta would have been buried and forgotten, there would have been no Bosworth Field, no Tudors, no Reformation and you might well be reading these words in French.

WILLIAM MARSHAL

The hero of Lincoln Fair was the seventy-year-old William Marshal, the earl of Pembroke. He was a sort of cross between Oliver Cromwell and Winston Churchill yet today hardly anyone has heard of him. In his day he was regarded as England's, and possibly Europe's, greatest knight earning the epithet *prud'homme,* meaning a man of high honour, from no less a person than King Philip Augustus of France. He served four kings – Henry II, Richard I, John and Henry III - five if you include Henry II's second eldest son, the Young King, who was crowned but never reigned. When King John died in 1216 William became Regent until his death three years later. His name, which originated with his father, derives from humble origins as the marshal of the king's horse. It lives on today in the hereditary title of Earl Marshal of England, one of the great offices of state, currently held by the Dukes of Norfolk.

ARTHUR

Arthur was the name of the eldest son of Geoffrey, Duke of Brittany, the fourth son of King Henry II of England. When Richard the Lionheart died in 1199 leaving no natural heir, by the rules of primogenitor Arthur was next in line to the throne. But at the time he was a child of twelve and so his uncle, John, was favoured by the barons of England. That didn't put an end to Arthur's ambitions however and after a short protracted war he was captured and then disappeared from view presumed murdered by John.

ELEANOR, FAIR MAID OF BRITTANY

Eleanor was Arthur's older sister by three or five years and next in line to the throne after him, but as a woman she was never likely to reign. That didn't stop her trying. She too was captured by King John but he was kinder to her than to her brother. Instead of murdering her he allowed her to live in captivity in various places all over England until her death, presumably from natural causes, in 1241 aged 57 or 59. But she never gave up her claim to the throne and escaped several times to pursue it, all to no avail. It is unlikely she made it to Lincoln in May 1217 much less with a pretend Arthur at her side.

FAWKES DE BRÉAUTÉ

Fawkes was an obscure knight from Bréauté, a village a few miles north-east of Le Havre in Normandy. His name derives from the French for a scythe (*faux*) which is the implement he is supposed to have used to commit his first murder. He was one of the most feared and ruthless mercenaries (*routiers*) of the first quarter of the thirteenth century. He served both kings John and Henry III under whom he acquired an estate in south London. The house was called Fawkes Hall which then became Fox Hall and finally Vauxhall which is how that part of London is still known today. Later the Vauxhall car company built its factory on the site and still retains the Bréauté griffin as its company logo.

SWW July 2020

FALLEN ANGEL

Summer 1225. Change is in the air. There is a new religious force in the world: the preaching friars. When the first of these arrives in Bury he is greeted with suspicion by some of the monks. What does he want? Why has he come to Bury?

Their mistrust seems justified when strange things begin to happen. The abbey comes under attack from a plague of rats and deadly poisonous gas.

Then one of the monks is murdered.

The prior attempts to calm nerves by appealing to the saint whose name the abbey bears. Is it the new friar who is doing these things or is there some supernatural power at work?

Walter is not convinced and decides to investigate. Only when all the children of the town suddenly disappear is the truth at last revealed.

NINE NUNS

Summer 1219. A group of nuns from England set out to travel to the south of France in order to found a new convent. Against his better judgement Walter agrees to accompany them to ensure they arrive safely at their destination.

But they never get there. Instead, one by one the nuns disappear in mysterious circumstances.

What happened to them? Were they murdered? If so where are the bodies? Or is the ship on which they travelled simply cursed as some believe?

Vanishing nuns, shipwrecks, pirates, murder. Walter becomes embroiled in matters he does not understand that will place his own life in peril not once but several times before the end of the adventure.

WALTER'S GHOST

Summer 1206. Before it was renamed, Bury St Edmunds was known as Bedricksworth after the ancient family who lived there. Now the last surviving member of the Bedrick clan, Arnulf Bedrick, wants an heir to carry on the family name. Marrying for a fifth time, this is his last chance to achieve it. But Arnulf has a secret.

Now jump forward seven hundred years to New Year's Day 1903. The antiquarian and celebrated writer of ghost stories, M. R. James, is excavating the graves of five medieval abbots of Bury. But in one of the graves he discovers something that shouldn't be there.

How are the two events connected? What is the secret found buried in the abbot's grave? Over it all hovers the ghost of Brother Walter who drives the investigation on to solve not only a seven hundred year old murder mystery but also another in the twentieth century in the way only Walter can.

Printed in Great Britain
by Amazon